SO-AII-657

Di Morrissey is Australia's most popular woman novelist. Her first book, *Heart of the Dreaming*, launched her bestselling career and paved the way for *The Last Rose of Summer*, *Follow the Morning Star*, *The Last Mile Home*, *Tears of the Moon*, *When the Singing Stops*, *The Songmaster* and her latest novel, *Scatter the Stars*.

Well known as a TV presenter on the original 'Good Morning Australia', Di has always written – working as a journalist, advertising copywriter and screen-writer.

Di has two children and lives in Byron Bay, NSW, where she devotes herself to writing, in between travelling to research her novels.

Also by Di Morrissey

Heart of the Dreaming
The Last Rose of Summer
Follow the Morning Star
Tears of the Moon
When the Singing Stops
The Songmaster

DI MORRISSEY

The LAST MILE HOME

PAN
Pan Macmillan Australia

In association with

Selwa Anthony

First published 1994 in Pan by Pan Macmillan Australia Pty Limited
St Martins Tower, 31 Market Street, Sydney

Reprinted 1995 (twice), 1996 (twice), 1997, 1998 (twice)

Copyright © Di Morrissey 1994

National Library of Australia
cataloguing-in-publication data:

Morrissey, Di.
The last mile home.
ISBN 0 7329 0804 3
I. Title.
A823.3

Typeset in 11.5/14.5 pt Bembo by Post Typesetters
Printed in Australia by McPherson's Printing Group

*Dedicated to families everywhere...
who are linked by those members present,
those past who are still with us across the circle of time,
and those yet to come... in the hope that respect and
affection for our own family might forge us all into
one international family.*

*And for Poppy who always said,
'The last mile home is always the longest... but isn't it
good to get there!'*

ACKNOWLEDGEMENTS

For my children, Gabrielle and Nicolas, who continue to astound and humble me with their insight, their compassion for others, and their beautiful free spirits.

For my mother who lost a husband and a son and still raised a daughter to believe in the beauty of the world.

For Jim, Ro, David and Damien Revitt . . . only family could be so giving.

And especially for my best friend, for his gifts of love, strength and belief in me.

CHAPTER ONE

1958

THE DARK WOOD DOUBLE-DOORS INTO THE library opened slowly, and the mustiness of old velvet, leather and furniture oil seeped through the narrow slit. For a moment, a slice of light was visible, then small hands carefully turned the brass handles to minimise the click as the doors interlocked and closed off this private world.

The room was dim, but the small figure moved surely, going to the great fall of wine draperies, giving a little tug to one side, dragging them apart. The slash of bright light was as sudden and unexpected as a rifle shot.

The lance of light illuminated the room so that

the furniture — a bulky desk, a standing lamp and a coffee table — was thrown into relief against the shadows. Two walls were lined with bookshelves; a third had bookcases with leadlight doors standing either side of a fireplace. Behind the wall of drapes were high windows whose view across landscaped grounds had been hidden. Like curtains moving across a grand stage set, the world of the library room and the beauty of the gardens was revealed, awaiting an audience that never came.

The little figure in short pants, neat shirt and woollen socks pulled straight up his legs, shuffled the small stepladder into place before the second wall of books. He took three steps up and leaned across without hesitation to a red leather book with gold lettering on its spine. Three books further along was a black book and this too was pulled from its place. A quick trip to turn the key of the glass door of one of the fireside bookcases and three more books were added to those at the boy's feet. The pile was transferred to the window where he settled himself against the loops and swathes of the velvet drapes, leaning back and lifting the first book into the sunlight that beamed over his shoulders.

First he held the book, reverently running his hands lightly over the front; then he opened the heavy bound cover, leaning down to sniff the tang of leather and old paper. Then came the tingle of anticipation as he tenderly peeled back the tissue over the frontispiece.

The boy studied the pictures, his mouth curving in a slight smile. There was a family gathered around a long kitchen table with a jolly looking father holding a carving knife ready to plunge into a steaming baked brown bird set before him. The boy had studied the faces around the table before — the kindly smiling mother, the eager faces of the children — and wondered, as he always did, what their names were and what they said to one another. He closed his eyes and drew a deep breath, inhaling the warmth of the kitchen, the smell of roast turkey and chestnuts roasting on the fire, and for an instant he imagined that laughter and chatter echoed in the silent library.

The boy closed that book and lifted the next. This one had pen and ink etchings through it and he turned the pages slowly until he found his favourite. This family was gathered in front of a simple hearth where a fire burned brightly; the father was lifting a cup without a handle to propose a toast. Beside him on a stool, very close, sat a little boy. He was so frail, his limbs supported by an iron frame, a little crutch resting at his feet. The man held the withered hand of his son tightly in his, as if he loved the child so much he didn't ever want to let him go. The little boy was saying something to his family, gazing up at his father with eyes that shone with love.

Beneath the picture, letters formed words and words formed the sentence, *'God Bless us every one!' said Tiny Tim*. But these were hieroglyphics to the boy with the book. How he longed to know what the poor little boy was saying. And did he get better? His questions would have to remain unanswered until the day came when he could read and all the treasures within the covers of these books would be revealed to him.

Guiltily he looked up, and suddenly, as if he'd willed the wrath upon himself, the library doors burst open.

'Caught! You wicked boy!' the voice boomed. A figure loomed in the doorway as the boy scrambled to his feet, trying to hide the books behind his back.

A tall man advanced on the boy, grabbing him by his collar. 'You've been told before not to come in here. Not to touch these books. These are valuable books. Not books for children.' The man raised his voice even further. 'Mrs Anderson,' he shouted. 'Mrs Anderson!'

The child was propelled towards the door as a worried voice and hurrying feet echoed down the hallway. 'Coming, sir.'

The housekeeper bustled into the room looking flustered, strands of greying hair spraying from the bun on top of her head. Her plump pink face was damp with perspiration and she was wiping her hands on her apron. 'Oh Richie, what mischief have you been up to now?' she chided.

Phillip Holten was holding the boy by the back of the shirt collar as if he were an errant puppy. He thrust the boy towards her. 'Take him to his room; he is not to come down until I say so.' He angled the boy's head towards him and glared at the downcast face. 'Look at me when I'm speaking to you, Richard.'

Hesitantly the boy lifted his chin, his mouth quivering, gazing up at him, his blue eyes humbled.

The man spoke in low, carefully measured tones. 'You are forbidden to touch these books or to come into this room. Is that understood?'

The boy nodded.

'Answer when spoken to, please.'

'Yes, sir,' he quavered. 'I wanted to look at the books with the pictures . . .'

'That's enough. You will learn to read when I say so, and you will read books appropriate for children. You will have a governess who'll prepare you for a good school. Until then, you do as you're told. Understood?'

'Yes, sir.' It was a meek voice.

'Say sorry, dearie,' prompted Mrs Anderson, taking his hand and giving it a gentle squeeze.

'Sorry, sir.'

'Off you go. Mrs Anderson, see this room is put to rights.'

'Yes, Mr Holten. I'll just settle him in his bedroom first.'

Holding his hand, she led the boy upstairs. When she heard the door of the study shut, she stooped, picked the boy up and carried him. 'Why do you go in there, luv? You know you aren't allowed. You have lots of toys and pretty books in the nursery. I suppose you like climbing up that ladder. I know you didn't mean any harm, but it's not worth getting him upset and cross at you.'

The boy nestled his face into the warmth of her shoulder. 'Never mind, luv, I'll bring a nice supper to your room. Maybe a treat if you're good.'

She was breathing heavily as she deposited him inside the door of his bedroom.

Back in the library, Mrs Anderson drew the drapes, put the stepladder back in place and picked up the books. Idly she glanced through them, wondering why the boy had chosen these. The pictures in them brought a lump to her throat. 'Poor little lamb,' she sighed. 'He must wish his life was like this. If only it were . . . for all of us.' She slipped the books back into the spaces on the shelves and went to make supper.

Far from being a punishment, Richie enjoyed his solitary supper. Mrs Anderson sat a tray on the low table with his soft-boiled soldier egg sitting under its knitted cosy, fingers of toast on one side. A bowl of sago custard with stewed apple, a mug of warm Cadbury's chocolate and, as a special treat, a little cupcake sprinkled with hundreds and thousands in a pleated paper cup accompanied the egg.

Richie was left alone to eat and he ate slowly, with enjoyment, dipping his toast into the egg just far enough so the yolk didn't dribble over the edge, just as Mrs Anderson had shown him. He played with his food; he hummed; he licked his fingers; he blew bubbles in his milk. This was far more fun than eating in the formal austere dining room as he did most nights.

Usually he would be seated at the long rose-wood dining table, his legs swinging, the table uncomfortably high, making it even more difficult for him to manoeuvre his knife and fork; while at the far end of the table, Phillip Holten would sit and meticulously eat his meal. Pausing occasion-ally, he'd sip a glass of claret and interrogate the small boy, who found it difficult to give more than short answers as he tried to concentrate on keeping the peas on the back of his fork. When a longer answer was required, he'd learned to rest his hands in his lap, respond, looking directly at his calm inquisitor, then turn his attention once again to the complicated business of eating while minding his manners.

Mrs Anderson served the courses, giving her little chap, as she called him out of hearing, encouraging smiles and little hints. Carrying the plates back into the kitchen, she'd sigh to Jim, her husband, 'Poor wee mite. Should be sitting on his mamma's knee, not struggling with great silver forks and knives at his age.'

'If he passes muster in there, he'll be able to deal with anything life throws at him,' Jim would advise. 'Leave matters be. You know the rules — no discussion about what might or might not be.'

The evening dinner ritual was observed as it had been when Phillip Holten was a boy, and he believed in carrying on the tradition. But for little Richie, uncomfortable in good clothes, lace-up shoes, and best manners to the fore, it was an ordeal. At the end of the meal, when given the nod by Mrs Anderson, Richie would recite, 'May I be excused, please?' And Phillip Holten would nod as he lit up his cigar. Mrs Anderson waited discreetly in the doorway as he slipped down from his chair and bid, 'Goodnight', before escaping to his bedroom.

But tonight, being 'punished' with supper in his room, he wore his pyjamas, and didn't worry if crumbs or egg yolk spilled. All alone, he acted out his little fantasy of a family Christmas party, pretending that there were relatives and friends gathered around and he was offering portions of turkey and pudding and joining in the laughter and the hearty togetherness he only could imagine from the silent pictures seen in forbidden books.

Later, Mrs Anderson came to take away Richie's tray and see that he washed and brushed his teeth. She smiled at his cheerful disposition.

'Do you want a story, luv?'

Richie nodded eagerly, settling himself on the bed and making room for Mrs Anderson to sit beside him.

It was a slow plod as she laboured over the sentences in a flat voice, but Richie followed the story closely, running his fingers along the lines of words as she read, memorising each one. He had heard the story so many times, he could 'read' the book himself, word for word.

This was a book from a previous generation, deemed suitable for little boys by Phillip Holten. One Christmas Mrs Anderson had given Richie a brightly coloured picture book of boys' adventures. Phillip Holten had thanked her but said he preferred that Richie be given more worthy reading matter, adding, 'It is not necessary for you to give the boy Christmas gifts. He is amply provided for.'

'It'll be Christmas soon,' said Mrs Anderson out loud, thinking of the books Richie had been looking at in the library earlier. 'And then a whole new year — 1959. I wonder what it will bring. You'll start school for one thing.'

But Richie looked wistful. 'Why don't we have Christmas like the people in those books?' he asked, for Christmas was no celebration in this household.

Richie accompanied Phillip Holten to church on Christmas morning but paid little attention to the service, although he knew better than to fidget. He liked the singing but spent his time studying the festive decorations of beribboned wreaths looped over the handles of the church doors, and the tinsel and flowers massed inside where candles burned. It was different to other Sundays and overflowed with happy people dressed in their best clothes. Everybody wished each other 'Merry Christmas', and children's eyes burned with excitement.

Phillip Holten always stood solemnly at the

front of the simple Presbyterian church for the service and afterwards Richie trailed behind him as he departed with a nod to several people and a shake of the minister's hand.

At dinner there was Mrs Anderson's plum pudding for dessert, but no other concession was made to the festive occasion.

Once Mrs Anderson had suggested the boy might like a little Christmas tree and some 'treats'.

'I am raising the child, thank you, Mrs Anderson. Besides, he is too young to appreciate the fripperies and nonsense people go on with ... a waste of hard-earned money in my opinion.'

Mrs Anderson had held her tongue, but she railed to her husband against the strict frugality of the man and the spartan childhood for the boy.

Jim Anderson knocked his pipe on the edge of the oven and tipped the dregs into the ash box of the fuel stove. 'Well, he might seem mean to some, but you can't interfere, Rene. If that's what he thinks is best, then that's how it will be. You can't really blame the man for not being joyful at Christmas.'

But instinctively Richie knew he was missing out. There was some other world where people went and he longed to find the secret door to it. He watched Mrs Anderson put the book away.

'What did you do at Christmas when you were little like me?' he pestered.

At first Mrs Anderson prattled on cheerfully about her brothers and sisters and how they'd played jolly games together and what fun they'd had on Christmas morning with their stockings filled with sweets and silly toys. But seeing Richie's wistful eyes and sensing his hungry heart made her catch her breath and she ended limply, 'Well it wasn't all fun and games. We didn't have much money and times were hard. Bread and dripping days they were. Now, you're the lucky one, living in such a grand place. And later you'll go off to the best school and become a clever fellow so you can read all the books in the world. Maybe even write one!' However, her words had a hollow ring and Richie didn't look at all convinced that he was better off.

Mrs Anderson tucked him in and kissed his cheek. 'Happy Christmas, Richie.'

In the silence beneath the cool white sheets, the little boy hugged his pillow. Like moving pictures beneath his tightly squeezed eyelids, he watched the scenes from the books glimpsed in the library unreel before him. And saw himself, laughing, in every one.

Perhaps whatever angels or dancing reindeer sped across that sleeping moonlit countryside, they could be forgiven for bypassing the big house. For no light glowed, no welcome candle called. It was not a house that invited visitors. It seemed to withdraw into itself, shielding itself from the outside world...remembering. For while the shadowy grand house was never a joyous or sunny place, there was once a family within.

CHAPTER TWO

1953

THE SUN SLANTED ACROSS THE LEVEL GREEN PAD-
dock where the freshly cut grass served as cricket
oval for the Graziers versus Townies quarterly
match. From a distance, the white figures were
placed like chessmen on a rough baize cloth
fringed by the colours of motorcars, trucks and
horses, and the bright patterned clothes of wives,
girlfriends and children. The spectators sat on
rugs and blankets, perched on car bonnets or held
umbrellas to shield the last of the sun's heat. Trees
drooped in the breathless air and all seemed as
tranquil as an oil painting entitled 'Summer's
Afternoon'. The occasional flurry of activity

when a whacking sixer headed for the roughly marked boundary caused attention to refocus on the game and produced a round of polite applause.

The doctor bowled out the last man and clinched the match for the Townies. As the two teams left the field, Phillip Holten met his tall son striding towards him.

'Well done, Barney. Good game.' He shook his son's hand formally.

'Thanks. Good game even if we lost.'

'Play to win but enjoy the game. It is how one plays the game after all,' said Phillip Holten as he turned to congratulate the other player walking beside him.

Barnard Holten wiped a hand across his damp brow and then rubbed it dry down the side of his cream flannels as he strode to the small group of women near the Holtens' car. His mother hadn't come: she didn't like sitting in the sun for any length of time and avoided his polo matches for the same reason.

The women, still chatting about the match, eyed the handsome young man as he and his father opened the boot of their car. Phillip Holten was tall and solidly built, and if it hadn't been for the wind and sunburned face, his features would have looked more patrician than the Roman nose, arched brows and firmly defined mouth already were.

Barnard, at twenty-four, was taller than his father, more fine-boned, with grey-green eyes; and where his father had a russet tint to his thick head of hair, Barney, as he was known, had sunstreaked brown hair. While his father was considered somewhat dour, Barney had a ready smile and mischievous eyes. Many a girl in the district was smitten by him, and as his father's property, Amba, was one of the best wool producers in the area, he was definitely a good catch.

Players and spectators stood outside the makeshift tearoom where women dispensed cups of tea through a counter window. Everyone helped themselves from plates of homemade cakes, biscuits, scones and pikelets while they discussed the finer points of the match and made social arrangements for the evening. The talk soon drifted to the record wool prices and some wondered how long this boom was going to last.

'Wool's here to stay, Frank. Country'd be bust without the wool industry.'

'The world will always need wool.'

'Can't produce enough of it, mate.'

The optimists were in the majority and the mood was buoyant. While no one would openly admit their wool cheques were the biggest they'd ever imagined, being paid just over a pound per pound, they did laconically agree that they'd done all right this year.

The district was prosperous and there was plenty of employment. The wool revenue flowed into new equipment, new fences, higher wages and more cattle, or overseas travel and home improvements.

Barney carried his cup inside to where two ladies were washing up, large aprons tied over their skirts and blouses.

'Thanks, Barney. How's your mother?'

'She's doing all right thanks, Mrs Graham. How's your family?'

'They're very well indeed,' came the quick response. Especially her twenty-year-old daughter. 'Are you going to the woolshed dance at the Frenchams tonight?'

'I haven't decided. I suppose so. Nice to see you, Mrs Andrews.' He nodded to the two women and escaped.

'Such a lovely boy. Not a bit like his father.'

'Gets his looks from his mother, I suppose. Enid must have been very pretty when she was young.'

'I wasn't thinking so much of his looks. It's the personality. Barney seems more down to earth.'

'He's not a snob like his father, you mean,' said Mrs Andrews bluntly.

'It's not snobbery so much. Phillip Holten just

seems such a cold sort of a fellow. Barney is a bit warmer, if you know what I mean.'

'Yes, I do. Surprising he's like that really. I don't think life at Amba is a barrel of laughs.' Bettina Andrews wiped her hands and untied her apron. 'I hear it's a pretty miserable household. Not that I want to gossip of course.'

Barney and his father drove home in near silence after exchanging a few pleasantries about the match.

'I was thinking I might go down for the Royal Easter Show this year,' said Barney casually as they turned off the familiar bush road and headed up the dirt track past the first of Amba's paddocks.

'Waste of time and money,' grumbled his father. Everyone they knew went to the annual agricultural show in Sydney but Phillip Holten steadfastly went against the trend. He hated the socialising and the camaraderie of the bushies let loose in the big smoke. He was a loner and he ran his business his way and detested anyone knowing what he bought, what he planned or what he sold.

'It's good to see what's new. Maybe we could pick up a good ram or two, mix with other people,' said Barney.

'That's what I said — waste time and spend

money. You're better off doing what we did today. You can learn from some of the older and wiser woolgrowers in the area, and you saw other young people there. Stick to your own, Barnard.'

Barney didn't answer. He thought the old established woolgrowers in the district that his father was referring to were conservative, not only in their politics, but in their thinking and attitudes. Something new had to be well proven before they'd take it on board. And as for the young people, there had been a few daughters from prosperous families at the match as it had been a social game, but he knew them all and none struck him as special. Barney was aware that every mother in the area had him lined up to put his feet under their dining room table beside their daughter. He knew his life was mapped out and, being the only child, that his future lay in the footsteps of his father.

They turned into the driveway leading past the home gardens and Phillip drove the car under the carport at the side of the front entrance. Barney got out and bounded around the side of the gracious verandah to the rose garden and neat flowerbeds surrounded by tall herbaceous borders and pruned shrubs.

His mother's straw hat was visible as she bent low, clipping, pruning and cutting off dead flower heads. Her constant companions, two white noisy and active Pomeranian dogs, began leaping and yelping at the sight of the familiar interloper into their mistress's territory.

Enid Holten looked up as Barney waved and headed to the wing where his bedroom, bathroom and small sitting room gave him his own privacy. His mother lifted a pair of secateurs vaguely in his direction and went back to her pruning.

Once inside his bedroom, Barney pulled off his sweaty cream pants and shirt, grabbed a clean towel off the wooden towel rail and stepped under the shower. He felt his tense muscles relax as the needles of spray bounced off the back of his neck.

He stayed in the shower longer than normal without feeling guilty about being extravagant with the water. He finally turned off the taps, wrapped the towel around his waist and padded into his bedroom to find clean clothes. He was grateful for his own area where he could relax and feel he was free to do as he wished. While all decisions were made by Phillip Holten, Enid had quietly suggested the wing addition for Barney might be a nice idea. Seeing he worked such long hard hours on the property.

Starting from holidays from boarding school, Barney had worked his way in stages through every part of the place, learning how it was run.

He now had his own responsibilities, but his father made the decisions and would do so until he either retired or dropped dead at the helm. It was the way of the land. The thought of following any other path in life simply never entered Phillip's head. His life and his son's life were mapped out.

After showering and changing, Barney went to the kitchen in search of Mrs Anderson, the housekeeper.

'Any chance of a cup of tea?'

'I would have thought you'd had your fill after the match. Didn't the ladies' committee give you afternoon tea?' she smiled as she filled the electric jug.

'Yep. But that was an hour or more ago.'

'I'll make a pot, maybe your mother would like a cup too. I'll bring it out to the verandah.'

'Dad in the study?'

'Yes. He doesn't want to be disturbed.'

Barney nodded. His father always took to his study at sunset; he wouldn't appear now until dinner. Barney took an apple as he went out of the kitchen door and through to the gardens once more. He found his mother inspecting the new growth on the hydrangeas against the shady wall of the bedroom wing. The two white bullets charged him as if they'd never seen him before and his mother turned around.

'Hello, dear. Good game?'

'Yes, despite the fact we lost. Close though. Mrs Anderson is making tea. Be ready on the verandah if you want a cup.'

Enid scooped up her two dogs whose fuzz-ball tails twitched in pleasure as they gazed at her adoringly. 'Hear that? Tea. Maybe we can wangle a biscuit or two for you. You'd like that, wouldn't you, eh? Maybe even a Monte Carlo ... num num!' She nuzzled their shiny black button noses; then, with her garden gloves and secateurs protruding from the pocket of her skirt and a dog tucked under each arm, she headed for the house.

Barney trailed after her with a bemused expression. He was used to his taciturn mother bursting into baby talk with Tucker and Diet. One dog was a piggy eater who loved his tucker, the other a picky eater who ate little, hence the names. Visitors observing the reserved and somewhat vague Mrs Holten with her dogs had to restrain their surprise and amusement. Barney had never been any trouble and with home help she'd scarcely had to lift a finger. Now her only child was grown she devoted herself to the dogs. Even Barney conceded she seemed to care for the dogs more than people.

Barney had been away at boarding school when his mother had acquired the dogs so he was unsure how she had managed to get his father's approval for Phillip Holten detested his wife's playthings. He didn't consider them real dogs and wouldn't allow them near the working dogs. He had told her they would be taken by a fox or a dingo but so far they had survived for years by rarely leaving the house or the side of their mistress. They slept in a large washing basket in the laundry and, as soon as they heard movement in the kitchen in the morning, they waited patiently on the doormat for Mrs Anderson to let them in. They then scurried down the hall to the master bedroom and waited outside the door until Phillip Holten opened the door and stumbled across them on his way to the bathroom. They then leapt onto the twin bed occupied by Enid where they were petted and whispered to until Mrs Anderson brought tea and toast. Each was given tidbits of toast and then let out into the garden from the bedroom side door.

Enid was careful to keep them out of her husband's way, and he simply refused to see them, speak to them or acknowledge their presence unless they irritated him more than normal. Generally he acted as though they were invisible, though Mrs Anderson had once come upon him stepping out of the library as the dogs trailed past the door in search of Enid. He'd given a swift kick with his boot and caught Diet between the back legs and sent her screeching down the hall. Mrs Anderson turned away and busied herself with the pile of ironing she was carrying, and pretended not to see the incident or his expression of grim satisfaction.

That evening, Barney came into the sitting room where his parents were having a pre-dinner sherry. His father was seated in the leather arm-chair that had belonged to his grandfather and his mother was seated on the sofa with Diet and Tucker on either side of her, their snouts resting on her lap as they eyed the Sao biscuit smeared with Peck's Paste which she was nibbling. Barney was dressed in dark grey slacks, a pale blue dress shirt and his Kings School old boys' tie. His hair was slicked down in place, the Brylcreem making it look darker than normal. His shoes were, as usual, highly polished. Phillip Holten had taught him that a man maintained a certain standard no matter where he was or what he was doing and that was epitomised by shined shoes. Even before setting out for a day's hard and dirty work around Amba, the riding boots had to be polished. A small wooden box with a flip-up lid was kept by the back door and it was a ritual before breakfast for Barney to take out the Kiwi polish, smear it on the boots on his feet with a rag from the box, take the brush, close the lid and rest his foot on its lid as he buffed the wrinkled leather to a shine.

'Dad, Mum, I'm going over to the Frenchams' for that woolshed dance tonight. It's turned into quite a big do.'

'Be a long drive back . . . late, I assume. I trust you'll drive with due caution. And not imbibe too much, with that in mind,' said his father, looking around the corner of the *Land* newspaper.

'I thought I'd stay over. Most are. There's a big breakfast on in the morning. I'll take my swag.'

'That sounds like a lot of trouble,' said his mother, snapping a cracker in half and giving a bit to each dog.

'It should be rather fun. It's an organised thing; you know, a committee and everyone pitching in,' said Barney, thinking of all the other families involved. Phillip and Enid rarely attended social gatherings.

'Don't forget we have to get ready for shearing soon. Start mustering on Monday.' His father turned back to his newspaper.

'Well, cheerio then.'

His father didn't answer and his mother was murmuring to the dogs.

'Bye, Mother.'

His mother didn't look up. 'Oh. Goodbye, Barney. Don't grab, Tucker, there's a good boy,' she admonished the dog, reaching for another biscuit as Barney left the room.

He threw his swag and knapsack with a change of casual clothes into the back of the Holden utility and drove through the last of the day's sun. He passed the black soil cultivation paddocks and drove out along the red clay road to the turnoff to the Pembertons' farm next door, which was marked by a rusting milk urn nailed to a post with *Anglesea* painted on it. He drove on through a stand of grey gums screening a small seldom-used timber mill, past the line of sheoaks marching along the banks of the creek bed, over the broad cement ford that became a floodway in heavy rains, until, three miles on, the dirt road hit the bitumen. After an hour and four mailboxes, he turned into the Frenchams' property.

The light had faded, the watercolours of the sunset running across the pale canvas of the sky. By the time he arrived at the gates of the Frenchams' homestead, lights were beaming into the twilight, the band could be heard tuning up and headlights from cars bounced from the woolshed to the house as food, grog, visitors, last-minute extra tables, chairs and gear were ferried between the buildings.

Further out on the deserted highway, coming from the direction of Glen Innes, an early model

Buick, towing a trailer, its engine rattling roughly, turned onto the dirt road heading towards Anglesea, the Pembertons' property.

The wide-bodied car, approaching twenty years of age, with deep seats now almost springless but sinkably comfortable, seemed ready to burst at the seams. Inside was a crush of people, a dog, parcels, laughter and singing. The Buick meandered on steadily, its headlights glancing off the unfamiliar terrain. Bob McBride drove with an arm hanging out of the window, patting the driver's door like a jockey urging on a thoroughbred.

'Come on, Betsy, we're nearly there. You can make it.'

The twin girls on the back seat were bouncing and singing, 'Zippety doo da, zippety ay, my oh my what a wonderful day . . .'

'It's not day, it's night,' came a fourteen-year-old boy's know-it-all voice.

'Hush, Kev, let them sing. I'd rather that than the "how-much-longer" whine,' came a young woman's placatory murmur.

'Come on, count the mailboxes,' called the cheerful mother. 'Only four they said.'

En masse the car counted, 'One . . .' Then, after what seemed longer than a watched kettle coming to the boil, they all shouted, '*Four*! We're here.'

'Not quite, we have to find our house,' came the young woman's voice. Heads hung out of windows, the dog barked and the car swung through the gate onto the track up to Anglesea.

'I bags doing the gates.' Kevin sprang from the car as the gate loomed into the headlights. The engine idled with an ominously tired cough as the boy struggled with the gate that was dragging in the dirt.

'Help him lift it, Abby,' said the father, wiping his hands around the big circle of the fat steering wheel as if trying to energise the car over this last hurdle. A tall slim girl of twenty, her long dark hair tied in a ponytail, wearing a full-skirted, faded flowered dress and old sandshoes, helped her brother lift the gate and then stood back expectantly.

But Betsy the Buick was pooped. She'd come this far and that was close enough. Like a plump matron suddenly relieved of the constraints of her corsets, the doors burst open and crammed passengers rolled out into the cool night air as Betsy steamed and heaved and refused to start.

Bob McBride understood her moods. 'That's it, Mum. She won't budge till morning now.'

Wails replaced the excited chatter and laughter. Gwen McBride stood with a small child on one hip, his three-year-old head leaning sleepily against her shoulder. In her other hand she held back the excited Border collie on his leash. 'So what are we going to do? How far to the house do you reckon?'

'One way to find out, eh? Shut the gate, Kev. Everyone grab a bag, roll up the windows. We'll hoof it from here and bring Betsy up after breakfast.'

'Grab some food, that Rinso box from the boot has bread and eggs in it,' directed Gwen McBride. 'Just in case there's nothing in the cottage. Though Mrs Pemberton said she'd have it ready for us. But you never know what that means.'

Amid mutterings, moans, giggles and admonishments, the McBride tribe of seven plus a dog and silkworms in a shoe box, straggled up the track, the slowly rising moon lighting their way. Bob McBride soon had them heartily singing, '*If I knew you were coming I'd have baked a cake . . .*' as they made their way towards their unknown new home.

CHAPTER THREE

BARNEY DROVE BACK TO AMBA LATE SUNDAY morning. It felt like a Sunday too: a lazy, sun-ripened day stretching ahead without any commitments. However, he knew his father would insist they have everything ready for the start of mustering the next day.

The Frenchams' party had been fun, and had virtually continued through until the breakfast barbecue. Some of the boys had hit the keg pretty hard and were the worse for wear in the morning, but all had hoed into the sausages, chops, eggs and bacon sizzling on the barbecue in a grove of gum trees. Sitting around on logs, with their plates on their laps, the girls toasting slices of bread on sticks before the fire or dishing out thick slabs that had soaked up the grease on the barbecue, all agreed it had been a great party.

The two dozen partygoers had all known each other for years. Friendships had been renewed after stints at boarding schools, trips abroad, or work out of the district. Most would now stay in the area on their parents' properties in readiness for putting down their own roots. Although the girls would move to wherever their husbands might be, few would marry outside this resident circle.

Barney glanced up at the fresh pink gumtips translucent against the blue light of morning. How Australian. How he'd missed the clearness of the light, the smell of the bush, the sound of the native birds in the years he'd been living in the city.

He had graduated from Kings School at Parramatta and like many promising and well-to-do country lads had joined the staff of one of the big wool broking houses in preparation for returning to work their own places. In the wood-panelled offices and cavernous warehouses of Goldsborough Mort he had learned much about the business of classing and selling wool, as well as servicing the farmers and graziers with everything from finance to shearing machines.

They had been years of mixed feelings. He had missed the land terribly. Every holiday and long weekend he caught a crowded steam train from Central Station and went home to Amba. Mrs Anderson would always make one of his favourite meals; he would have a sherry with his father before dinner and they would discuss business matters before he took his place at the long rosewood dining table. His mother was glad to see him he knew, but apart from asking him general questions about his life in Sydney, she simply assumed he was doing well and was happy. He had given up trying to persuade her to come to the city and shop or go to the theatre. His parents had visited Sydney only twice while he lived there. His father had come down on one other occasion to see a solicitor and they had lunched together at the Australia Hotel. It had not been a happy dining experience. His father had complained about the service, the standard of the food and the cost. When Barney offered to pay for the lunch, Phillip Holten had curtly remarked that he hoped this wasn't how he spent his money in Sydney.

There were compensations. The postwar years in Sydney were stimulating. Migrants, many of them misplaced persons from refugee camps in Europe, were starting to arrive. Often when on errands to the waterfront, Barney would watch the huge ships with decks crowded with passengers being nudged in to the wharf by tugs. He looked at the travellers' faces and tried to imagine how they felt about arriving in a land that was so strange and different from their homelands. While some looked eager and hopeful, others still had the pain and horror of what they'd left behind etched into their faces.

In the office, on the beach at weekends and at parties, Barney met some of the younger migrants from Britain and Europe. He was particularly attracted to the girls with their accents and very different look. But it wasn't easy to make friends with them for they seemed aloof and uncomfortable with a lifestyle where young men abandoned them on a scorched beach while they spent hours in a dangerous looking ocean. Nor were they at ease when their companions plunged into wild terrain with haversacks to go bushwalking.

The Australian girls were easier to get along with and although he made good friends with many and had a lot of fun, he didn't get serious with any of them. Nor could he imagine being married to any of them. In the heady days of postwar booming Sydney they were all obsessed with the material joys of peacetime living. He couldn't visualise any of them being content to ride the boundary fences with him. While Amba was a gracious homestead and wealthy property, Barney would live simply though comfortably until the day came when he took over the reins from his father. The daughters of other graziers understood how it worked, unlike the city girls who rarely expressed interest in his country background anyway.

He was glad to quit the city and return home to his special country, the miles of New England land that encompassed Amba's five thousand acres. The actual homestead, the physical trappings that established their credentials to be there, didn't mean as much to him as the indefinable quality of place, of belonging.

The unravelling of the landscape — its rocks and trees, ridges and gullies — was as recognisable as his own face in a mirror. He felt he understood the Aborigines' affinity with the land, even though he knew little about them. There were none living in the immediate vicinity; some properties had itinerant Aboriginal stockmen but there was little contact. Phillip Holten distrusted them and had no time for what he called 'the lazy blacks'.

Barney shook his head and concentrated on the road. He started to think through the gear he would need and what had to be accomplished before the shearing was under way. It was good country that carried two sheep to the acre. His father set exacting standards and it was up to Barney to see they were carried down the line.

He tried not to compare his father with the men who had been at the Frenchams'. They were rugged and hearty and he enjoyed their laconic humour, their teasing banter and long solid discussions on politics, wool and farming. Exchanges with his father meant more listening and little chance to put across his own viewpoint. There wasn't much banter or wit. Barney quickly cut off any thoughts of wishing his father were different. He'd sorted that out as a boy, realising his father would never be like those of his friends. He knew his father was honest, believed in what he was doing and was proud of his achievements. But Barney wished that his father would acknowledge his own achievements and deep down longed to hear his father tell him he was proud of him.

Barney turned off the bitumen onto the dirt road to the homestead, hoping there wouldn't be a big Sunday roast waiting for him. He couldn't eat a thing. Suddenly he noticed something different — a car was parked at the entrance to the Pembertons'. No, not parked. The bonnet was up and someone was tinkering under the hood. It wasn't a car he recognised as belonging to anyone he knew — a thirties, at least, Buick. He turned in and stopped.

'G'day. You stalled, are you?'

'She ain't going anywhere, that's for sure. Not for the moment anyway. Temperamental old biddy, but I know what makes her tick.' Bob McBride grinned at Barney. He wore a patched khaki shirt, old army pants and boots, and he wielded a spanner in grease-stained hand. A cheek was smudged with black.

'Can I give you a hand? I've tools in the ute. Or do you want a tow?' offered Barney.

'Thanks, mate. We'll be right, I think. But you could get in and turn her over for me.'

Barney sat behind the wheel, sinking deep into the old seat. He turned the ignition once, then again, and she finally spluttered and caught. 'Keep her going, rev her up a bit. That'll do us.' McBride slammed the bonnet shut with a bang and tucked the spanner in his hip pocket.

Barney fiddled with the gear lever, made sure it was still in neutral and edged out of the car. McBride was rolling a cigarette.

'She picked a bugger of a time to call it quits,' he said.

'You on your way to the Pembertons'?'

'Last night we were. Been a long day's drive and she couldn't drag herself up to the house, could she? No, she karks it at the gate. Had to hoof it up to the cottage in the dark. Bit of a lark really,' he added cheerfully.

'You're staying with the Pembertons?'

'Nah. Staying in the other house. Doing some work for him, plus looking for a bit in my own line. Bob McBride, by the way.' He held out his hand then withdrew it and wiped it on the side of his pants. 'Grease, sorry.'

'Barney Holten,' he took the stained hand and shook it firmly. 'What's your line, if you don't mind my asking?'

'I'm a shearer. Brought the family over to settle in one place for a bit. A mate put me on to Keith Pemberton.'

Barney nodded. He'd heard the Pembertons had been looking for someone to stay on the place as a kind of caretaker, handyman and rousabout.

'Are you sure your car will keep going now? I'm happy to follow you up the track a bit in case she conks out again.'

'She wouldn't bloody dare. No, once she's running she's right. Just needed a good night's rest and a bit of a kick in the guts,' grinned McBride, sticking his hand-rolled cigarette to his bottom lip and getting into the car. 'Righto then. Thanks for stopping. You a local?'

'Yes. My father owns Amba. We're neighbours.'

'Well, I'll probably see you round then. Cheerio.' Bob McBride cautiously slipped Betsy into first gear and eased up the track.

'I'll shut the gate,' called Barney and McBride gave a thumbs-up and a wave without looking back. Barney grinned to himself as he got in the ute and resumed the trip home.

The McBrides were settling into the manager's house at the Pembertons' amid much confusion and laughter. Rooms were shared, and after a tussle over which of the ten-year-old twin girls got the top bunk, relative peace reigned. Abigail, who was twenty, had the single bed in the room with the bunks for Shirley and Colleen. Brian, the three-year-old, had his cot in with teenage Kevin. Gwen McBride pulled down the heavy faded cotton curtains and left their bedroom window bare so she and Bob could lie in bed and look at the paddocks and the stand of trees in the distance.

'No one's going to be snooping around here peeping in windows, so what's the point,' she smiled.

'Sun'll wake us up,' grumbled Bob, only half serious. He was up at sunrise most mornings anyway.

Sarah and Keith Pemberton had welcomed them warmly, offering to lend any supplies or gear until they were settled. 'There's plenty of linen, china, cutlery, kitchen utensils and so forth on hand. You know how you keep accumulating stuff,' Sarah Pemberton told Gwen, who had never been in one place long enough to acquire more than very basic necessities.

The children were gone at daylight exploring their new domain. Rules were established about letting young Brian get anywhere near the dam in the top home paddock.

'Too far for him to walk,' said Kevin.

'Listen, he's stowed away in the back of a truck or on a tractor before today,' their father reminded them.

The twins found an overgrown kitchen garden which they commandeered as their own, promising to keep it weeded and watered. Their father warned them not to repeat an earlier habit of pulling up quarter-grown carrots and potatoes to see how they were coming along. The twins scoffed at him. 'We know how to grow things *now*, Daddy,' they insisted.

As Abigail helped her mother unpack and sort things out, she wondered whether she'd be able to find work in the area. She'd done her St John Ambulance course and had worked as a hospital aide. She had been a general office hand in a seed and grain store, and when not near a town had worked as a hand around the shearing sheds.

Gwen worried about her eldest daughter, wishing they could give her a bit more help to develop a career so she'd have some financial security and be able to buy the things they couldn't afford to give her.

Bob McBride was less concerned. 'She'll make her way. She's bright and pretty and can turn her hand to most things. She'll find a nice bloke soon enough.'

'Not the way we've been moving around,' sighed Gwen.

Abby was aware her parents discussed her future and wondered herself where her life was going, but she wasn't too worried just yet. She really hoped that this time they would be staying longer so she might be able to make friends and even have a social life. She had heard there were a lot of young people in the district and her father had hinted they might be staying on for a fair bit. It was an exciting prospect and Abby already sensed a nice feeling about their latest home and the district.

After two days, Abby took a break from the house, borrowed the small truck her father had for his use, and went exploring some of Anglesea's three thousand acres. She took a sandwich and a bottle of soft drink and drove through several paddocks. Some had been ploughed over and the dark black soil showed a build-up of years of topsoil being washed down in floods. Another had been seeded with feed grass which was sprouting in a haze of green clumps. Stolid Hereford and black Angus cattle watched her progress with little interest.

She left the truck in the shade of some gumtrees and walked a mile along the lightly wooded creek until she came upon a perfect swimming hole. Rushing floodwaters had at some time gouged out the side of the bank so that it was now a wide still pool through which the creek flowed. This was no secret find — an old tyre swung on a rope tied to one of the overhanging weeping willows. The dark pool looked cool and inviting, so Abby decided to have a swim before eating her lunch. She peeled off her dress but modestly left on her bra and 'scanties', as her mother called them, even though it was doubtful there was another person for many miles.

The water was cold and felt like pinpricks on her skin. It smelled of disintegrating leaves, sodden twigs and faintly of tea-tree oil — an earthy, not unpleasant tang — and her white skin took on a rusty hue beneath its surface.

She swam around the pool, disturbing several frogs; then, glancing at the tyre, decided to get out and try it. Gingerly she pulled in the rope, put one foot on the tyre and pushed off from the bank with the other. The tyre swung out towards the centre of the creek and as she was about to let go and drop into the deep water, the rotten rope broke with a crack and she plunged unceremoniously into the creek. She came up spluttering and burst out laughing at her stupidity, glad no one had witnessed her ungainly descent into the water.

She sat in the dappled sunlight drying off as she ate her sandwich, her long hair splayed down her back. It felt good to be on her own — a rarity in the McBride family — and for once not to have to set an example to the others.

She pulled her dress back on, laced her sandshoes and started back along the narrow track sheep had made beside the creek. After a while she heard the sound of a horse. She stopped and saw a dark brown horse cantering through the trees towards the creek. As she watched, the horse turned on to the track and slowed to a walk as the rider saw her.

Barney Holten pulled up the horse, touched his hat and grinned down at Abby.

'Hello there. How was the swim?'

Abby had been shyly waiting to see who it was, prepared to chat for a minute or two. But at the sight of the handsome young man with faintly amused eyes, a cheeky grin and a well-bred voice, she was overcome with embarrassment and blushed deeply. He must have seen her cavorting in her underwear in the creek. She lowered her eyes and started to stammer then simply turned and fled to the safety of the truck. She quickly got in, started it, jumped the clutch, started again and drove away as fast as she safely could, still cringing at the memory of those dancing grey-green eyes.

Barney stared after her, quite flabbergasted. What had he said to make her take off like a startled rabbit? He'd merely assumed from her wet hair streaming down her back and leaving a dark damp patch on her dress that she'd been at the old swimming hole. Did she have a guilty conscience over something? She could scarcely have been trespassing way out here. He nudged the horse forward to the Pembertons' but the image of the girl stayed with him.

Barney found Keith Pemberton by the machinery shed, then dismounted and shook Keith's hand.

'G'day, Mr Pemberton. Dad tell you I was coming over?'

'Yeah, he rang a while ago. You made good time.'

'I took the shortcut across the ridge and along the creek,' said Barney.

'So, you want to talk to McBride. He seems a good worker, good references, affable bloke. Decent shearer, I hear. I've hired my team and frankly I don't want to rock the boat by taking on an outsider. Some outfits get a bit narky.'

'Well, that suits us if he's available — we could do with another hand in the shed... that is if it doesn't interfere with what he's doing for you.'

'I've hired him long term so we can work something out for a couple of weeks during shearing. He's settled in with his family. Quite a crew of them.' The grazier pushed back his hat and smiled. 'It's like Muldoon's picnic down at the old house now.'

'I ran into a girl down by the creek, suppose she was one of them. I didn't get a chance to talk to her. Took off like a scared rabbit,' grinned Barney. 'Pretty she was, too.'

'Not like the girls to run away from you, Barn,' replied Keith Pemberton with a half-smile. 'That was probably the oldest girl. Sarah had them all up for tea. Anyway, you'll find McBride — Bob — down at the boundary dam. He reckons he can fix that dicky pump. Tell him you've spoken to me. Give my regards to your father.'

Barney thanked him, remounted his horse and went to the dam close to the boundary with Amba.

Barney greeted Bob McBride, who once again was oil-stained and wielding a spanner. 'I'm not officially a mechanic, but you always seem to catch me at it, don't you?' he said, grinning.

Briefly, Barney explained that he'd spoken to Keith Pemberton, who'd cleared the way for the Holtens to offer McBride some shearing if he was interested.

Bob McBride straightened up. 'Well yeah, that'd be good. I'm a better shearer than I am mechanic. When do you need me?'

'More or less straightaway. We've almost finished mustering. The other three fellows are arriving tomorrow night.'

'I'll finish up the urgent stuff here tomorrow then. How many you got?'

'Ten thousand. That's why we'd appreciate another hand. And seeing as you're right next door, it could work out well. Of course, you're welcome to stay in the shearers' quarters with the others if —'

'Not likely. Not when I can sleep in my own bed.' He paused then smiled. 'Besides, the tribe would miss me.'

'Well, that's settled then.' Barney held out his hand. 'You'll meet my father when you come over. By the way, how many in the tribe?'

Bob McBride acknowledged Barney's grin with a big smile. 'Enough...enough to give every day a few laughs.'

At the end of the day, after he'd cleaned up, McBride found Pemberton and thanked him for the opportunity to do some shearing.

'I'll still keep an eye on things here, never fear. So will Gwen. Holten seems a nice young fellow. He's the oldest son, I take it?' McBride knew the tradition of the owner's eldest son working beside his father.

'No, the only one,' replied Pemberton.

'No girls?'

'No.'

McBride took the hint and didn't pry further.

'By the way,' said Pemberton, changing the subject, 'do your girls want some fowls? Ran into a bloke in town who had a crate of chickens.'

'They'd like that for sure. The eggs would be handy too. Gwen bakes stuff.'

'Send someone up to collect them then. Mrs Pemberton has them round the back of the kitchen somewhere.'

McBride ambled back to the cottage where smoke was rising from the chimney. The smell of a freshly baked cake wafted from the kitchen, and the twins were taking turns pushing young Brian on the newly erected swing under the mulberry tree. Abby was sitting on the back steps with her chin in her hands, watching them.

'Howdy, gang. Where's Kev?'

'Chopping kindling for Mum,' said Abby. 'You look pleased with yourself, Dad.'

'Move over.' He squeezed onto the old weather-etched wooden step beside her and dropped an arm about her shoulders. 'Like it here? I know there's not much for you to do, work like, but help your mum for a bit and I'm sure something will come along.' He gave her a slight squeeze.

Abby smiled fondly at him. 'It is nice here. Mum really likes it. Once the kids are in school, I'll start looking around. Don't worry about me, Dad.'

'You're a good girl, Ab. You always go along with things. Don't always put yourself last though, luv. You have to think of yourself occasionally.'

'I will if I need to, Dad.'

'So what did you do today then?'

'I went exploring. Went up the creek a bit. There's a nice swimming hole . . .' Abby stopped, cringing inside a little as she imagined that boy, or rather man, sitting on his horse and watching her antics. What a baby, what a silly fool he must think her. Then, as she thought about it, she realised he'd probably been spying on her. Hoping she was going skinny-dipping she supposed.

'Hey, what are you thinking about, sweetie? You look mad as a hornet. You got a problem?'

'Oh no. I saw a fellow go by on a horse while I was down there. He gave me a bit of start that's all.'

'Oh, that'd be Barney Holten. He came over to see me actually.'

Abby bristled. 'What for? Who is he?'

'His dad runs Amba next door. They've offered me some shearing work. Pay'll be good. Haven't told your mum yet.'

'What about your job here at Anglesea?' Abby looked worried at the thought.

'Don't worry, luv. Mr Pemberton has given me the okay to work at Amba until shearing is finished. Very good of him.'

'He's figured out you're a good man to keep about the place, Dad,' said Abby affectionately. She knew her father could turn his hand to all manner of work and he'd just been a bit unlucky with the way so many of the jobs had tailed off, forcing the family to keep on the move. She admired her mother so much for the stoic and good-humoured way she supported their father. The way she stuck by him no matter what and rarely complained. Wherever they were, there was a loving, happy and stable environment. She hoped that one day she would find a husband who would inspire such loyalty and devotion.

Bob McBride got to his feet. 'I'd better go find your mother and tell her the news. Something smells good, eh?' He looked over his shoulder. 'By the way, we've got a bunch of fowls to add to the family. You'll have to help me build a chook pen, okay?'

Abby clapped her hands together. 'Oh great, the kids will love that.'

Bob McBride turned indoors, a contented man.

CHAPTER FOUR

THE SHEARING SHED WAS EIGHTY YEARS OLD. Great grey walls of rough timber supported a high, peaked, rusting corrugated-iron roof. Inside, the floorboards had a patina of age, oil, and hard use. Smooth pillars of tree trunks supported the soaring roof. The board had four shearing stands, a small pen with bat-wing doors behind each. Chutes ran into the outside pens. The big solid wool-classing tables smelled of lanolin, and the wool press was an antique contraption but it did the job of compacting the wool into hessian packs.

The shed was high enough off the ground to

push sheep beneath it in case of rain during shearing. Most of the year it was empty and unused, except by nesting swallows and sparrows. But now it throbbed with life and energy. Voices rang out over the buzz of the shears and the bleating and rattle of hooves as shorn sheep were pushed down the chute to stand dazed and denuded in the pen. It was hard and sweaty work.

The metallic clanging of an iron bar on a plough disc brought the activity to a standstill. As each sheep was finished, the shearers straightened and headed to their quarters for a lunch prepared by the team's cook.

Bob McBride stretched and rubbed his back as he walked to the enamel dish of water outside the quarters. He washed his hands, face and arms with the Solvol soap, took off his old sweat-stained felt hat, held it under the water, then plonked it on his head. The water ran down the sinews of his neck, making dark stains on his navy singlet. Refreshed, he joined the others at the long bare table. Despite the heat, a steaming shepherd's pie, pumpkin and peas were heaped onto plates and liberally doused with gravy. Thick slices of bread and butter mopped up the plates as the cook brought out tinned peaches and custard. The men lit up cigarettes as the large tin pot of tea was passed around to refill mugs.

Barney Holten appeared and poured himself a mug of the tea. 'How's it going?' he asked.

'We're a rouseabout short in there. That boy you organised didn't show,' announced one of the men.

'Yeah, we need a kid in there to give a bit of a hand. Any chance of digging one up? Like by tomorrow?'

'I'll see what I can do,' promised Barney.

As the men headed back to the shearing, Barney fell into step beside Bob McBride. 'You haven't got a strapping son in your family, have you?' asked Barney.

'To work in the shed?'

Barney nodded.

McBride flicked his cigarette into the dust. 'No, but I do have a hardworking daughter though. Abby has worked in sheds before. She'd be happy to take it on if the blokes don't mind.'

Barney hesitated. He didn't know anyone else who could come at such short notice. If she'd worked in a shearing shed before, she wouldn't be fazed by the men and would know what to do. The last thing they wanted was a useless girl around the place. 'Righto, I'll ask her if she's interested.'

Abby took the utility truck to the Pembertons' and a couple of sacks to put the fowls in, and Kevin went along to lend a hand.

Mrs Pemberton led them down to where the birds were in temporary residence in a small pen. 'They're mostly bantams, a few Australorps and a couple of roosters,' she said, pointing to the mixed group peering anxiously through the wire mesh.

'What's that big brown thing?' asked Kevin.

'Oh, that's a bronzewing turkey. He's still only a teenager but he's five times the size of his little mother. Apparently he was hatched by that white bantam. From what I've observed, she doesn't want a thing to do with the great big freaky son she's produced,' laughed Sarah Pemberton. 'When you're done, come and have a cool drink.'

Kevin squeezed into the pen and eagerly cornered each bird as it shrieked and fluttered. Abby tied their feet together, dropping them into the bag. 'Why bother tying their legs, Abby? It's not far back to our place,' said Kevin, pouncing gleefully on the last rooster. 'Gotcha,' he hissed triumphantly.

'The spurs on their legs could rip into each other if they fight or panic,' explained Abby. 'This is safer.'

A short time later, Abby and Kevin appeared at the Pembertons' kitchen door and were invited inside, where glasses of cordial and slices of fruit-cake were set on the table. 'Help yourselves. So, are you settled in all right down there?'

'Yes thanks, Mrs Pemberton. We really like it here,' said Abby with genuine warmth. 'The kids start school next week and I'll be looking for work. You don't know of anything going in town, do you?'

'No, dear. But I'm sure you won't have too much trouble.' She was thinking what a pleasant girl Abby was. 'What sort of work are you looking for?'

'Anything really. I've done a lot of different things.'

'You saving up for a trip overseas, or just your nest-egg?'

'Oh gosh no, nothing like that. I just want to help out at home. I've never thought of travelling overseas,' said Abby. Then, in case she was thought unsophisticated, she added quickly and brightly, 'Maybe one day after I'm married.'

'A honeymoon trip,' smiled Sarah.

'Yes. That would be lovely.' Abby suddenly noticed Kevin surreptitiously reaching for another slice of cake. 'Kev, ask Mrs Pemberton if you can have a second piece!'

Kevin snatched his hand away in embarrassment as Abby and Mrs Pemberton laughed.

'It is awfully nice cake,' said Abby.

'It's a bought one, I'm afraid. I didn't have time to bake this week — not that I'm much of a baker.

Help yourself, Kevin. Now, do you have chicken feed? No? Well, take some of our grain with you to get your lot settled in.'

Back at home in the makeshift chicken coop, they untied the sacks and began taking out the chooks, cutting the string around their feet. As Abby held an irate rooster, Kevin struggled with his blunt knife to cut the string. Then suddenly let out a cry. The turkey had wiggled his way out of the bag and, with a nasal squeak, had spread his magnificent wings, taking flight despite his bound legs.

'Oh dear, watch the others, Kev, I'll get the turkey.' Abby took off after the wildly flapping bird that was cruising at an altitude of three feet above ground level. About every ten yards the turkey made crash landings but just as Abby reached out to grab it, it made another floundering takeoff.

'Come back, Tom Turkey, you stupid creature!' shouted Abby in frustration.

Across the paddock the turkey hiccupped from ground to air with Abby in stumbling pursuit. She was desperate to catch the poor creature, afraid if it got away it would never survive with the handicap of its feet tied together.

Then into its shuddering flight-path loomed the small dam and the turkey landed in it with a skidding splash. Flapping its wings, the turkey just managed to stay afloat, but as it became water-logged, under it went.

Abby reached the edge of the dam on the run and launched herself with a magnificent bellyflop onto the spot where the bird had landed. Wildly reaching under the muddy water, she felt the bird and hauled it to the surface, staggering to her feet in the murky shallows.

'Got you, you crazy bird!'

Tucking the dripping turkey beneath her arm, she struggled from the water. Her cotton slacks and blouse were soaked and glued to her body; her ponytail dripped over her shoulder, and when she rubbed the water from her eyes, it left a muddy streak down her face.

As she trudged from the dam, the sound of an approaching car made her pause. As it drew up to her, she stopped and saw Barney Holten grinning through the windscreen.

He leaned out of the window. 'That was a good catch.'

'How come every time I get in the water you're spying on me?' she demanded.

'I've never spied on you...I just saw you taking off across the paddock here...' Barney suddenly stopped and flushed. 'When I saw you on the track by the creek, I just assumed you'd been swimming. I didn't actually see you in the water.'

'Assumed?' said Abby archly.

'Well yes, you were coming from the direction of the swimming hole and your hair was wet. Or were you diving for birds then too?'

Abby looked down, realising she had misjudged him.

'Er, do you mind if I ask how come the turkey was in the dam?' he asked.

Abby smiled slightly. 'It was the one that nearly got away. Its feet are tied up because I just got it from the Pembertons. It actually thinks it's a bantam,' she grinned.

'And a duck,' said Barney, flashing a big smile. 'Look, you're Abigail, aren't you? I was coming over to see you. I spoke to your father a little while ago. I'm Barney Holten from Amba.'

'I know. Dad's shearing for you.'

'Yes, that's right. Well, we're short a rouseabout in the shed and your father suggested you might be interested in the job. You know, sweeping up the boards, the locks and bags, the loose wool, helping with the fleeces, getting the sheep into the pens and . . .'

'I know what's involved,' said Abby. 'I've worked around sheds before.'

'So would you be interested? I need someone to start as soon as possible. I'll pay you the same as the other fellow who's helping.'

Abby was uncomfortable at being offered a job while she stood there dirty, wet and clutching a bedraggled turkey, but she knew it would be good money for at least two weeks.

'All right, I'll get cleaned up and be over this afternoon.'

'No need to rush, the day is about finished. Start first thing tomorrow. And good luck with that turkey, hope he lasts till Christmas!' Chuckling, Barney drove off.

Abby watched the car disappear in a cloud of dust, then headed back to the coop where Kevin and the twins were scattering grain amongst the still ruffled chooks.

Abby turned up early the next morning dressed appropriately in old overalls and boots, her hair tied back and no lipstick on. Her father introduced her to the men and, without any fuss, she set to work sweeping up and running around with the red antiseptic paint to dab on the occasional cut from a careless nick with a blade. She knew how to be unobtrusive, quick and quiet. She was used to handling sheep and when she was told to put another dozen from the yard into the pen, she did so without drama.

She sat quietly next to her dad at morning tea, tucking into the sweet tea and lamingtons. Later, she helped the wool presser and asked the wool classer about the different wools and properties he'd worked. At the end of the day, driving home with her father, she was exhausted.

When they arrived at the house, Gwen was there to greet them. 'The chip heater is going like a steam train. Off you go and have a good old soak, Abby.'

'Oh, lovely. Thanks, Mum.'

'How'd she do?' asked Gwen, slipping her arm around her husband's waist.

'Good. She's a great little worker. Doesn't make any fuss. The blokes said she was a nice kid. She'll be fine. Now, what about a bit of a back-rub? I always forget shearing is another word for backache.'

Over the next ten days, Barney worked close to the shed, branding, bringing in sheep and sending out the finished ones to other paddocks. The shed was his responsibility, although his father did come down once to inspect some of the fleeces. He asked the wool classer several questions, nodded curtly to the men, who glanced cautiously at him, then left.

As he went about the place, Barney found himself subtly observing Abby at every opportunity. She was unobtrusive but she intrigued him.

He thought she was more than pretty — she exuded a sweetness, a naturalness, which he found entrancing.

She seemed in some ways younger than she was, being unspoiled and unsophisticated; yet compared to some of the other girls he knew, she was far more mature. She had a strength about her and an obvious sense of responsibility.

Barney watched her work around the shed and saw she didn't shirk hard labour. Once he'd watched her struggle with a stubborn sheep and as she'd finally dragged it towards the pen, he'd hopped over the railing and helped her lift it.

'Thanks. That's a big one. Weighs a ton,' Abby had panted gratefully.

He'd been tempted to tell her not to lift heavy things, but thought better of such a personal remark. She was smart enough to know her limitations, he figured. Her smile had been thanks enough and he'd hummed as he'd gone about his own work.

Out of Abby's earshot the men made a few jesting remarks to McBride about the boss visiting more than normal and always stopping to have a word with Abby. Bob knew they were only joking, but their comments worried him. So one evening, on the way home, he broached the subject.

'Young Holten seems to go out of his way to have a few words with you. I know you haven't led him on at all, Abby, but . . . well, watch it. We don't want to cause any talk.'

'Dad! I haven't said boo to him! If he stops to say something, I can't be rude and ignore him, can I?'

'No, of course not, Ab. But you did say he'd spotted you about the place before this. I just don't want you to get led up the garden path. You are close at hand, so to speak; not to mention being the prettiest girl in the State as well.'

'I can look after myself, Dad. I did think he'd been spying on me one day when I went swimming, but I was mistaken. He seems all right. Anyway, let's face it, he's not going to ask someone like me out.'

'Well, not in public,' said her father bluntly. 'Just keep your distance.'

'Oh I am, don't worry.'

Bob McBride patted her knee. 'You'll find a nice young fella soon enough. When you get your pay from this job, why don't you and your mum go into town and you treat yourself to a new frock? Something pretty you can wear to a dance. There'll be plenty of dances coming up. And once the boys catch sight of you, you'll have more beaus than you'll know how to handle.'

Abby laughed and lifted her chin in mock arrogance. 'I can handle 'em, Dad; just let me at them!'

They laughed and Bob broke into song as the old truck bounced along the rutted road — *'I'm looking over a four-leafed clover that I overlooked before . . .'*

But Abby was silent as her father sang, thinking over what he'd said. She knew he was right, yet it had never occurred to her that someone like Barney Holten would be interested in her. She'd heard stories before of rich boys who fooled around with the girls in town or girls who worked on their properties fruit picking, girls her mother described as common. These were not the girls they married — they married from their own class — and while they might have a few laughs and a bit of a fling, everyone knew the unwritten rules. Abby, however, was not going to be one of the goodtime girls the ladies loved to gossip about at tea parties.

Once or twice when they'd been living close to a town, her mother had gone to teas and once to a card party. She'd come home after one occasion, pulled out her hatpin, held her hat up as a shield and pretended to fence with the long pearl-handled pin, jabbing and lunging at imaginary opponents in the kitchen.

'And then she said, that Mabel Clarkson is being such a snob.' Jab, jab. 'And did you hear Tom Ogilvy had a drinking problem they say?' Dart, lunge. 'Of course those clothes of Betty Smith's all come from the Red Cross.' Joust, score, point!

The children, seated around the table, had laughed and clapped as she fell into a chair fanning herself with her hat. 'That's it, I'm not going to another one of those dreadful hens' parties.'

Talk was big time in a small town where the trivial assumed unnatural proportions, and Abby had observed and learned that what caused most gossip was the overstepping of one's 'place'. There were status levels that, while never called class, existed in rigid and long-established rules. Income, job, family background, all dictated one's level in the hierarchy and the barriers were strictly observed, each sticking to 'their own'. So there was no way Abby was going to take any notice of Barney Holten other than observing the social niceties. He was out of her class — her father was working for him after all.

When the shearing was over, Barney went in search of his mother. He found her in the cool dimness of the sitting-room, the lightweight curtain linings drawn against the sunlight. Diet and

Tucker were curled around her footstool and she was absorbed in her crewel work, using the light from the fringe-shaded standard lamp behind the settee.

'Mother . . .?'

'Yes, dear?' She didn't look up and frowned slightly at an unaligned pink stitch in the rose petal she was working on.

'We'll be finished shearing tomorrow.'

'That's nice, dear.'

'I was thinking it might be nice to have cut-out drinks and a bit of a barbecue for everybody before they leave.'

Enid looked up in surprise. 'You mean, like a *party*? For the *workers*? Whatever for, dear. They're being paid, aren't they?'

Barney was defensive. 'Nothing fancy. They've got through quicker than we thought.'

'Dear me, ask your father. I wouldn't have to go to it, would I? I mean, the shearer's cook is still on the payroll, isn't he?' Enid looked distressed.

'Don't worry about it, Mum. I'll handle it. I just thought . . . Oh, never mind.' Barney headed for the kitchen where Mrs Anderson was pulling bread from the oven. Jim Anderson was sitting at the small table, his hat resting beside his mug of tea.

'G'day, Barney. Join us for smoko?' He rose to his feet, reaching for an extra mug that hung on hooks along the mantelpiece above the stove.

'Don't mind if I do. Any cake, Mrs Anderson?'

'Under the flymesh cloth on the table there. Only a pound cake,' she answered as she banged the loaf pans onto the side of the fuel stove.

Barney poured milk from the blue-and-white-striped jug into his tea. 'I thought I'd have a cut-out barbecue tomorrow before everyone leaves,' said Barney, and the Andersons looked at him in surprise. 'Would you make a cake, Mrs A? The cook will do everything else.'

'Of course I will. I'll do two big fruitcakes.'

'You're both welcome to come down, of course. Nothing fancy, a few steaks and chops and drinks.'

'Thanks, that'd be nice.' Jim Anderson drained his tea. 'Good clip this season?'

'Yes. The wool classer reckons we'll get a good price for it. Just hope the market stays up. Well, I'll be off, got a few things to see to.' As Barney went out of the screen door, Rene and Jim Anderson exchanged a glance with raised eyebrows.

'We have never had a cut-out affair before,' said Phillip Holten sternly. 'It is quite unnecessary. Pay them off and let them cut out and go into the pub in town.'

'Oh, I'm sure they'll do that too,' said Barney. 'I just thought as I've been so involved with them all, I'd like to make the gesture. Just a few beers and a barbecue.'

'Barnard, just because this is the first time I've allowed you a free hand to manage the shearing doesn't mean you owe these men anything. You did them a favour in hiring them.'

'They didn't have to work as hard and as fast as they did.' Barney knew dissension among shearers, dissatisfied with conditions, could create havoc in the shed. 'And it makes it easier to get a good team back next year. They talk amongst themselves, you know.' Barney had heard the talk and knew the men had their own blacklist of properties and owners.

'Very well then. But it's your show. I might put in an appearance, but that's all. And while I'm still head of Amba I'd appreciate it if you ran your ideas past me first.' He turned and strode towards the library.

Enid heard the exchange between her husband and her son, and she felt her heart constrict with sadness.

She walked onto the verandah, her heart beating erratically, and stood there watching the dogs sniff around on the grass as the dusk crept in. The confrontation between Barney and Phillip troubled her enough to penetrate the veil of vagueness that usually kept her from seeing the world too clearly. When Barney asserted himself, Phillip regarded it as a challenge to his authority. If Barney flowed along without making waves or taking any initiatives, Phillip criticised him for being weak. She knew, and with a pang realised Barney also knew, that he would never measure up in Phillip's eyes. The bitterness and resentment Phillip felt, quite unreasonably, towards his son had coloured and clouded their relationship. And it was her fault.

Phillip's dissatisfaction with his marriage had been transferred to his son. Images of the past she tried so hard to ignore came flooding back. The pretty young woman she'd once been who'd fallen in love with her schoolfriend's brother. The passionate romance, the First World War, their engagement, his enlistment and departure. Then the news of his death near Damascus with the Light Horse. She shivered, not because of the coolness of dusk, but because the pain returned to rack her thin frame. She struggled for another deep breath, trying to control her irregular heart-beat as another series of flashing pictures reeled through her mind . . . the Sydney Show, the intro-duction by mutual friends to the handsome and wealthy grazier, Phillip's persistent if somewhat stodgy courtship, and the recognition of a safe escape from grief and insecurity.

It was nearly dark when Enid called the dogs back to her. The strange beating of her heart made her feel a little nauseated. Phillip was right, she told herself, they must not put off too much longer going to Sydney to see a specialist.

She turned and walked indoors, the two white shadows at her heels, their nails clicking on the polished wood floor. As she passed the library, she paused and looked in. Phillip was in his usual leather chair reading his Stanley Gibbons catalogue, spectacles perched on the edge of his nose.

Phillip noticed his wife out of the corner of his eye but did not acknowledge her presence. He listened to her walking down the hall, following the steps into the kitchen. God, she was becoming hard to live with! Ever since her heart murmur had been detected by a very worried local doctor, she had become increasingly vague.

Phillip walked to the sideboard and poured himself a port from the crystal decanter and returned to his chair. He sipped his drink and put his head back, staring into the darkness of the high wood-panelled ceiling. The doctor had said the trouble began with the strain Barney's birth put on her heart. It was an unexpected and difficult pregnancy, and a harrowing birth — a miracle of survival was how the doctor had put it because it had nearly killed both mother and child.

Well, the child had grown into a stout lad, but his mother had never recovered fully. In a way, neither had Phillip. He never quite got over the resentment of a child whose birth had taken away the wife he loved, leaving a woman obsessed with tending a baby that nearly killed her. He had hoped that things would change when Barney was sent to boarding school, but Enid had retreated further into her own little world.

Phillip wished he could relate better to his son, but somehow his resentment could never allow him to get too close. He felt his son had robbed him of his wife.

Phillip Holten finished off the port and walked out of the French doors of the library onto the verandah. He leaned on the railing and looked up into the sky with its eggshell moon and profusion of stars, searching for the answer to a question he often asked the heavens. 'How can a family lose itself like this? Is there a way to connect with each other again?' He never heard an answer.

CHAPTER FIVE

GWEN PULLED THE STEW OFF THE STOVE AND SET it to one side. The long kitchen table had been laid by the twins, with everybody's plate in place save for Bob's and Abby's. The tablecloth was blue-and-yellow-check oilcloth, thick and easy to wipe clean. In the middle of the table sat a large bottle of Rosella tomato sauce, a bottle of Holbrooks Worcestershire sauce, pepper and salt shakers that looked like little lighthouses — 'A Souvenir of the South Coast' — a slab of butter on a plate, a pile of thick slices of milk loaf, and a pot of homemade mulberry jam.

'Kevin, go and get the twins inside for their

bath while I get Brian out,' sighed Gwen, already missing Abby who normally bathed little Brian and got him ready for bed.

She hurried through the house to the bathroom, hoping Abby was having a good time with her dad at the cut-out barbecue. Maybe there was a nice young shearer there she'd make friends with. Not that she'd wish the life of a shearer's wife on her daughter. At least with Abby in tow, Bob wouldn't be tempted to go into town to the pub with the others. Gwen knew what the men were like once they got a few quid in their kick. Bob had never blown a pay cheque the way some of the men had, but in his younger days he hadn't said no to a drink or two. Gwen knew he'd have a few beers and bring Abby home safely.

It was nice for them to be out together like this, she thought, for soon enough Kevin then Brian would be out with their dad, and hopefully Abby would have a man and a life of her own. Father and daughter would treasure these times.

Once in the bathroom, she picked up the worn enamel saucepan from out of the bath and poured a panful over Brian's soapy head.

'Okey dokey, out we get.' She lifted him over the edge of the old tin tub onto the floor mat and wrapped him in a towel. She staggered slightly as she lifted the chubby child. 'My, you are getting a big boy. Almost too heavy for Mummy to pick up.'

'Where Abby?'

'She's at a party, darling. With Daddy. They'll be home soon. But *we* are going to have a party of our own.'

Outside, the twins were nowhere to be seen. Then Kevin heard their muffled squeals coming from the back of the water tank where they'd set up their little garden. There he found Shirley and Colleen running about the edge of their garden bed, flapping their arms and chanting, 'Shoo, shoo!'

'Quick, Kev, help us! The chooks got out and they're digging up our plants,' wailed Colleen.

Kevin lunged and clapped his hands at the merrily digging hens and rooster. Tom Turkey flew up to perch on the tank stand and, with a startled screech and whirr of wings, the rest scattered from the garden bed across the straggly grass lawn.

'Don't frighten them! Now look what you've done!' Shirley began to run after them, sending them in all directions, a rooster crowing in alarm.

'Come back, stop chasing them, you're frightening them,' called Kevin. 'They'll come back. Come inside. Mum says to have your bath.'

'We can't leave them out, it's getting dark.' Colleen looked worried.

'Leave them alone. Leave the coop door open and they'll find their way back inside.'

'Do you think so?' asked Shirley.

Kevin looked at his twin sisters, their almost identical blue eyes looking trustingly up at him. He grinned. 'Yeah. Take my word for it. They'll all be there in the morning.'

Brown-haired Colleen and fair-haired Shirley walked beside their teenage brother, comforted by his know-it-all voice.

'Why do we have to lock them up at night anyway?'

'Well, you sleep in a house, don't you?' Colleen said to her twin.

'There could be a fox or a dingo or a cat about that would grab them. Or a big bad wolf!' teased Kevin, pretending to grab them both. Squealing and laughing, the girls took off as he chased them, growling and calling, 'Who's afraid of the big bad wolf...?'

They thundered into the house and the girls fled to the bathroom, slamming the door as Kevin began, 'I'll huff and I'll puff and I'll blowwww your house down...'

'*Kevin*, stop that racket and come and help in here please,' Gwen shouted from the kitchen where she was lifting a saucepan of milk, which had boiled over, off the stove. Brian was perched on a cushion on his chair eating a chunk of bread. 'Wash your hands, I'm about to dish up.'

'I can't, the girls are in the bathroom.'

'Use the laundry; but before you do bring in some more wood, please.'

Eventually, after much toing and froing, they were all seated at the table, Brian and the twins in their pyjamas, all with shiny scrubbed faces.

Gwen brought the big pot of stew to the table and put it down on a bread board; then she clasped her hands and looked around the family. They all recognised Mum's 'announcement' pose.

'Dad and Abby are having a party at the shearing shed, so we'll have a party too. I have a little surprise.'

She went to a kitchen cupboard and got out a pile of paper hats shaped like boats, made from coloured pages of the *Women's Mirror*. They were handed around to squeals of delight from the children, though Kevin disguised his feeling of awkwardness as he put his hat on.

'What's the party in aid of, Mum?' he asked with genuine curiosity.

'Our good fortune, Kev. Our good fortune.' She smiled and ladled out the meat and vegetable stew thickened with barley.

Brian picked up his spoon and echoed happily, 'Party!'

They all laughed and Gwen wondered how the other party was progressing.

The cook was passing around seconds of the steak, chops and sausages. The Andersons had joined the shearing team at the table and were handing round a roasting pan piled with baked pumpkin and potatoes. Barney put another couple of bottles of draught beer on the table and glasses were topped up.

'How about you, Abby?' asked the shearer beside her. 'Want a beer instead of that lemonade?'

'No thanks,' she smiled.

'Would you like a shandy, luv?' asked her father, who was sitting opposite.

Abby shook her head. 'I'm supposed to keep a clear head to drive home, remember.'

'Thanks for helping out,' said Barney, slipping onto the end of the bench next to Abby.

'I was glad of the work. Now I have to find a proper job.'

Barney nodded and raised his glass. 'Here's to finding a proper job.'

She acknowledged him with a quick smile and sip of lemonade, stealing a glance at him over the top of her glass.

Barney picked up the conversation across the

table, but he was thinking of the girl beside him. Abby intrigued him and he didn't understand why. They had only talked briefly and while she was certainly attractive, it was a subtle kind of prettiness which crept up on you. He'd found he couldn't help watching her, the way she moved with easy grace. Her voice was soft and musical and it made him want to listen to her tell him all about herself. She was different from other girls he'd known. And it wasn't because of their class. Abby exuded a poise and gentle confidence, despite her more humble background.

He wished he could get to know her better. Obviously she had to help out financially, being the eldest of a big family. It was an imperative that few of his female friends would understand since they came from rural families enjoying boom times; for them, work was an optional way of filling in time until Mr Right turned up. It wasn't considered necessary for girls to have a fancy education. They had to be a good hostess, wife and mother. Still, he had to admit more and more of them were quitting the bush and picking up jobs in the labour-starved cities. Barney turned his attention back to Abby.

'You thinking of heading off to the big smoke too? Seems to be the thing to do these days.'

'Oh, I wouldn't like that. I hate cities, what I've

seen of them. I guess I'm a country girl and always will be. Anyway, it would be odd being away from the family.'

'I prefer the country too. Have you been to the city often?' he asked.

'I had to go down to Sydney two years ago for an operation on my eye. Nothing serious, but it couldn't be done in the country. We were out near Gilgandra at the time. After I got out of hospital, Mum and I looked around Farmers, Mark Foys and Horderns; didn't buy anything, but it was fun to window-shop.'

Barney looked at her sparkling eyes and wondered what had been wrong. She certainly had stunning eyes. He realised that there wouldn't have been much spare money for a shopping spree in Sydney, unlike some of the girls he'd met who were always going on about 'the latest' from Sydney.

'There's certainly a lot more to look at in the shops now compared to when I lived in Sydney. Took a while to get over the war but the country is on a roll now, that's for sure. So tell me where else you've lived. You've probably seen more of the country than I have.'

They chatted comfortably and Abby relaxed, feeling safe in the large group and realising he probably preferred to talk to someone closer to his own age. She'd noticed there was restraint when the men spoke to Barney compared to when they talked amongst themselves. Unlike the others, she didn't regard him as a 'boss' as this job had been a one-off for her and probably for her father too.

Barney finally glanced at his watch. 'Struth, I'd better hand out the money or I'll have a riot on my hands.'

'I doubt it. Everyone seems to be having a good time,' said Abby as Mrs Anderson came over.

'I'm going to bring the cakes and a sweet down now, okay, Barney?'

He nodded and swung his leg over the bench and stood. 'Righto.'

'Do you want a hand, Mrs Anderson?'

'Yes, Abby, that would be nice. Come on.'

As they headed back to the homestead, Barney picked up his jacket and took out envelopes marked with each man's name and began handing them round.

It was only a minute's drive to the house and as the high roof and tall chimneys came into view behind the beautifully landscaped gardens, Abby gulped. 'Oh my, how lovely.'

Mrs Anderson glanced at her, then back to the imposing facade. 'Yes, it is, isn't it? When you live in a place you sort of stop seeing it. Come on round the back, we'll go past her rose garden.'

Inside the kitchen, Abby looked around at the large work area, the benches, the extra table, the high cupboards and the pantry that was as big as a small room. 'My mum would love a kitchen like this. She likes to cook and never has enough room.'

'Is she a good cook?'

'We think so. She likes baking and making jams and pickles. She wins prizes for her cakes.'

'And do you cook?'

'Yes, but I'm not a baker, I'm afraid. Mum says I'm too heavy-handed. Though I always get the job of beating the eggs,' said Abby.

'Well, I'm a pretty average cake maker. But the men always like my fruitcakes. Wait a sec while I go get the cream from the other refrigerator.'

'I'm sure your cakes are delicious,' called Abby, wondering at a kitchen that had two fridges. At their house there wasn't even an ice chest. As she stood gazing at the array of pots and pans, there was a flash of white at her feet, followed quickly by another. She squealed and jumped, then gazed at the small creatures in astonishment. They, in turn, began a frenzied yapping, dancing about on their short legs and pointy feet.

Abby burst out laughing. 'Golly, what sort of mug dogs are you? Who squashed your face?'

She bent down and peered at their pug noses and black raisin eyes. Giggling, she held out a hand and Tucker boldly inched forward in case this was an offer of food. Abby grabbed him and scooped him up before he had a chance to run away. She stood up and held the surprised dog up to her face so they could eyeball each other. Diet continued to yelp around her ankles.

'What do you think you are you doing?'

Abby spun around in shock at the icy voice. Enid Holten stood at the door, a look of horror on her face.

'Who are you? Give me my dog at once.' She advanced on the stunned Abby, who meekly handed over Tucker. Enid bent down and scooped up Diet and swiftly inspected them, then glared at Abby. 'No one touches my dogs. They don't go to strangers,' she said accusingly.

For a minute Abby thought this woman must have thought she was going to throw the two mutts into the cooking pot. 'I'm sorry, they just came in. I've never seen dogs like these before.'

'These are pedigree dogs. They are sensitive and special creatures who are easily upset.'

Abby glanced down at the dogs under each arm, glaring back at her with a similar expression to that of their mistress. Abby had the feeling the two of them were about to poke their tongues out at her.

Thankfully Mrs Anderson came hurrying in with a bowl of whipped cream. 'Oh, Mrs Holten. This is Abigail McBride. She's been working at the shed.'

'Then what is she doing here?'

'I came to help Mrs Anderson take down the dessert for the party,' said Abby soothingly. So this was Barney's mother.

Enid swung around and glared at Mrs Anderson. 'Dessert for the party? I thought the cook was doing everything.'

Mrs Anderson thrust the bowl of cream into Abby's hands and picked up the two cakes. 'Barney asked me to make a cake or two, nothing special. Come along, Abby, don't want to keep them waiting.' She shot Abby a look and Abby headed swiftly for the door.

'Nice to meet you, Mrs Holten.'

'Bring back the leftover cake, Mrs Anderson,' called Enid.

'So she can stuff it into those spoiled little beasts,' muttered Mrs Anderson.

Abby couldn't hold back her giggles. 'Goodness. When they ran into the kitchen I thought they were some sort of monster rats!"

'They're the bane of my life, I tell you. She even has me cook special things for them. I told Jim I had this dream once where they were stuffed with food till they were as fat as a Christmas goose and I roasted the pair of them and took them to the table on a silver salver, lifted the cover and said, "Dinner is served, madam". He thought that was a dreadful thing to dream.'

Abby burst out laughing. 'I didn't think Barney's mother would be like that. For a minute I was a bit scared of her.'

'She isn't normally that feisty. She mostly drifts around in a dream world. Well, come on, let's serve up the cake.'

Back at the barbecue Bob McBride smiled at Abby and slipped an envelope across the table to her. 'Here's your pay, luv.'

'Thanks, Dad.' She slipped the envelope into the pocket of her skirt and ate a piece of cake. Some of the men were moving around, gathering up their gear ready to cut out. They came up to shake hands and said goodbye to Abby, saying she'd been a real help and a breath of fresh air around the shed.

'It was good having a girl around the place, made us watch our p's and q's,' said the boss of the team with a grin.

While her father was saying goodbye and politely refusing invitations to meet the others in town, Abby picked up a pile of dishes and carried them in to the cook. 'It was great. All your meals were, Tommo. I don't know how you keep up with it all.'

'This job's an art, Abby. Specially when you're out on the track and got a limited plant so you have to cook everything in a camp oven and in the coals. I'll let you in on a secret, d'ya know what my nickname used t'be?'

Abby shook her head.

'One Pot Tommo. Cause everything from a cake to a roast came outta one pot!'

'Like the magic pudding!' exclaimed Abby and they both laughed. She went back to the deserted table and opened her pay packet. There was a neatly folded wad of pound notes with the hours worked and the amount tabulated in pencil on a piece of paper. Pinned to it was a new five pound note with another note. *Thanks for helping us when we needed it. Buy yourself something pretty next time you're window shopping. Cheers, Barney Holten.*

Abby gasped in surprise. He must have slipped it in after talking to her about shopping in Sydney. She blushed and put her pay in her pocket; then, curling her fingers around the five pounds, hurried outside.

She waited until she saw Barney shake hands with two men who were about to drive off. He saw her standing in the twilight and came over to her. 'You and your dad setting off now too?'

'Yes. Thank you, it's been a nice dinner. And

thank you, but I can't take this.' She thrust the blue note at him and turned away.

Barney caught her wrist and stuffed the money back in her hand. 'Look, I don't want to embarrass you. You did more than your share. Call it a bonus. Really, I won't take no for an answer.'

Abby didn't want to feel under any obligation to Barney Holten. 'I don't feel right about it. I didn't do anything more than anyone else.' She was looking down, feeling uncomfortable, and was relieved when she heard her father approaching.

'We're all set to go, Ab. Our stuff is in the ute.'

'Hop in, Dad.' She turned away, not looking at Barney. 'Goodbye. Thanks again.'

Barney stopped Bob McBride. 'You have a stubborn girl there, Mr McBride. I gave her a bonus and she won't take it. Here, put this away for her.' He handed the five pound note to him.

Bob McBride glanced at the money and at Abby. 'You got your right pay, luv?'

'Yes, Dad. I didn't do anything extra. Really.'

'Then if you don't feel you've earned it, don't keep it.' He handed the money back to Barney. 'We appreciate the gesture. Thanks.'

Barney nodded, suddenly aware he had made Abby feel beholden or had somehow demeaned her, and he regretted it. 'I just wanted to say thanks. I appreciated her pitching in at short notice,' he said softly.

'A handshake's all the thanks that's needed,' replied Bob McBride. He shook Barney's hand. 'Be seeing you round no doubt.' He strode over to the ute.

Abby glanced up apologetically at Barney. She hadn't wanted to embarrass him. She held out her hand and he shook it looking again into her wide eyes.

'Thank you,' he said.

Abby smiled at him and gently drew her hand from his. 'Thank you. See you again.' She hurried after her father and didn't hear Barney's soft response.

'I hope so.'

Abby's father nodded off to sleep as she drove home. She wished Barney Holten hadn't offered her that extra money — though it would have been nice to give it to her mother — because it had spoiled the ease she'd felt when talking to him. Suddenly, instead of being two young people simply chatting together, he had reinforced his position as the wealthy one, able to dispense favours. For a moment she was angry with him, thinking he was trying to buy his way into her good graces. Then she laughed at herself. Who do you think you are, Abigail McBride? As if Barney

Holten would even want to go to that much trouble. He probably felt he only had to snap his fingers and she'd come running. Well, he was wrong on that score. Sensibly she realised he had probably felt a bit sorry for her and figured with such a large family and her looking for work, extra money would be welcome. Now she was angry with herself. She should have kept the money. 'Oh well,' she sighed aloud as she turned towards the house.

The dog leapt to his feet, rattling his chain against the little tin humpy, but he didn't bark as he recognised the ute.

'Wake up, Dad, we're here.'

Bob McBride stretched, then peered into the darkness. 'What's that, Abby? That light over there?'

'Where, Dad ?'

'By the tank. I could swear I saw a light.'

'You're seeing min min lights, Dad.' She turned off the ignition. Lights glowed from inside the house and all was silent in the yard. Then Abby saw it too. A quick flash of light. They both got quietly out and walked towards the plump silhouette of the water tank. Rounding the corner, they stopped. Two small figures in white were on their hands and knees shining a torch into the chicken coop.

'What are you up to?' asked Bob McBride loudly.

'Eek!'

'Oo-er!'

The twins jumped to their feet, stumbling over their nighties, Colleen hiding the torch behind her back. 'You scared us,' she said.

'You gave us a bit of a start too,' said Abby. 'What are you doing with the chooks?'

'We just wanted to make sure they were there,' said Shirley. 'They got out when we were feeding them.'

'Kev said if we left the coop open they'd go in.'

'And are they in?' grinned their father.

The girls broke into large smiles. 'Yep.'

'Well, let's get you girls back inside. Does Mum know you're out here?'

'No, we climbed out the window,' said Shirley, and Colleen punched her in the ribs for giving away their secret.

'Okey-dokey. Abby, you take one, I'll get the other and we'll smuggle 'em back inside.' Bob McBride bent down and Colleen leapt onto his back as Shirley hoisted herself onto Abby. Abby grasped Shirley under the knees, lifted her up higher on her back, and set off. Their father galloped ahead with Colleen clinging on as he piggybacked her to the bedroom window, trailed by Abby with Shirley. Panting, they tipped the giggling girls through the window onto the bed beneath.

Gwen looked up from her mending as Abby and her father strolled in, arms linked, smiling broadly. 'You two look like you've had a good time.'

'We have.' Bob reached into his shirt and dropped his unopened pay packet into her lap. 'There you go, luv.' He kissed the top of her head. Gwen smiled up at him. 'Anyone for a cup of tea?'

'I will, Mum. I'll put the kettle on,' said Abby.

'Think I'll go get cleaned up,' said Bob. He yawned and headed for the bathroom.

'He'll be out like a light in five minutes flat, Abby,' said Gwen, sticking the needle back in the reel of thread. 'Come and sit down and tell me all about it.'

Abby dropped onto the settee next to her mother, picked up a loose cushion and hugged it to herself, and started to laugh. 'I met Mrs Holten . . . and friends . . .'

As Abby and her mother talked softly, their light laughter occasionally drifting through the peaceful cottage, the twins sleepily whispered to each other, glad Tom Turkey and the bantams were in bed. Kevin and Brian breathed slowly and deeply, both fast asleep. Bob McBride kicked off his boots, pulled off his leather belt and fell back on the bed, and promptly went to sleep.

At Amba, Barney Holten sat in a chair on the darkened verandah. His mother was in the sitting room listening to a play on the radio, her two dogs curled in her lap. His father was in his study with the door shut. Reading, doing the books, or looking at his stamp collection, Barney assumed. On impulse, he stood up, went to the study door and tapped lightly. Hearing his father's voice say, 'Yes?', he opened the door.

His father sat at his desk, peering through a magnifying glass at a page of stamps. 'Yes, Barney?'

'Er, nothing. I just thought I'd see what you were doing. The barbecue went well. You should have come down.'

'Like I said, it was your affair. I hope everything is cleaned up and no damage was done.' He continued to stare at Barney in the doorway. 'Well, if you'll excuse me, I want to sort through a few more of these.' He looked back down at the neat rows and carefully adjusted the alignment of one of the stamps. Picking up the glass, he studied them intently and didn't notice the door close quietly behind Barney.

CHAPTER SIX

THE TWINS CAME RUNNING IN TO BOB AND GWEN'S bedroom and jumped on the bed.

'Rain's gone,' Colleen announced brightly.

'Are we going out today?' asked Shirley.

'They said at school everyone had to go,' elaborated Colleen.

'Go where, my little sausage?' asked Bob, ruffling Colleen's hair as she bounced on his chest. 'Ouch! I don't like schoolteachers bossing me around.'

Gwen wrapped her arms around Shirley, who was snuggling under the bedclothes between her parents. 'Now, Bob, don't be disrespectful about their teacher.'

'It'll be fun, Dad. Can't we please go, Mum?' asked Shirley.

'Go where?' demanded Bob, pretending to shake Colleen, who squealed and laughed.

Kevin appeared in his pyjama bottoms at the door, rubbing his eyes. 'What's going on?'

'Tell them, Kev, about the picnic.'

'Oh yeah. It's the town community day picnic.'

'A picnic! Why didn't you say so? That's different. I like teachers who recommend *picnics*,' said Bob with exaggerated enthusiasm. 'What d'ya reckon, Mum?'

'Gosh, I'd forgotten. There was something about it in the local rag. We'll call Mrs Pemberton, she'll know all about it. So it's today, eh? If the rain has stopped, I suppose we could go. I'd better get cracking and bake something.' She flung back the covers and jumped out of bed, pulling her chenille dressing gown over her nightie.

'There she goes, the mad baker.' Bob let out a wolf whistle and the children laughed. 'Go tell Abby and Brian, gang.'

Gwen had a cake in the oven, was dressed, had made the bed and was dishing up bacon and eggs and porridge by the time Bob had spent a little time in peaceful contemplation in the throne room down the back, showered, shaved and emerged in a good pair of slacks and a white shirt.

He looked around his family at the table. 'We'll go to the picnic, but we're going to church first. We haven't been since we got here and that's over a month ago. The priest will think us a bunch of heathens.'

'I haven't got a dress to wear to mass,' wailed Colleen.

'Me neither,' joined in Shirley.

'Of course you do,' said Abby. 'I ironed those pretty blue and white dresses myself. We don't have to get too dressed up if we're going to a picnic afterwards. Where is it anyway?'

'In the town park. They're setting up a tent and there'll be rides and things, I think,' said Kevin enthusiastically.

'What a good thing the rain has stopped,' said Gwen.

'We needed it, luv, don't complain,' said Bob, a typical countryman who'd welcomed the rain after the preceding long dry months.

'Right, mass then the picnic. As soon as you've finished breakfast, make your beds, get cleaned up and into Sunday clothes,' directed Gwen. 'Abby, as soon as you're ready, help me with the sandwiches.'

'I'd rather do that first, then get dressed. I don't want food on my clean clothes,' said Abby, carrying the empty porridge plates to the sink.

When everyone was finally dressed and ready, Betsy was backed out of the shed she shared with stacks of feed, tools and drums of diesel fuel. The picnic food and blankets were stowed in the boot, and the family scrambled noisily for positions on the well-worn leather seats in her soft interior.

'Don't crush my dress, Brian.'

'Here, Shirley, pass him over, he can sit on my lap in the front,' said Gwen.

'Doesn't Kevy look nice.'

'Don't call me that. My name's Kevin.'

'Kevy, Kevy, Kevyyyy . . .' sang the twins.

'Ignore them, mate,' said Bob, loosening his wool tie as he got behind the wheel. 'Now, what's the priest's name again?'

Betsy behaved beautifully and as they drove, Bob warmed up the McBride choir with a spirited rendition of *Faith of Our Father*.

All was going well until they came to the dip where the floodway was running a small stream. Bob McBride stopped Betsy and contemplated the flowing water.

'Ooh, Daddy, how are we going to get across?' wailed Shirley.

'Do you want me to get out and test it?' offered Kevin, keen for adventure.

'It looks a bit deep, do you think she'll stall?' asked Gwen with a worried frown.

'I don't think so,' declared Bob, letting out the clutch and giving Betsy a bit of a rev-up. She sailed valiantly onto the concrete channel and with a cough, an intake of water up the exhaust pipe, she stalled. Dead centre.

'All right, everybody out.'

'Daddy! We'll get wet!' squealed Colleen.

'We've got our best clothes on,' echoed Shirley.

'Well we can't just sit here,' said Abby.

'Why not?' muttered Kevin.

'You want us all out?' Gwen double-checked.

'Absolutely. We're not pushing you lot *and* Betsy. Right, Kev?'

'No fear,' said Kevin.

The twins started to cry.

'That's enough, you two. Take off your shoes and socks, stick your dress in your undies and wade over. And don't trip,' dictated their father.

Abby and Gwen were already taking off their shoes. Gwen pulled off her gloves, pushed them in her handbag, looped it on her shoulder, and lifted up Brian.

'I'll take him, luv. Kevin, you go first. Go slowly,' directed Bob.

Sniffing, Shirley and Colleen took off their white socks, stuffing them down into their patent leather shoes, wiggled around and stuffed the skirts of their spotted muslin dresses into their white cotton undies and gingerly opened the car door. Abby was beside them and helped them down. Taking a hand each, she led them carefully through the knee-deep water as they clutched their prayer book in one hand and hat in the other. As soon as they reached dry land, they quickly fluffed out their skirts, smoothing the wrinkles.

Kevin held out a hand to his mother as she stepped up on the dry road, letting down the bunched skirt of her frock. 'Good thing I wasn't wearing nylons, eh, girls?'

Bob McBride deposited Brian on dry ground and turned back to the stranded car. As the somewhat bedraggled family watched, he tried the starter, but to no avail.

'Righto, Kev,' Bob called after a few tries, 'bring your muscles over here. Abby, you get in and steer.'

Abby, who had been treading carefully, her skirt hitched up into the elastic legs of her pants, glanced back at her father and Kevin as she opened the car door. Her attention was momentarily diverted, causing her to miss her footing on the running board. She slipped and fell to her knees, soaking the bottom of her skirt. Gritting her teeth in annoyance, she got behind the wheel.

Father and son put their shoulders to it and

slowly pushed Betsy through the short strip of water.

'Give her a minute or two,' Bob panted, 'and we'll give her another go.'

Gwen opened her handbag and handed him the red packet of Ardath cigarettes. They both lit up while the girls peered at themselves in the tiny square mirror Gwen produced from her bag. Hats were adjusted, hair touched up, Peter Pan collars straightened, dresses smoothed and shoes put back on. The twins paid particular attention to folding over the tops of their socks so the ruffle edging sat just so.

Abby shook out her mud-stained skirt. 'Not much I can do about this, I guess.'

'Rinse it out in the bathroom at church,' suggested Gwen. 'At least it might get the mud out.'

'It'll dry in the sun,' said Colleen.

'Right, let's give her another go,' said Bob.

Gwen looked anxiously at her small marcasite watch as Bob got behind the wheel. One, two, three turns of the ignition and then, with a burble, she caught and turned over. Everybody cheered, Brian clapped and they all piled back into the car and set off once again.

They were late but the service hadn't started. They genuflected quickly and shuffled along a rear pew as several people turned to watch the newcomers get settled. Abby followed last and there were a few raised eyebrows at her bedraggled skirt.

Gwen nudged Kevin and showed the girls which page to turn to in their missal. Father O'Leary settled his vestments and Kevin closed his eyes as the long Latin service began.

By the time it came to the sermon, Brian was very bored. He'd been sitting on the floor between their feet, crouched on the hassock. Gwen handed him her rosary beads, which he pulled over his head, playing with the silver cross. With Brian quiet, Gwen settled back to listen to the sermon.

'Today,' began Father O'Leary loudly, 'as we celebrate with God on this day of rest, we can rejoice in the hard work we have done this past week. But while there are those of us who toil honestly and obey the lessons of the Lord, there could be among us, right here, evil at work. The filthy and dangerous idea of Communism, which is a blight on our world today, is spreading. Its seeds are carried into our precious country by those who come from other places and seek to destroy what they have never known or enjoyed. We must guard against this insidious disease. Be watchful of those who espouse the overthrow and change of our democracy and all that our parents and grandparents held dear, fought and died for. Communism will undo our way of life!' thundered the father, raising his hand and shaking it.

Kevin didn't understand this talk of the Cold War and Communism and atomic bombs. It all seemed so far away. He stifled a yawn as the priest continued.

'Communism is the death knell of decency, safety and morality. Stand firm against this threat. Today in many parts of Europe, Catholic families like yours are no longer able to attend the holy mass or pray publicly. We can only pray that the faith of these families can survive the years to come. I beg you all to keep the holy Catholic faith strong in your families. Pray together, stay together. Mother, father, children, kneel down together every night and say the rosary, attend confession and the sacrament together.

'Instruct the children well in the holy Faith, have them marry within the Faith and it will stay with them forever. Let us now pray for the souls of the heathens, unscrupulous leaders and evil-doers that they will see the light and follow the true path of God's righteousness.'

There was a scrabbling and banging as the congregation knelt to pray. Gwen clasped her hands together and rested her forehead on them on the back of the pew in front. She felt Colleen snuggle closer beside her and knew she was scared. While the ten-year-old hadn't fully understood what the priest was saying, she knew there was a danger out there that could sneak in and rattle the walls of her safe home. Shirley loved going to church, she loved getting dressed up and collecting the holy pictures and repeating some of the Latin mass. Colleen, however, always found the experience frightening: the threat of punishment, the curses that would come raining down from heaven if she disobeyed God, and always some dire warning from the priest. She put her fingers in her ears and tried to think about the picnic instead.

Abby, who'd been daydreaming, suddenly became aware that the service was over. While her mother untangled the rosary from Brian's neck, she helped get the twins ready, collecting an assortment of gloves, handkerchiefs, dislodged ribbons and religious cards. The large congregation filed slowly from the church to the accompaniment of an enthusiastic rendition from the organist. There were so many children in the family groups that the aisles soon became jammed with jostling, joking youngsters more committed to having fun pushing and shoving than in making a prompt and decorous exit.

On the neat lawns outside the church, Father O'Leary circulated, shaking hands, patting children on the head and taking jocular care to single out newcomers or infrequent worshippers for special attention.

Bob McBride watched him at work, waiting for the inevitable. 'Workin' the mob like a good sheepdog,' he said to himself, and smiled.

'Tis good to see you all,' said the priest as he shook hands with the McBrides, winning a smile from each of the children as he teased them. 'Of course I understand you've had the settlin' in and shearin' to keep you busy of late, but I trust we'll be seeing more of each other in the future,' he said warmly, making it sound more like an invitation than a recognition of religious backsliding.

'You know we'll do our best,' said Gwen reassuringly.

'Indeed I do...indeed I do...Now are you coming to the picnic? I'm in one of the mixed cricket teams you know.' He winked and lowered his voice, 'The Church of England minister is on the opposing side.'

'And whose side is the Lord on then?' shot back Bob, and got a sharp nudge in the ribs from Gwen.

'Oh ye of little faith,' replied the priest with a laugh, and moved on to another family group.

At the same time, several blocks away from where the Catholics had their towering red-brick church, a smaller congregation gathered outside the modest white wooden Presbyterian church. They exchanged news on the weather, stock and family, generally in that order of priority. Most were from the land or small businesses.

Phillip Holten took his wife's arm after a brief and perfunctory round of greetings, and steered her towards the car, only to be confronted by an attractive young woman all florals and smiles.

'Hi, Mr and Mrs Holten,' she gushed.

Enid smiled back as she felt Phillip tense. She knew he hated the 'Hi' greeting which he believed had been left behind by the American army.

'Good morning, Cheryl,' he replied formally. 'I trust that you are well.'

'Unbelievable, Mr Holten. Are you coming to the picnic in the park?'

'No . . . It's not really what we are accustomed to on a Sunday.'

Over Phillip's shoulder Cheryl was relieved to see Barney, who was moving slowly through the family groups shaking hands and making small talk. 'Oh, there's Barney. See you later, Mr and Mrs Holten.' And she bounced away.

Barney saw the floral dress coming from out of

the corner of his eye and was ready with a smile. Although Barney was somewhat shy himself, he enjoyed the times he chatted to Cheryl.

'Hello, Cheryl.'

'Hi, Barney,' she said. 'I'm hoping you're coming to the picnic. I've put you down for my team for the mixed cricket.'

'I thought it was mainly for kids. I had planned to go home with Mum and Dad.'

'Oh come on, Barney. It's a charity fundraiser. They're running a sweep or something on the number of runs scored or whatever . . . Do come, you'll find a lift home.'

Phillip Holten opened the car door for his wife and looked questioningly at Barney chatting to the girl. Barney turned and caught his eye.

'Look, Cheryl, I'll see. Maybe I'll come back in to town.' Barney hurried to the car. As they drew away from the kerb, he raised his hand to Cheryl.

'Why don't we drop in on the picnic?' asked Barney quickly.

'Whatever for, dear?' queried his mother.

'Well, I thought I might go. Cheryl Maddocks has put me in her cricket team.'

'In what, dear?'

'Waste of time. And it is Sunday,' cut in his father.

The traffic entering a side street leading to the

park forced them to stop at the intersection. They were sitting in silence when Barney spotted the unmistakable round brown beam of the McBrides' Betsy in the line of traffic going to the park. He started to smile and peered closer, looking for Abby.

'Hang on, Dad. I think I'll get out and walk down to the park. Might just have that game of cricket. I'm sure I'll get a ride home. Don't worry about me.' He opened the back door and quickly got out.

'You're not dressed for cricket, dear,' observed his mother, then added, 'and I have roast pork for lunch.'

'I'll eat it for tea, Mum. See you later.' He sprinted off, leaving his tight-lipped father to drive home in silence.

Many people had come straight from church to the picnic. Some had casual clothes on but most were still in their Sunday clothes, and it gave the outdoor setting a festive air. Several tents and marquees had been erected and there were pony rides and a small merry-go-round for the children.

The Red Cross ladies were selling soft drinks, cups of tea and homemade pastries. A Legacy stall had a hot plate going for sausage or steak sandwiches or the ever-popular Jaffles. Groups were setting up picnic sites, spreading tablecloths and blankets. The sportsmaster from the school had a loud-hailer and was announcing that the first of the children's races would be under way before lunch. This would be followed by the mothers' and fathers' three-legged race.

Barney bought a creaming soda and a sausage roll and wandered happily about, looking at all the activity. He suddenly came upon the McBrides under the shade of a gumtree in a big sprawl of tablecloths, blankets and picnic paraphernalia.

Bob McBride hailed him. 'G'day, Barney.'

'Hello, everyone,' said Barney. 'Looks like you're settling in for a big day out.' His eyes met Abby's and she quickly looked down at her skirt. She was relieved to find that the worst of the damage was hidden. At least the dress had dried out, but it was still stained with mud around the hem.

'Yeah, it's a great treat something like this,' said Bob warmly. 'Why don't you join us for a bite? Got masses of tucker. One thing about this mob, we never travel short on rations. Abby, move over and make room for Barney.'

Barney hesitated briefly and was about to accept when Cheryl Maddocks grabbed his arm.

'Barney,' she smiled, 'you're here to captain my team. You're absolutely wonderful.'

'Ah...oh...hello again, Cheryl. I was just having a yarn. I don't suppose you know the McBrides. Mr McBride has been helping us with the shearing.'

He turned to the group which had become almost like a tableau, everyone frozen by the sudden arrival of the smartly dressed and bubbly girl. Abby was already on her bare feet following her dad's example as Barney began introducing each member of the family to Cheryl. She was still standing when Barney said, 'And this is Abby.'

'Hi,' said Cheryl casually, her eyes quickly taking in the state of Abby's dress. She gave Abby a quick sympathetic smile.

'Hello,' said Abby quietly.

Barney also noted the slightly muddied dress, felt her embarrassment and found himself saying, 'Abby helped out with the shearing as well. She's a good hand in the shed.' Abby and Barney exchanged glances. Abby was clearly mortified.

Bob McBride sprang to the rescue. 'Not this morning though... Today she was the heroine of the great Nine Mile Creek flood rescue.' As Abby sat down, her father gave a greatly exaggerated account of the whole episode that soon had everyone laughing.

When the story was over Cheryl tugged at

Barney's arm. 'Come on, we're about to eat and you're going to need lots of energy for that match. See you all again perhaps. Bye.'

'I'll see you later. Thanks for the invite anyway,' said Barney to the McBrides.

The younger McBrides spent little time over lunch. They were soon dragging Abby off to sample every ride and game they could afford. Abby lavished some of her earnings on the children, including buying pink fairy floss all round. The promise of such ecstasy was the only bribe that could get Brian off the merry-go-round where he had clung to the pole of his horse demanding loudly, 'One more...one more...' By the time they all flopped down sleepily at the picnic site, the cricket match was well under way, and the crowd was enjoying the light-hearted match enormously.

Gwen nudged Abby as she settled down beside her. 'Barney is in fielding. There he is with his back to us. Cheryl is bowling. And would you believe, Father O'Leary has hit three fours. He's quite the hero of the moment.'

Cheryl gave an excellent delivery of good length straight down the pitch to Father O'Leary, but he had its measure. Not for nothing had he been captain of the cricket team during his final years at the seminary. He got right under the ball with a bold sweeping stroke that sent it high and hard towards the boundary. The crowd cheered and then went silent as they watched Barney take off under the ball, looking over his shoulder as he raced towards the boundary. Still running, he half turned and reached up with both hands to intercept the ball and hold it. But the final reach made him lose his balance and he fell backwards into a picnic party on the boundary. Their shrieks and shouts were drowned by the huge cheer that was raised right around the ground.

Barney was a little winded by the fall and saw a star or two, but was soon more conscious of two big and beautiful startled blue eyes looking down at him. He had come to rest in Abby's lap.

'Hello again,' he said with a silly grin. 'Sorry to drop in on you like this.'

She smiled then gave him a shove. 'Play on. Play on and play the game,' she recited with mock heroics.

The game was eventually declared a draw and, for most, its end signalled that it was time to head home. The McBrides were loading up Betsy when Barney arrived looking quite dishevelled, coat and tie over his shoulder.

'I was wondering if I could cadge a ride home with you. I kind of stopped off here on the spur of the moment.'

'Be a bit of a squeeze but if you don't mind, we're happy to have you along,' said Bob.

'Great. Thanks a lot.'

'There's a catch to travelling with our mob,' said Abby. 'Dad sings.'

'That's all right. The Irish usually have good voices.'

'Ah, yes, but you have to sing too,' said Abby grinning. 'And if you don't put enough into it, you might get dumped halfway along the track.'

'Oh dear. Maybe I'd better start walking now.'

Gwen sat in the front, Brian on her lap, with Kevin between her and Bob. The twins, Abby and Barney were in the back. There was much jollity as everyone shared their experiences of the day and admired the toy panda and kewpie doll that Bob and Kevin had won for the girls.

'This has been better than the Easter Show in Sydney,' said Barney. 'Everyone certainly went to a lot of trouble.'

'This is a nice town. With nice people,' said Gwen, patting Brian's sleepy head.

Once they were out of town heading homewards in the late afternoon light, Bob began, *'When the red red robin comes bob bob bobbin' along . . .'*

Abby nudged Barney. 'See, I wasn't joking,' she whispered.

'I don't hear you lot in the back,' called Bob

over his shoulder, and Barney made a feeble attempt to join in.

Abby sang loudly and well and he gave her a grateful wink. He wondered what they would say if he admitted he'd never sung in his family's car in his life. In fact, he'd never been with a family quite like the McBrides before. His parents wouldn't approve of their behaviour at all. Running in a three-legged race — Bob had fallen over and he and Kevin had rolled about in fits of laughter as they tangled together and had ended up crawling over the finishing line last — telling silly stories and singing in the car would all be considered very déclassé. But Barney was having a wonderful time. Especially feeling the softness of Abby pressed against his side and smelling the sweet tang of her skin and hair.

Barney threw upbringing and inhibition to the wind and joined in, '*Wake up, wake up, you sleepy head, get up, get up get outta bed, cheer up, cheer up the sun is reddddd . . .*'

CHAPTER SEVEN

ABBY SWUNG THROUGH THE GATE TO THE PEM-
bertons' back garden, balancing the cake tin so as
not to disturb the passionfruit cream sponge
nestling on greaseproof paper inside. She tapped
at the kitchen door and poked her head around the
flyscreen door.

'Yoo-hoo, Mrs Pemberton . . . It's me, Abby . . .'

'Hello . . . Come in,' came the reply.

Abby stepped inside and put the cake tin on the
kitchen table as a young woman came through the
dining room doors. The smile on Abby's face
faded as she stared at her. She was her own age,
with light honey-coloured hair and deep brown

eyes. She wore lipstick and white daisy earrings, and her hair was set in neat waves turning under at her ears. Abby was struck by the white pedal-pusher pants, elastic top blouse and multicoloured heeled sandals. To Abby she looked the height of casual elegance as seen in the women's magazines she glanced at swiftly in the newsagents.

'Oh. I was looking for Mrs Pemberton. I'm Abby, I've brought up a cake.'

The girl looked at Abby, who felt uncomfortable at being scrutinised so openly. 'Cake? I adore cakes. Has it got lots of cream?' She inched off the lid of the cake tin and Abby noticed the bright red fingernail polish. 'Ooh, this looks scrumptious. Passionfruit. Oh, I'm Shannon by the way. Mum is on the telephone. I think I'll have a piece of this.'

'My mother made it for Mrs Pemberton, she said it was for a special occasion,' said Abby, feeling self-conscious in her faded slacks with turned-up cuffs, sandshoes and one of her father's old blue work shirts hanging out. Her hair was in its usual ponytail. She studied Shannon Pemberton more closely as she took the cake and placed it carefully on a cut-glass cake stand she took from a cupboard. Abby saw she was wearing powder and a mauve shade of eyeshadow, as well as the lipstick.

Sarah Pemberton bustled into the kitchen. 'Shannon! Don't you get into that cake, it's for your tea party! Did you meet Abby?'

'Of course, Mother. Can't I at least sample my cake?'

Sarah Pemberton laughed. 'Shannon is hopeless around cake and sweets. Well, girls, let's have a cup of tea at least.'

Shannon sat on one of the four chairs at the small Laminex kitchen table. 'So, you're one of our new residents. I hear you have brothers and sisters. I only have a ghastly little brother. He's at boarding school.'

'I have two little brothers. And twin sisters. I'm the oldest.'

'Shannon has been travelling and living in Sydney since she finished at Pymble Ladies College. She came home rather unexpectedly,' explained Sarah Pemberton.

Shannon shrugged. 'That's me. Up and off. Suddenly decided it was all too boring. I'd done everything and my flatmate decided she wanted to go to England and the girl who was going to move in got engaged instead. So I wasn't going to hang around any more. Time to come home. Especially now Barney is home too.'

Shannon's mother set out the tea cups. 'So, Abby, your mother tells me you are looking for a job.'

'Yes. I'm not too choosy but I'd like something that is interesting and where I could meet people.'

'I was thinking I might work if the right thing came along,' said Shannon nonchalantly.

Sarah Pemberton turned to Shannon with a teasing, 'Your father thinks after that expensive education you had, you should be running the country at the very least!'

'How boring. That's the men's job. We women get to plan the parties, be hostesses, spend money, and look beautiful,' said Shannon cheerfully, and Abby couldn't tell if she was joking or not.

Abby finished her tea and rose to leave. 'It's been nice to meet you, Shannon.'

'Thank you. I'm sure we'll see each other around.'

'Maybe you girls could go for a ride or something,' suggested Sarah.

'I haven't got a horse, I'm afraid, though I've ridden a bit, working mainly.'

'Well, I suppose we can scrape up an extra horse sometime,' said Shannon unenthusiastically.

Gwen's heart lurched as she heard Abby describe Shannon and she wished Sarah and Keith's daughter had been more friendly.

'I mean, she's so pretty, and smart, and up to date and everything. A bit snobby, I suppose because she went to a posh school and has money and stuff. I feel such a dag next to her.'

'Now listen, Abby, it breaks my heart that your dad and I can't give you those sort of advantages. But you listen to me, my girl, she's no better than you because of it. You are a truly special girl. I mean this, not because I'm your mother, but because I'm a woman and I know there are some girls God gives special qualities to... maybe to compensate for other things.

'Abby, you don't know how beautiful you are... Yes, you're pretty, but inside, you are a precious gem. You're caring and giving, funny and sensitive and have great depth of understanding. If only you knew how I pray that someone truly deserving of you will come along...' Gwen suddenly faltered with the passion of her words and Abby rushed to her and hugged her tightly.

'Oh, Mum. How good you make me feel. If I can be half the mother you are, I will feel I've achieved so much...' They clung together, the mother wanting so much for the daughter, the other asking for so little.

Barney hooked off his boots on the iron boot-rest by the back door, padded along the verandah in his socks, and went to his bathroom to clean up. As he changed clothes he peered from his bedroom window at a strange car in the main drive. He wondered whom his mother had invited around. People didn't drop in at Amba unexpectedly.

He met Mrs Anderson coming from the sitting room with the tea tray. She beamed at him. 'Your mother has a guest. Someone you'll want to see. I set an extra cup for you.'

She said no more and so Barney quietly opened the door. For a moment he didn't recognise the back of the blonde head seated next to his mother on the lounge. But as she swung around he exclaimed, 'Shannon! You're back. How nice to see you.'

'Do sit down, Barney. I'll pour,' said his mother as Barney gave Shannon a big grin. She gave him a knowing smile, preening at his attention.

'So, what's new? Glad to be back? Are you staying?' he asked Shannon.

'I'm home to stay, Barney. No more shilly shallying around, as my father says. I had thought about going overseas, but Dad says it's time I settled down.'

Enid handed Barney a cup of tea. 'Shannon has travelled though. She was telling me what an interesting place New Zealand is,' said his mother, passing the plate of biscuits to Shannon.

Shannon bit into the shortbread, gazing at the

boy she'd known all her life. He'd always been a friend; they'd been thrown together for social occasions since they were young and it had always been in the back of her mind that if she didn't get a marriage proposal from some fabulously wealthy, exciting foreigner or movie star, there was always Barney and Amba in the wings. She'd never thought of Barney as wildly dashing. He wasn't like her romantic teenage idols — he was a solid, sweet, but sophisticated, Australian country boy. She studied him through lowered lashes as he stirred his tea and she had to admit that in the year she'd been away she'd forgotten how handsome and charming he was. Or was she now better able to compare having met other men in other places?

Barney too was assessing Shannon. She'd certainly acquired a veneer of glamour and worldliness with her fashionable clothes and new hairstyle. He didn't care for her heavy make-up, and Abby's natural beauty came to mind in comparison. Images of her sweeping the woolshed with her hair in a ponytail, coy and damp after her plunge in the swimming hole, laughingly chasing the chooks and playing with her brothers and sisters, contrasted with the immaculate and artificial look of Shannon. He realised a lot of it had to do with personality too. Abby was unaffected, down to earth, and obviously sweet-natured. He knew only too well Shannon's temper and spoiled affectations.

Barney was aware Shannon was staring at him. He gave her a swift smile. 'So, what are you going to do with yourself, Shannon?'

'I'm going to take up showjumping. Daddy has bought me a really super horse.'

'That sounds interesting, Shannon,' said Enid with feigned interest as she fondled the two dogs curled beside her. 'More tea?'

'No thank you. It was lovely. I should be getting back.' She rose and picked up her shoulder bag. 'Thank you so much for the tea, Mrs Holten. Do give my best to Mr Holten.'

'I'll walk you out to your car,' said Barney, following her outside.

He opened the door of the new Holden and Shannon sat behind the wheel scooping in the folds of her full skirt. Barney shut the door and leaned through the window.

'Life is going to seem a bit dull back here, isn't it?' he asked.

'You settled back down all right,' she retorted with a smile. 'Are you glad I'm back? You hardly looked me up at all in Sydney like you promised. Twice, at most.'

'I didn't want to cramp your style,' grinned Barney.

'I'm glad we're friends and neighbours again. We have been most of our lives, haven't we?' said Shannon softly. 'Maybe it's time we got to know each other again, seriously.' Barney didn't answer.

'Be seeing you then,' he said as she started the motor.

'Soon, I hope.' She gave a wave and drove off faster than was necessary. Barney hoped his father was away from the house and didn't see or hear the spray of gravel from the Holden's whitewall tyres.

Shannon had been a part of his life by locale, family association and social standing since he was a boy. He felt some pleasure, but no great excitement at seeing her again. She was familiar and they understood each other. There were very few young women his mother would entertain. The Pembertons' property adjoined Amba and that was a significant factor in tightening the links between the two families. Shannon would marry and move to her husband's property, her brother would inherit Anglesea. However, it had not escaped comment in the district of the possible merging of the two families and land should Barney and Shannon marry. Not that Shannon was short of suitors. Like matchmaking royalty, the families of large holdings with eligible sons and daughters kept track of each other.

Abby gossiped with Colleen and Shirley, admired their paper dolls, listened to the story of Fred the border collie mustering the chooks, rounding them up like a mob of sheep, and heard how there was a concert coming up at school and how they would be in it. She stood on the bottom bunk to kiss Shirley in the top, smoothed Colleen's hair and said goodnight, putting out their light.

Brian was fast asleep and Kevin was sitting up in bed reading a Phantom comic for the tenth time.

Abby sat at the foot of his bed. 'So, kid, what's new and exciting in your life?'

'Dad's teaching me to drive the ute. Just round the farm.'

'That's handy, mate. I know you won't break the rules and get out on the highway. And once you can drive you'll be out chasing after girls soon enough.'

Kevin looked down and fiddled with his sheet. 'How do you learn about girls, Ab? The other boys are always teasing them — sometimes they're really mean, putting their hair in the ink and stuff — but they just giggle and sort of like it even though they pretend to be mad.'

'Learn what sort of things about girls?' asked Abby carefully.

'Some of the boys were talking about a film

they'd seen, said it was dopey cause there was so much kissing and stuff that spoiled it. But I just sorta wondered . . . like, how do you know how to kiss, Ab?'

Abby smiled gently at him. 'You mean where to put your nose and what you do with your lips? I used to wonder about that. Not that I'm any expert, Kev,' she cautioned him, 'but you know, the funny thing is, it's like a lot of things you worry about — when the time comes, you find it just comes naturally and there you are, doing it perfectly. When you find a girl you want to kiss, you'll find it's easy.'

Kevin accepted this explanation, relieved it hadn't led to any embarrassing discussion, and sleepily pondered whether he should swap his marbles — his blood alleys and favourite connie agates — for Ted Johnston's Superman and Prince Valiant comics.

After she had said goodnight to Kevin, Abby thought further about their conversation and fleetingly wondered what it would be like to kiss Barney's smiling mouth. Abby's kissing experience had been limited: swift and clumsy kisses snatched in the darkness of the picture theatre or in dark corners at a dance. There had been one boy she'd liked a lot back in Gilgandra, a jackaroo working his way around the country before settling down on his parents' orchard in Victoria. He had been so shy, she had finally leaned close and lifted her face so he couldn't escape the lure of her sweet mouth. It had been everything she'd read about in books — her knees trembled and her heart beat faster. But the next time they'd been together he'd kissed her ardently then drawn away protesting, 'We shouldn't do this.'

'But we're only kissing,' she'd answered.

He'd dropped his arms. 'It's hard for blokes to . . . stop. You know . . .' But she didn't know. Instead she had been hurt, thinking he hadn't really liked kissing her. Then suddenly he'd got a new contract and was gone without a good-bye. Being a farm girl she knew about sexual reproduction but she was not worldly. She had a vague knowledge of contraception from her St John Ambulance course and simple questions she'd asked her mother. The Wedding Night — girls whispered about it, giggled and groaned and said it was worse than having a baby. But like she'd told Kevin, Abby just hoped that when the time came it would all come naturally and be as her mother had promised — special and wonderful.

Two days later, when Abby was helping her mother peg out the huge pile of washing, Shannon appeared and asked Abby if she would go riding with her the following morning.

'My horse is frisky and Mum and Dad won't allow me to go alone, can you come along? You can take Jolly the stockhorse out, he hasn't been exercised for a bit.'

Abby hesitated as it seemed more of an order than a request. Gwen spoke quickly. 'You go ahead, luv. It'd be nice for you. I can manage around here.' She adjusted the fork of the wooden clothes prop under the sagging line, and Abby helped her push it upright and brace the heavy line of sheets, towels, shirts and trousers.

'I'm supposed to be looking for a job, but I'd like that, Shannon.'

'Good. Come up to the barn after breakfast. You'll probably have a devil of a job catching Jolly.'

But when Abby arrived at the Pembertons' barn which served as a stable, she found Jolly saddled and standing quietly next to a dark brown thoroughbred and sleek black Arabian.

'Shannon?' called Abby.

'Coming, Abby.' Shannon came out followed by Barney. 'We have company. Barney couldn't come two days ago, now he can.' She gazed flirtaciously at him.

'Oh. That's good,' said Abby, suddenly feeling

like the unwanted third that made a crowd. She eyed Shannon's smart beige jodhpurs, tartan shirt and elegant boots and felt uncomfortable in her faded jodhpurs, cotton jumper and old elastic-sided work boots. But Barney's gentle smile, which seemed to say 'I'm glad you're here,' put her at ease.

They swung into the saddles and Shannon led the way as the horses lifted their heads, anxious to step out in the fresh morning air. Once they'd left the pasture and trotted along the dirt track that led towards the scrub-covered ridge, Shannon rode beside Barney, chattering all the while. Abby, bringing up the rear, relaxed and began to enjoy herself; she hadn't ridden just for pleasure in a long time. Generally she was on a horse to work and although she enjoyed it, riding for the sheer pleasure of it was a rare treat.

They rode for forty minutes then stopped and dismounted at the head of the small ridge. They sat and rested, admiring the view.

'How you feeling, Abby? You've been very quiet,' commented Barney. He gave her a quick wink behind Shannon's back.

'I've been enjoying the ride. It's pretty up here.'

'Well, let's make a move,' said Shannon abruptly. 'What say we take the steep side of the hill back? Be a bit of a challenge rather than going down the way we came.'

'You're dying to give that horse a bit of a test run, aren't you?' said Barney.

'Why not? You game, Abby?'

'Jolly seems sensible; we'll be right,' answered Abby, not about to be put down by Shannon.

The three set off, each finding their own trail down the steep hillside towards the gully and the road. Abby leaned back in the saddle letting Jolly have his head and find his own footing. When they reached the flat, they were flushed with exhilaration.

Shannon swung around in her saddle and shouted, 'Race you home!' She kicked the horse into a gallop and Barney and Abby took off behind her.

They grouped together, the pounding of their horses' hooves and the cracking of twigs echoing through the bush lit by the strands of sunlight and melting dew.

Shannon rode close behind Barney, who glanced back at Abby and reined into a canter. 'You all right, Abby?' he called.

She gave a wave and nodded. Shannon, who had been carrying a broken twig as a crop, leaned over to Barney's horse and teasingly whacked it under its arched tail. 'Come on, Barney, get a move on!'

Barney's horse, highstrung and toey at the best of times, didn't race off as Shannon expected, but jammed its tail down and bucked in annoyance. It happened swiftly and Barney, caught unawares, lost his balance, and fell heavily to the ground.

Abby wheeled about and was off her horse before Shannon realised what had happened. By the time she turned and raced back, Abby was gently examining Barney, who appeared to be unconscious.

'Oh my God, Barney!' Shannon screeched, sliding from her horse.

Abby lifted his limp hand and ran her hands over his neck and shoulders.

'Is he all right? Oh God, he looks dead!' gasped Shannon.

'He'll be all right, he's just knocked himself out for a minute,' said Abby.

'Are you sure?' Shannon was shaking as she patted his hand. 'Oh dear, what'll we do?'

'I'm just seeing if anything is broken before we move him.' Abby lifted one of Barney's eyelids and, as his eyes gradually focused, he groaned.

'Barney, Barney, are you all right? Say something.' Shannon started again. She wrung her hands, knowing she was responsible for the accident.

'Please, Shannon, go and get a car. We'll have to take him in to the doctor.'

'Shouldn't he go to the hospital? What about the Flying Doctor?'

'Shannon, go and get a car,' said Abby in exasperation.

Shannon silently remounted and galloped off.

After a minute or so, Barney stirred and lifted a hand to his head, mumbling, 'Good grief, what happened? Did I take a spill?'

'Don't try and get up. We'll get you in to the doctor, I think you've dislocated your shoulder.'

Barney tried to move and winced. 'Feels broken.'

'No, you'll be right. Be a bit of a painful trip in, unless you want me to snap it back in place now. I've done it before, but if you can wait, it will better for the doctor to do it with a needle. It hurts otherwise.'

'You know something about all this then?'

'I did a St John's course and I've had a bit of practice here and there,' smiled Abby.

Barney lay his head back down and closed his eyes as Abby stroked his forehead.

Soon the Pembertons' utility truck bumped erratically towards them.

'That'll be Shannon. She was a bit hysterical. I think I'd better drive.'

Barney nodded.

Shannon stopped the truck and jumped out,

talking so fast they could barely understand her. 'This is all I could get, couldn't find anyone, should I have phoned, what are we going to do, how are we going to get him in, are we going to fit?'

'Listen, Shannon,' said Abby calmly, 'I'll drive him in to town, he's damaged his shoulder, maybe his collarbone. Only two of us can fit in the seat of the ute. You look after the horses.'

Shannon didn't look pleased. She felt flustered and insecure in the face of Abby's calm and authoritative manner. She didn't like the idea of Abby taking control of Barney. 'No, let me help.'

'Please, Shannon, let Abby, she knows about medical stuff,' said Barney feebly.

The two girls helped him to his feet and, with Abby directing, they got him into the cabin. 'Take the horses back, Shannon, and call the doctor and tell him we're on our way, and if you wouldn't mind, phone the Holtens and my mother as they might wonder where we are.'

Shannon nodded and turned her attention to the horses, looking very put out.

Doctor Malone concurred that it was indeed a dislocated shoulder, gave Barney an injection and relocated the shoulder. He was impressed with Abby's calmness and practical skill and looked thoughtful as they chatted. 'I've seen you and your family in church and at the community picnic. How about a cup of tea?'

'That wouldn't go astray, that's for sure,' said Barney.

'Can I help, Doctor Malone,' offered Abby. 'Don't you have an assistant?'

'Did have till three days ago when she took off for the city. Not a word of warning.' Doctor Malone suddenly looked at Abby. 'You want a job? Can you type?'

Abby stared at him. 'I am looking for work actually. My typing is a bit rusty, but I just need to practice a bit.'

'I can recommend her nursing skills,' added Barney.

'Bring the patient back in a week for a checkup and we'll talk about the details. I'll struggle on till then. It's nothing glamorous, no Florence Nightingale stuff, I'm afraid, Abby. Mainly making appointments, writing up files and so forth.'

'It sounds perfect. I'm very grateful, Doctor Malone. I'll do my best.'

The doctor smiled at her. 'Righto then. Get him home. Keep the arm in the sling till I see you next week, Barney, and take these painkillers — one now and one just in case you need it tonight.'

Despite his drowsiness in the car driving home,

Barney was enthusiastic about Abby's job offer. 'If I hadn't fallen off, you wouldn't have been offered the job. So I'm glad this has happened.'

'I'm glad about the job too. I hope it comes off.'

'Listen, we have a typewriter in the shed; I'll look it out for you. It's an old Remington that came out of the ark, but you're welcome to bash away at it. How are you going to get into town every day? Drive Betsy?'

'I've been thinking about that. I think I'll get the school bus and ask Doctor Malone whether I could leave at four to get the bus home if I took a short lunch break.'

'I'm sure he'll agree. People are pretty accommodating round here, knowing the distances people have to travel.' Barney's head began to droop and soon he fell asleep, his head lolling and coming to rest on Abby's shoulder. She drove slowly, savouring the sensation of his closeness.

When they reached the gate leading to Amba, Abby sat in the car, reluctant to disturb Barney in order to get out and open the gate.

He stirred and glanced up at her, asking sleepily, 'Are we home?' He realised he was leaning against her and he straightened up, looking into her eyes.

'Yes, Barney, you're home,' she said softly. Barney leaned over and gently kissed her lips.

Surprised, a flush swept over Abby's cheeks. Before she could respond, Barney reached to touch her hair but winced in pain as he moved his shoulder.

Abby got out of the car and opened the gate, drove through, closed it and drove to the house in silence. She helped Barney down, he squeezed her hand and went into the house. Abby drove back to Anglesea, the taste and memory of Barney's kiss lingering on her lips.

CHAPTER EIGHT

ABBY PLACED THE LAST PATIENT'S FILE IN THE filing cabinet and slid the drawer shut. She smoothed her hair, unused to the neat French roll, and picked up her bag. The bell above the door tinkled as it was opened. Abby turned to say the doctor was out but instead gave a big smile as Barney came through the door holding his hat.

'Hello, Abby. How's it going?'

'Great. Are you here to see Doctor Malone or to make an appointment?'

'Neither, actually. I was hoping you might be free at lunchtime. I'm in town today.'

'I was just about to walk out the door for my lunch. I bring my own but eat it in the park.'

'How about I pick up a sandwich, a couple of milkshakes and we eat together?'

'That would be nice,' said Abby. 'By the way, thanks for the loan of the typewriter. And how's the shoulder? I see you've dumped the sling.'

'I'm coming along fine now.'

They strolled along the street, shaded from the midday sun by shop awnings.

'So you're enjoying the job then?'

'Yes. Doctor Malone is very nice. I'm learning all sorts of things and I'm meeting lots of people.'

Barney turned into the Athena Cafe. 'What flavour milkshake?'

'Chocolate, please.'

In the park they spread their little picnic between them on a broad bench shaded by a jacaranda tree.

'Want half my corned beef and tomato?' offered Barney.

'No thanks, I'll stick to my tuna. It's Friday,' smiled Abby.

'Friday? Oh yes, no meat... So tell me who you've been meeting. Been invited out by all the young men in town?'

'Not yet. I'm mainly meeting old blokes with crook knees and old ladies with arthritis.' Abby gave a mock grimace, then brightened. 'I have met Cheryl Maddocks again, though. She's asked me to join the local hockey team. I haven't played for years but I said I'd think about it. Though it would mean making time to train and for games every Saturday.'

'Go on, be in it,' said Barney encouragingly. 'You've got to have some fun too, Abby.'

Abby looked at him over her milkshake and smiled. 'And what do you do for fun then, Barney?'

Barney stared into her large dark blue eyes. For a moment he couldn't think. He didn't seem to have much fun in his life, unlike the McBrides, who seemed collectively to get so much fun out of everything. 'Well, I . . . er . . . play tennis and cricket occasionally. Get dragged to the odd ball.' He hesitated then went on, amazed at the rashness of his sudden decision. 'I'll tell you what, though, I'll come and watch your first hockey game. Promise. Let me know when your first match is on.'

'Watching girls' hockey might be seen as a bit odd, wouldn't it?' said Abby with a raised eyebrow. 'People might get ideas.' She didn't add 'about us' as it seemed presumptuous, but she knew how people liked to gossip in a small town.

'I couldn't care less what people think. It'll be fun . . . if not funny perhaps.'

Abby gave him a playful shove. 'Time to get back to work. Thanks for the company.'

He walked her back to the surgery and as she thanked him, he added, 'Look, I'll be in town for a bit, appointments and such. Do you want a ride home?'

'Oh, the bus is working out all right. Thanks just the same.'

'But I'd like the company. You'd be doing me a favour. Phone the bus office and tell them you've got a ride so the kids won't worry and hold the bus for you. Please, Abby.'

She felt her resistance crumble. What was the harm? She did enjoy his company. 'All right, Barney. Thanks.'

'I'll be waiting here a bit after four.'

It was a pleasant ride home. Each felt relaxed and comfortable. They chatted easily and laughed often. As Barney recounted an anecdote about his first day on the job in Sydney, it suddenly struck Abby that she'd never felt so at ease with anyone before. By rights there should be something of a barrier between them, that unwritten, unspoken law of position in the town. Someone in Barney's position didn't socialise equally with the likes of Abby, pretty and pleasant as she may be. Of course there was friendly peer rapport, manners and courtesies observed, but on a serious date, each class kept to their own.

Are we dating? Abby wondered. No, of course not. They were just two young people being friendly. Yet she knew that with anyone else with Barney's background she'd feel uncomfortable. With Barney she felt the deep pull of attraction coupled with a feeling of natural affinity which was hard to explain. She decided not to question it and instead relaxed in his company.

Barney felt the same. He found Abby unaffected, natural and easy to be with. He could tell she was not a girl to play games or be devious. Her freshness enchanted him and for the first time in an age he felt he was able to be himself. It was a heady feeling.

Both were in a buoyant mood as Abby waved him goodbye from the homestead garden gate and turned to chase after Kevin who had arrived home in time to give a loud wolf whistle as Barney drove off.

Abby's lunch with Barney and the lift home did not go unnoticed. Before the sun had set, almost the whole town knew about their meeting — thanks to party telephone lines and a few addicted gossip peddlers.

Shannon Pemberton heard it from a girlfriend

in town who couldn't wait to be first to tell her. Shannon dismissed it lightly. 'You know Barney, he's always trying to help people...' But underneath she was furious and within a few days she found an excuse to ride over to the Holtens'.

Barney greeted her warmly and inspected her horse with a keen eye. 'How are things going with your showjumper?' he asked cheerfully, bending down to run an expert hand over one of the horse's legs.

'I was doing just fine till I heard you've been squiring your own little show pony around town.' Shannon said it lightly but the words were sharp. Barney stiffened and turned to face her. 'What's going on, Barney?'

Barney looked utterly confused. Then suddenly he realised she was referring to Abby and his mouth and eyes hardened. 'Listen to me, Shannon, what I do or do not do is my own business.'

'Well it affects me too, Barney. I mean, what will people think? I don't like being treated this way. People think of us as a pair.'

'Well I don't. Behaving like this is a pretty cheap shot, Shannon. You and I are friends but that's all. There is *no* commitment between us. I can see whom I want.'

'Barney, you can't be serious!' Looking at his face she saw he was deadly serious. 'It's all very well to play around, but be discreet. I mean, if you're going to see someone seriously — other than me, then at least have the decency to make it someone from our circle — this is embarrassing for me. Everyone has always taken it for granted that you and I...'

'Shannon, I will see whom I want. And you should do the same,' interjected Barney.

Shannon's temper snapped. 'But she's a nobody! A paddy shearer's daughter! I thought you had more taste than that, Barney Holten.' She stormed off as Barney stemmed the retort that sprang to his lips. But as his anger cooled he did try to analyse his feelings for Abby. There was no doubting there was a strong attraction between them. He enjoyed her company, he delighted in the warmth and humour of her family, but there was no getting around the fact they came from opposite sides of the tracks. He knew his parents wouldn't approve, but then, in their eyes, there'd never be a girl good enough for the son of Amba. Best not to think beyond the present, and if that didn't include Shannon, it didn't bother him one bit.

Cheryl peeked around the surgery door. 'Hi, Abby. You coming to practice this arvo?'

'Yes. I brought Betsy. Dad said I could drive in two days a week.'

'I'm really glad you decided to join our team. You can really whack that ball around. I reckon you're going to be a very useful winger.'

Abby grinned at her. 'Just call me Speedy McBride.'

'Yeah, you certainly are a speedy worker. I hear you've already snared Barney Holten for a date or two.'

Abby gasped. 'What do you mean?'

'It's all over town that you had lunch together and he drove you home for starters,' grinned Cheryl. 'The rumours are flying thick and fast. I bet it's put Shannon's nose out of joint. Watch her, Abby, she's always had first claim on him.'

Abby flushed and turned away. 'You can't beat a small town for gossip.'

Later, Abby drove home from hockey practice as the soft dusk turned the trees violet. She hated the idea of people in town gossiping about her, but she had lived in enough towns and outlying districts to know that small communities thrived on everyone else's business. However, it presented an extra dimension to her problem. Being practical, she knew she shouldn't see Barney again. Her head told her there was no future in it, that she was building Barney's neighbourly interest into more than it really was. But then she remembered the look in his eyes, the tenderness of his smile and the warmth of his voice, and she tingled all over. She knew she couldn't help herself — she had to see him again.

Then, as if she had wished him there, when she drove up to the gates of Anglesea Barney was sitting on the fence, his horse tethered to the gatepost. He waved, jumped down and opened the gate for her. She stopped Betsy, her heart leaping at the sight of him, and got out as Barney closed the gate behind her.

'Thanks, Barney. You're out for a late ride.'

'Just heading back. I was hoping I'd catch you. I was wondering if your mum would like a fridge? Once I got into the shed for the typewriter I found an old Silent Knight kero fridge we had for the shearers for a time. It's old, a few nicks in it, but it runs well. What do you think?'

'Why didn't you ask my mum?' She gave him a smile.

'Because I'd rather talk to you.' He reached out and touched her hair.

'I don't know if I should be talking to you,' she said quietly, suddenly serious.

'Why?'

She took a deep breath. 'I really like you. But I don't want you to think I'm just some simple girl you can . . .' Her bravado faltered and she stopped.

'. . . fool around with?' he finished for her.

She nodded and he tipped a finger under her chin and tilted her face to look up at him. 'Abby, I won't fool around. Or take advantage of you. You're different...special. It doesn't matter about anything else. So if we like each other, why don't we just enjoy being together?'

'Because it's not that simple, Barney. If we were just fooling around it would be easier. But I like you...more than I should.' She glanced down, thinking that the word 'like' inadequately expressed the tumbling, powerful feelings Barney aroused in her.

She took a breath and continued. 'And let's be honest, I come from a different world to you. There's everything against us being more than casual friends — my family, my background, even my church.' She blushed. 'I know there's nothing serious between us, but...I don't want to get hurt,' she finished in a whisper.

'Oh Abby, I would never hurt you,' breathed Barney. He too was shaken by the surge of emotion he felt for this sweet and simple girl. He was starting to feel that they were in a small boat that had pushed off from shore without sail, engine or oars, and that they were drifting towards rapids. He was powerless to stop their inevitable flight forward; and in his heart, as he stared into her blue eyes, he was prepared to go wherever this path took them. Suddenly he wanted to take Abby in his arms and kiss her wildly, but her reserve and hesitancy held him back.

'And what about Shannon?' asked Abby.

'She's a family friend. She's always been there and maybe before she went away we all did just sort of think one day . . . Well, it seemed what our families wanted; it made sense that we might end up together. It's sort of traditional, I suppose. But not now. Definitely not now,' said Barney vehemently. 'We're different people.'

'But won't people talk?' said Abby.

Barney sighed. 'I wish people would mind their own business. Look, Abby, just let things be.'

Abby smiled. 'What will be, will be, right?' She spoke lightly, not wanting to make an issue of things. Instinctively she knew that to put any pressure on him or to expect anything more from him was inviting trouble. But an inner voice whispered, 'Tread softly, Abby, you're falling in love with this man and there can be no future for the likes of you and he.'

Barney gave her a grateful grin, feeling better for the openness of their discussion and surprised at its frankness. He was especially touched. 'I suppose you always talk like this in your family, being so open and candid. I'm not used to it. But I'm glad we cleared the air.'

'Come up to the house and talk to Mum about the fridge. She'd love it, I know. Stay for tea if you like.'

Barney rode behind Betsy as Abby headed for the cottage. He knew his dinner would be waiting in the formal dining room at Amba, but once he entered the warm, noisy and happy kitchen at the McBrides', he readily accepted their invitation to stay for stew and dumplings. Gwen put an extra chair between Colleen and Shirley; Bob opened a bottle of beer; and suddenly everybody was talking and laughing at once, telling highly embellished stories about their day.

Bob McBride rapped a knife on his plate. 'All right, settle down everyone. Abby, it's your turn to say grace.'

Silence fell around the table as heads were bowed. 'We thank thee Lord for all thy gifts, for our family, for our good friends, and our home, and for the food we are about to share. Dear Lord, we are truly grateful.'

Abby found she was stammering over words that usually fell so easily from her lips. She glanced across the table at Barney, who gave her a quick warm smile, their eyes connecting.

'Amen,' chorused the family, followed immediately by Kevin at the top of his voice: 'Two, four, six, eight, bog in, don't wait.'

The languid pallor of a small town Saturday afternoon hung over the sleepy town. There really is something special about Saturday afternoons in the country, thought Abby as she thrust shin pads inside her socks, then looked around the hockey field. The visiting team was already warming up, the sound of sticks thwacking against balls signalling the change of pace and mood. The morning shopping over, sport loomed as a popular communal way to relax until the town returned to work on Monday.

Abby studied the few small groups of spectators dotted around the field, but there was no sign of Barney. She was left with a hollow feeling which would have taken hold of her spirit had it not been for a rallying call from Cheryl that had the team trotting on to the field, passing the ball with practised ease as they took up positions for the start of the game.

Abby, on the right wing, was looking forward to the action. She felt a slight tensing and a tingle of excitement as she leaned forward on her stick, poised for a lightning reaction to the play. Within minutes she was totally immersed in the cut and thrust of the game; the fast-changing tactics, the aggression, the defence and every so often the breakaway on the wing that could give her the chance to put her team on the way to a goal. It wasn't until half-time when they stopped for a drink and sliced oranges that she suddenly saw Barney. Her heart leapt. He was standing beside Gwen and Bob who had spread a blanket in the shade of a tree.

Her delight suddenly turned to nervousness and she looked quickly around. This was madness on his part, thought Abby wildly. Joining her family to watch the game and cheer her on was making a very firm announcement of his interest in her. However, overwhelming her initial shock was a sensation of delight. Their eyes met and he gave Abby a big grin as she made her way over to him.

'So you did come then. Nice to know a man who keeps his promise to a girl.'

Barney continued her mock seriousness. 'Wouldn't have missed your first match for the world. Besides, I'm famous throughout New England for keeping promises — ask any girl.' They both laughed.

'Seen much of the game?' asked Abby, finishing her orange and accepting his handkerchief to wipe her hands.

'Missed the start, but I think I've seen the best of the action so far. You can run like a rabbit when you have to,' said Barney with genuine enthusiasm.

'Not to much effect so far,' said Abby lightly.

'We're down one-nil.' There was a sharp blast on the referee's whistle and Abby turned and looked at the teams running back on to the field. 'That's the call to battle.' She turned back to Barney briefly. 'Staying to the bitter end?'

'Wouldn't miss it for quids.'

The second half was hard fought and Abby found that the brief training had not prepared her adequately for the long tiring grind. More running around the paddocks in the evening is needed, she told herself midway through the half as she leaned on her stick, panting heavily.

Suddenly her front row was moving forward again; the ball was flicked out to her and, as she got into a rhythmic stride, she heard a shout from the sideline, 'Go, Rabbit, go!'

Abby would have grinned had it not been for a clash with a defender that required some deft stick and footwork. Quickly she was safely past the defence and snatching looks in-field at her supporting players as the opposition goal came within striking distance.

She heard a distant shout. 'Centre it, Rabbit!' And she did, right to where Cheryl was waiting in anticipation and then it was one goal all. As Cheryl and Abby ran back, arms around each other's shoulders, Abby caught sight of Barney, his hands clasped over his head in a victory salute, her mother clapping, Bob giving the thumbs-up and the youngsters jumping up and down. She waved her stick in acknowledgement.

The game finished with the score unchanged. Abby dragged herself off the field exhausted, and joined Barney and her family. Colleen and Shirley dashed on to the field to hug Abby.

Kevin handed her a peeled orange. 'It was a pretty good match . . . for a girls' game,' he conceded.

'Well done, lass,' said her father admiringly. 'Still got the touch.'

'Here, have a towel,' fussed Gwen. 'You're wringing wet.'

Abby wiped her face slowly and emerged from behind the towel to once again catch Barney's eye. She grinned. 'Thanks for the encouragement, but I'm not sure that I want to be known as Rabbit.'

'Let's talk about it over afternoon tea. I've cleared it with your mum and dad, you're excused from the delights of afternoon tea with Mrs Doherty.'

Abby once again felt her stomach somersaulting and her knees wobbling, not from physical tiredness but the anticipation of being with Barney.

'Well, in that case, I won't take long.' She ran off still feeling shaky with excitement.

The rest of the girls were meeting friends at the Athena Cafe and she certainly didn't want to go there. There'd be enough speculation over Barney joining her family to watch the match. While Shannon hadn't been there Abby had no doubt she'd hear quickly enough.

Barney drove to the river through the Saturday afternoon empty town. The puntman was sitting in the sun with his feet up on a wooden pylon, slowly reeling in a fishing line. He and Barney were friends and they exchanged light-hearted greetings.

'The dinghy is over there . . . help yourself.' He eyed Abby then winked at Barney. 'Don't do anything to rock the boat, Barney.'

Barney let the remark go without a response. He took a large paper bag and Thermos flask from the car and helped Abby into the dinghy. She sat gingerly on the seat at the stern. Barney pushed off from the bank, set the oars, and began rowing downstream.

'What a great idea, where are we going?' she asked happily.

'Anywhere . . . Keep a lookout for somewhere nice to go ashore for our picnic.'

'Aye, aye, captain. Say, I know what my dad would be singing now,' grinned Abby.

'I know, I know. *Row, row, row your boat gently down the stream,*' sang Barney as Abby joined in. '*Merrily, merrily, merrily, merrily, life is but a dream.*'

'Very good, Barney. We'll make an honorary McBride of you yet.'

Abby spotted the delicate mauve clusters of a jacaranda near an open stretch of bank and Barney steered in, leapt ashore and tied up the little boat.

They sat down and tucked into Mrs Anderson's cheese and cucumber sandwiches, Thermos of tea and fruitcake. They laughed and talked about Anglesea and Amba, the other places they'd lived.

Listening to Barney talk, Abby thought how clever and thoughtful he was. Many of the young men she'd met about town and talked to briefly, seemed empty in comparison. They were interested in beer, sport, having a few laughs at each other's expense, and making a decent quid out of the land. Honest, cheerful, down to earth, unromantic, Abby secretly thought of some of them as being a bit like the cattle they cared for — practical, useful and dull. How different Barney was. He made her laugh at nothing and feel warm and happy. He was caring and sweet, yet she detected a sadness in him, a sadness she couldn't explain. To anyone else he would seem to be a young man who had it all, but Abby suspected there was something missing in his life, some sense of loss that maybe he didn't understand either. Perhaps it came from being an only child. When she was little, when the McBride household, with its noise and clutter, seemed to leave no silent space just for her, Abby had sometimes wished she was an only child. Most of the time, however, she adored the love and support of her close-knit family.

Abby stretched out on the grass and looked at the sky through the trembling frail leaves of the delicate jacaranda. She wished she could paint and capture the pattern and shape of the leaves glazed with sunlight, silhouetted against the blue sky and drift of cloud.

Barney's shadow fell across her. He held out his hand and pulled her to her feet. Their lips met in a warm soft kiss and Barney kissed the tip of her nose as they looked into each other's eyes. 'I like being with you,' he said softly.

It was a light remark that barely cloaked the deep and disturbing feelings that threatened to overwhelm him. He took refuge in Australian understatement.

Abby recognised this and being a little unnerved by her own feelings and recognising they stood at the edge of some sort of precipice, she answered simply, 'Me too.'

They walked a little way, holding hands, looking at the sun reflected on the river where an occasional perch sent a bubble to the surface. It was comfortable being together, neither felt the need to make conversation; instead they just enjoyed the shared companionship. Abby felt as if she had known him all her life, there just seemed an inevitability, a special closeness between them, which she couldn't imagine experiencing with anyone else.

They rowed back to the punt where the puntman nodded to them, concentrating on the slight curve at the tip of his rod.

Barney and Abby drove back to town, and then wandered past the closed shops, the movie cinema where the final moments of the weekly serial's cliffhanger could be heard through the open doors, and past the blacksmith's forge, which was closed and silent. Leaving the Saturday afternoon stillness of the main street, they made their way along the rows of neat houses where hydrangeas flourished, sweet peas climbed over front fences, and short cement paths led to welcoming front doors. Occasionally they passed a man who raised his hat or a woman who smiled and nodded with obvious interest in the pair.

Barney and Abby waited by the park, holding hands as Betsy, laden with the McBrides, rolled to a stop before them.

'Had a good afternoon?' called Bob.

'Yes, we did,' Abby smiled shyly up at Barney and he kissed her lightly on the lips, then opened the rear door for Abby.

'Move over, kids. Thanks for a lovely time, Barney.'

'It's been a great day. See you soon.' He gave a wave as they pulled away.

Bob and Gwen exchanged a glance but Gwen gave Bob a look that stopped him making any comment about the tender scene they'd just observed.

Bob glanced at Abby's flushed and happy face in the rearview mirror and started to sing, '*If you were the only girl in the world and I were the only boy . . .*'

CHAPTER NINE

Bob McBride loved the end of the day best of all. With the day's hard work behind him, he could relax, replete after one of Gwen's hearty meals, his family around him.

The twin girls, smelling of Johnson's baby powder, wrapped in their dressing gowns, came into the little lounge room to kiss him goodnight.

'Who won the Monopoly game?'

'Kevin of course.'

'I think he cheats.'

'I never did!' Kevin grinned at his father and flopped on to the sofa beside his mother.

'Watcha knitting, Mum?'

'A vest for Brian. Goodness, he's turning into a beanpole. Have you finished your homework?'

'Not quite. The girls wanted a game. They know I always win and they always whinge.'

Abby looked up from the *Daily Telegraph* she brought home every night. 'How come you always win?'

'They're too scared to spend their money. I buy up everything I can.'

'I hope you won't be so free and easy with real money,' said Gwen.

'You don't need money, you buy on the HP nowadays,' replied Kevin cockily.

'Not this family,' retorted his father. 'If you haven't got the money in your pocket, you can't buy it.'

Abby didn't mention the dress she had put away on layby at McKenzies.

'Off you go to that homework, young man. Then you can listen to "The Amateur Hour",' said Bob, and Kevin headed back to the kitchen table, the workplace for all family projects.

Bob turned on the wireless and the family went quiet. Silence always reigned during the evening ABC news, just as it did at one o'clock each afternoon for Gwen's favourite serial, 'Blue Hills'.

Abby folded up the newspaper and stretched.

'Why do those announcers sound so plummy? Why can't they talk like the rest of us?' she wondered aloud.

'They're radio announcers,' whispered Gwen. 'They learn from the BBC.'

'Hush up, girls, I want to find out how the Redex Reliability Trial is going.'

Gwen and Abby exchanged smiles. 'Can you just see Betsy racing round Australia?' whispered Gwen again.

The news over, Abby went to make the last pot of tea while Bob and Gwen chewed over the events on the news.

'So they're still talking about bringing in this television. I reckon it'll be a bad thing,' said Bob, lighting up one of Gwen's ready-made cigarettes.

'Would be nice to see something like the coronation though,' said Gwen.

'Fancy sitting in your lounge room watching some goggle box. It'll kill reading, and the wireless and going to the pictures, you mark my words,' prophesied Bob.

'Talking of the pictures,' said Abby, coming in with a tray with the cups on it, 'I'm going out on Saturday night. Going to see *Rear Window*.'

'Who with?' asked Bob.

'Grace Kelly.'

They all burst out laughing.

'I'm going with Barney,' said Abby, setting out the cups.

Gwen and Bob exchanged a swift look.

'Just the two of you?'

Abby straightened up and stared at her parents. 'Yes. Why not?'

'We've been through this before, luv. Go out and enjoy yourself, by all means. Just don't expect it to lead to anything. He's a decent enough bloke and you're a good girl, but don't you start getting big ideas here,' warned her father.

'Why does everyone think I'm some sort of man trap and that Barney and I seeing each other is a real big deal?' demanded Abby angrily. 'I'm just as good as he is, you know.'

'Keep your hair on, Abby,' said Bob calmly. 'And yes, you are just as a good a person as he is. But there's a bit of a difference in your backgrounds and you know it.'

'And there's your faith, too, luv,' said Gwen gently. 'The Catholic Church doesn't like its members marrying outsiders, you know that.'

'The church should be understanding and forgiving, not punishing and cold-hearted,' said Abby. 'It's time things changed, it's supposed to be the age of the modern girl. It's not unheard of for people to marry who they want. The war was supposed to change things; women did their bit and now we're supposed to put on aprons and go back into the kitchen and do what our husbands and the church tell us!' declared Abby heatedly.

'Steady on,' said Bob. 'I'm first to say the ladies did a terrific job when the chaps were away at war, but now the men want to work and the women want to have families and enjoy peace-time niceties. And as for the church... well, you've broken the rules, Ab, and you're going to have to come to terms with that. We're not criticising, we just don't want to see you get hurt, luv.'

'It's a bit late for that. Let me worry about my life. I just wish everyone would mind their own business.' Abby hurried from the room.

'I'll fetch the teapot,' said Gwen. 'Let her be. She's sensible.'

'Sense sometimes flies out the window where the heart is concerned,' mumbled Bob, reaching for the paper.

Barney pushed the suitcase into the boot of the Ford, slammed it shut and turned to his mother and father, giving them a half smile.

'Don't you worry about me, dear. Everything will turn out all right I'm sure,' said his mother as she gave him a big hug.

'You take care, Mother. The specialist will

probably give you a big gold star,' said Barney warmly.

'I hope so, dear. Please keep an eye on Diet and Tucker...'

'Right, Enid, let's get on the road. It's a long drive to Sydney.'

Phillip shook his son's hand. 'We'll be at the Australia Hotel. Be back as soon as we can.'

'Take your time and don't worry. Take Mum to the Tivoli or something.' Barney leaned through the car window and kissed his mother on the cheek. 'Try and have a bit of fun. Go shopping, take in a film at the Prince Edward, live it up,' he said brightly.

Enid gave him a look that said, 'You know your father...'

Barney knew his parents would eat in the conservative hotel dining room, speaking little and retiring early. He wondered whether either of them ever longed to do things, see places, without the other. What had their life been like before they married? It occurred to him that he had never asked. Had their lives he'd observed in these recent years been how it always was?

As the shiny Ford V8 headed down the formal driveway, he wondered what Mrs Anderson could tell him about life at Amba when he was a baby. However, he had something better to think about at the moment — seeing Abby on Saturday night. He had suggested the movies and was now wondering where he could take her afterwards.

The New England Highway south was free of traffic. The occasional car flicked past in the opposite direction. Enid crossed her legs and angled her body slightly towards the window, gazing at the wall of forest gums and ironbarks that screened the road. Phillip was deep in thought. They never talked much in the car. If she made a comment about the scenery or something that caught her eye, they were past it before he responded, and she had the feeling she was intruding on his thoughts and disturbing his concentration on the driving.

Enid wasn't looking forward to seeing the heart specialist. She dreaded the tests and her nervousness made her heart seem even more fluttery than usual. She hated people fussing over her; she felt such a bother to them and especially to Phillip. She wished no one knew she had a heart problem. It didn't cause her a great deal of pain; the breathlessness and her heart's irregular rhythm were bothersome, but it wasn't as if she was an invalid. Yet she did feel like such an old woman. Where had her life gone? One day she'd been a young woman, in love and dreaming dreams that never became reality. When she thought about it she could still feel the pain of the day she'd been told of the death of her fiancé. If Ray had lived, would her life have been better, happier? Or was this all there was: raising a child, keeping an orderly house, standing in the shadow of a successful man? Now Barney was independent, her dogs and her garden gave her the most pleasure in life.

Life with Phillip was placid. He had long ago given up making sexual demands on her, and now they slept in separate beds. She had regarded sex as her duty but never understood why it was such a passionate force in other people's lives. She had only ever experienced sex with Phillip but she could recall the ardent kisses of her youth and she regretted letting her love go off to war, their union unfulfilled. 'Wait till I come home. We'll have our whole lives ahead of us.' But they didn't and she felt cheated. Ray remained strong and straight and youthful in her memory, while she was aging, no longer pretty or desirable.

Enid knew Phillip had regarded himself as second best in a competition he had lost without the chance to fight. But he had offered her security, a safe haven, and she had welcomed that. They had a pact and she had adhered to her part of it out of loyalty and, she realised now, gratitude. But with years stretching ahead with more of this sameness, a sadness crept into her soul. There would be no adventurous trips up the Amazon, no passionate love affairs, no large and boisterous family to occupy and interest her, and as she stepped into the unknown, she would leave no footprint on the world she left behind. Had there been a point in her life where things could have changed, been different? Was there a signpost she'd missed, some subtle gesture or indication from Phillip that she'd ignored? Enid closed her eyes against these unpleasant thoughts and tried to make her mind a blank. It was becoming a practised habit.

Phillip was aware she'd slipped into that nether region she inhabited so much of the time. He was more concerned than he showed about her 'condition', as he called it. He dreaded the idea that she could become an invalid, or suddenly leave him alone. Enid was a stoic if pliant buffer between him and his son, and the rest of the world. He didn't have to cope with socialising while he had the excuse of a reclusive wife in frail health. Those that knew him would be astounded at the idea that the formidable and often imperious Phillip Holten was, in fact, terrified of coping with normal social intercourse and the idea that strangers might breach his personal barriers.

Phillip had met Enid through mutual friends

at the Royal Easter Show when he had been showing his father's prize rams. She was fascinated by the huge merinos and, after a long conversation, he had invited her to morning tea. After that they met regularly, Phillip visiting Sydney as often as he could. He found her attractive, well bred and very intriguing. Beneath her bright and cheerful demeanour, there was a vulnerability that drew him to her.

It wasn't until he was courting her seriously that she told him of the loss of her fiancé in the War. Phillip thought he had understood but was convinced that his living love for Enid would win out over her love for a dead man; he had been wrong. Even after he had won her, he still felt second best. Still, Enid had been a good wife to him for a while. She wasn't the country woman that he'd been expected to marry, but she settled happily into the quiet rural life. All had been peaceful with them until the long-awaited arrival of a child.

He had expected a child but did not expect it to ruffle the smooth running of his existence. Which the child had not. What he hadn't anticipated was the withdrawal of his wife, a loss he blamed on his son. He had tried to bring Enid back to his world, but he could not fight the pull of maternal instinct and so he adjusted his life accordingly.

The car swung onto a long straight stretch of road and Phillip looked across at his wife. He was shocked at the sadness in her face. It sent a strange feeling through him, a feeling that stabbed uncomfortably at his stomach. 'You all right, dear?' he asked with genuine concern and warmth.

Enid was a little startled by his voice and turned from the window towards Phillip. She looked at him for a moment then said quietly, 'Yes, Phillip. I'm fine. Just thinking a bit.'

'About the past?' he asked softly.

'Yes.' Phillip nodded and after a pause Enid went on. 'I was just thinking about a few things and the trip we're making . . . another journey and we don't know just what it's going to lead to. I know it leads to Sydney, but what else? We really can't be sure of anything, can we? It's all a mystery. That's life, isn't it? A journey full of surprises. I read once that someone said it is better to journey than to arrive. Have you heard that, Phillip?'

Phillip was surprised. He couldn't remember when his wife had last talked like this and he was lost for an immediate response. Instead he simply nodded an acknowledgement.

Enid went on as if she had never asked him a question, or at least never expected a reply. 'My father used to say that the first step of any journey is the hardest. I'm not so sure of that now. I rather think that arriving at the end might be the hardest step of all.'

Phillip smiled at her. 'You might be right, dear. I've never really thought about it.'

For a while they drove in silence, Enid looking straight ahead but not really seeing anything. Then suddenly she spoke, not, it seemed, to Phillip, but to herself. 'I wonder if we're lost? People sometimes do get lost on journeys, don't they?'

Phillip reached over and took her hand in his, a great sadness sweeping over him. He had no answers to her questions. He gave her hand a squeeze, and she softly squeezed his in response — the first physical and emotional touching they'd shared in a very long time.

Sharing a homemade ginger beer on the verandah with Mrs Anderson, Barney decided to ask her about the old days. He took a sip as she shaded her eyes and stared across the gardens.

'Jim is out there somewhere. My goodness these shrubs have grown up since we've been here. I'll give him a hoy. Cooeee, Jim. Smoko,' she called.

'You came here when I was a baby. What were my parents like then?' asked Barney.

'Younger! Like all of us,' laughed Mrs Anderson. Then, seeing Barney's serious face, she said, 'They were pretty much as they are now, I suppose. Your mother was so taken up with you. You came along as a bit of surprise — she'd given up ever having a child. She was obviously delighted. Your father wasn't so fussed about there not being a child. More of a woman's need, I suppose. Not that he wasn't pleased at your arrival, of course,' she added hastily.

Barney sipped his drink. 'Do you really think so, Mrs A? I just look at the way my family is, compared to ... other families. There just isn't the closeness, between any of us.'

'Ah, families are strange creatures. We all have differences and we all have similarities. I came from a big family, so did Jim, yet we didn't have kids. Maybe it's God's way of balancing things out. Though I have to confess I feel I've shared in bringing you along. Jim and I have both got a kick out of your achievements over the years. From learning to walk, to graduating from university. My, we were so proud of you that day.'

Her face glowed with pleasure and Barney's heart lurched. He had always taken the Andersons' presence in his life for granted, though with gratitude and affection. It was always to Mrs Anderson he ran in times of upheaval. She had always been so giving and generous with her love and advice; Jim, too, in his stolid, quiet and helpful way. The time he'd taken in teaching him practical things like the basics of an engine or how to catch yabbies in the creek. Yet it suddenly dawned on Barney that his family had never reciprocated. Why hadn't he thought of asking the Andersons to be there on the day he graduated? They probably wouldn't have agreed, it not being 'their place', but they would have appreciated being asked.

'I've always thought of you as my second mum,' said Barney softly, and meaning it.

Mrs Anderson nodded and busied herself with pouring tea for Jim. Then after a minute, she said, 'I will say though, Barney, seeing as how you've asked . . . things did change . . . but slowly like. One day you suddenly look back and realise things are different. I think your dad felt a bit left out when you were born, so he tended to become more involved with the property and left the domestic side to your mum and myself. She didn't get her strength back for a long time after you were born. Jim and I settled in and here we still are!'

'What's that? My ears are burning.' Jim wiped his feet, took off his hat and sat on the step as his wife handed him a cup of tea with a biscuit on the saucer.

'Thanks, Rene. What are you two rabbiting on about?'

'Barney was wondering what it was like around here when he was a little bloke.'

'The place has improved a lot, but it hasn't changed all that much I s'pose.'

'We were talking about his mum and dad. How people change.'

'We just get older,' said Jim with a wry smile. 'You're not thinking of making any big changes when you take over Amba?' he asked suddenly.

Barney stood and shook his head. 'No. I imagine things will go on pretty much the same. Well, I'll be off.'

'Did you mention the weekend, luv?' Jim reminded his wife.

'Oh goodness me, I forgot.' She turned to Barney. 'Would you mind managing on your own this weekend, seeing as your parents are away? Jim and I thought we might take a little break. I'll leave some cooked food for you.'

'That's perfectly okay by me. Don't go to a lot of trouble. I can fix something and I'm going out Saturday night.'

The quivering words *The End* were obscured by the red and gold curtain pulled across the suspended screen. Abby drew a deep breath and turned to Barney, realising she was still gripping his hand. 'That was fantastic.'

'Good film for sure,' he agreed.

'I got so scared in parts, I was shaking!'

'I liked that,' grinned Barney. 'I liked you squeezing my hand.'

Abby blushed and dropped his hand. 'You were on the edge of your seat too.'

'You're right. Come on, let's escape.'

They hurried to Barney's car. As he opened the door for her he asked, 'Well, what do you feel like? We could still get a steak at the hotel, or there's the Golden Dragon if you feel like Chinese food.'

Barney slipped behind the wheel of the Holden FJ and looked at her pretty profile. 'What's it to be?'

'Whatever you think, Barney.'

'You don't sound too excited about either choice. I suppose we could go . . . Oh never mind.' He turned the ignition on but didn't put the car in gear.

He had thought he might ask Abby back to Amba as the house was empty and he liked the idea of them eating a meal in his home. However, he knew that such an invitation could be misinterpreted and Abby was too well brought up to go to a man's house alone. He had no intention of making any serious advances towards her, but she stirred disturbing emotions in him.

'Let's just enjoy the drive home,' suggested Abby.

It was a balmy night and the moon was full. As they reached the ridge that marked the boundary between Amba and Anglesea, Barney was about to point out the spectacular view down into the valley when a sound like a rifle shot rang out, and the steering wheel pulled to the left.

'Oh no,' groaned Barney. 'A blowout!'

It was the front tyre on the driver's side, which was almost flat. 'Must have been a sharp stone. Make yourself comfortable, Abby, while I change it.' Barney opened the boot and took out the spare tyre, a rusty jack and an old rug for Abby. 'Here, sit on this and look at the view.'

It was an unforgettable sight. The enfolding hills were a smudge against the clear sky and tree-lined creeks shone like silver plate in the moonlight. The fat butter moon and diamond stars hung reachably close.

Barney worked steadily, grunting once at a stubborn nut, but he soon had the spare tyre in place. He stood, wiped his hands, and sat down beside Abby. 'Whew! All fixed.' He paused and for the first time took in the view and the mood of the moonlit valley. 'My . . . it's magic, eh?'

'It certainly is. It looks better at night than day.'

'I didn't mean just the view. I meant, being here with you, Abby...' They reached for each other and their lips crushed together, blotting out all other thoughts.

Moments of time blurred as they were swept into a world of their own. They leaned back, their bodies entwined, surrendering to their deep true feelings.

Barney ran his hands along Abby's body making her quiver. They pulled a little apart and looked deep into each other's eyes. 'I've never done this before... kissed anyone like this... Oh, Abby.'

'Me either,' she whispered back and they reached for each other again, overcome by the power and ardent heat of their passion. Once unleashed there was no holding back their feelings.

It happened easily and naturally, with no collusion, no coyness. At one point he held her by the shoulders and looked at her sweet face. 'Abby... are you sure?'

She nodded and hugged him tightly.

Despite a little fumbling, a giggle, a gasp of pain that was soon replaced by soft sighs of pleasure, the first-time experience for both of them was sweetly satisfying.

Barney smoothed Abby's damp hair off her forehead, delighting in this intimate gesture. She ran her hands down his strong back and glanced shyly at his body, marvelling at the wonder of it all.

Slowly Abby became aware again of the world that was beyond their bodies and their passion. Over Barney's shoulder she found herself focusing on one particular star in a universe of stars.

'There's a star looking at us,' she whispered.

Barney lifted his head from nuzzling her hair, settled close and, holding her hand, asked with warmth, 'Which one?'

Abby carefully led him through the heavens to her star near the Southern Cross.

'Let's call it our star for the rest of our lives,' whispered Barney.

Both were overwhelmed with love. They kissed and then Abby pulled away. 'That friendly star may warm the soul but it doesn't do much for the body . . . It's getting cold.' She turned to him, took his hand and they looked into each other's eyes. They knew that neither of them really wanted to leave.

'Hard to come back down to earth,' said Barney quietly but with feeling.

Abby nodded.

'Nothing will ever be the same, Ab. We can't undo what's happened. I love you so much.'

'I love you too, Barney. Very much.'

At the gate to Anglesea Abby got out. 'Don't drive up to the house, we might wake them. I'll walk the last mile home.' The idea of walking along the track in the moonlight through the trees appealed to her. She wanted to savour all these special moments.

'Not on your own. I'll drive slowly a little way with the lights off and walk you the last bit,' he whispered, as if the McBrides could hear them.

He waited and watched her hurry along the last of the track to the house, till she turned and waved and disappeared from sight. For both of them the night was like a dream, and for the moment the promise of the future shone as bright and untarnished as the stars above.

The following morning Barney came into the surgery and placed a bunch of roses from Enid's garden on her desk. They smiled at each other, a warm, loving, knowing smile.

'Meet me for lunch in the park,' he whispered. 'I'll get us sandwiches.'

Screened by trees, they sat in the sunlight and held hands and ate their sandwiches. Barney turned to Abby and kissed a crumb from her bottom lip. 'Ab...I love you. And I'm not just saying that because of last night. I really do love you. So much that I won't let it happen again...get carried away like that. I just don't want you to think that was why I asked you out or anything. I want to keep seeing you, and I promise I won't let it happen again.'

She smiled tenderly at him. 'It wasn't anything horrible, Barney,' she teased. 'But I appreciate you saying that. I love you too. Do you think we should keep seeing each other though? I mean...' She stumbled to a halt, not wanting to say that she knew their love had no future.

Barney kissed her again, a long passionate kiss which she returned eagerly. He drew away and touched her cheek with his fingertip. 'Shush, Abby...Let's not say any more. Let's just enjoy being together. I just want to be with you.'

For the next few weeks they saw each other every moment they could, throwing caution to the wind, not caring what the town gossips were saying. Picnics, horse riding, hikes, movies — everything delighted them when they were in each other's company. They laughed; they teased each other; they shared secrets and grew closer and closer together. Barney was totally enraptured by this girl and Abby knew she would never love anyone the way she loved Barney.

But a shadow crept into her heart for she knew it couldn't last. One day their two different worlds would force them apart and she kept saying to herself, 'The next time I see him, I'll say we can't go on like this.' But as soon she saw his happy grin, felt the touch of his hand and tasted his sweet and stolen kisses, her resolve weakened. 'Next time, next time. One of us has to be strong and stop this before we break our hearts. It's wonderful but we have no future together.' But each time her heart overruled her head.

Barney didn't see any problems. He had found the girl of his dreams, he loved Abby and all he thought of each morning was when he'd see her next. Tomorrow was a long way away.

CHAPTER TEN

SHANNON LEANED ON THE WOOL-CLASSING TABLE, watching Barney write in his notebook, which was where he kept his figures, calculations, details of sheep and day-to-day activities about the property.

'So. How's your horse coming along?' he asked.

'Not bad. There's such a lot of boring drilling and practising for dressage. The jumping is more fun.'

'Can't do one without the other?'

'Not really.' Shannon gave him a shrewd look. 'So what have you been up to? Haven't seen you around lately.'

'The usual is keeping me busy, that's all.' Barney straightened up and buttoned the flap of his top shirt pocket over his notebook.

'Does the usual include Saturday night at the pictures, horse riding and picnics with a certain girl?'

He gave her a cold look. 'Perhaps. Now look, Shannon, we've been through this...'

'You're being a fool, Barney. And you're making her out to be just as bad, or worse.'

'And what does that mean?' Shannon's roundabout conversations irritated him. Abby was so straight to the point and uncomplicated.

'The general belief is that when boys like you take out girls like her, it's only for one reason.'

'And I'll tell you the reason, Shannon. It's because I like Abby's company. It's that simple.' He paused and took a deep breath. 'Look, Shannon, you're a pretty girl, you have a lot going for you. Don't spoil our friendship. Choose one of those blokes that are always hanging about, and have a good time. I'll see you around.' He stepped into the truck, gave her a slight smile and drove away. Shannon remounted her horse and rode back towards Anglesea in a fuming temper.

Gwen noticed there was something different about Abby and she decided to talk to her one

Sunday afternoon while they were doing the huge pile of ironing in the kitchen.

'Barney means a lot to you, doesn't he, Ab?' She continued to sprinkle water over a cotton shirt then roll it up for ironing.

Abby didn't let the remark interrupt her rhythmic sweep of the iron across one of Kevin's school shirts. She had been expecting her mother to say something like that for some time. 'Yes, Mum. I love him,' she said calmly.

'Deeply?'

Abby stopped ironing, stood the iron on its end and looked at her mother. Their eyes met. 'Desperately . . . I'm terribly in love with him, Mum.' Her eyes began to fill.

'Switch off the iron, luv, and sit down for a while.'

Over the pile of damped-down clothes, Gwen watched her daughter. It's going to hurt the girl, she thought, hurt her badly.

Abby sat across from her mother, arms folded on the table. She reached into her pocket for a handkerchief and wiped her eyes. 'I know what you're thinking, Mum . . . that it's an impossible situation . . . that it can't work . . . and . . . Oh God, Mum, what's the answer? You have no idea just how much I love him.'

'Yes I have. Remember, mums can be as deeply

in love as their daughters . . . and we have memories too, you know.'

Abby said nothing, but sniffed a little into her handkerchief and wiped her eyes again.

'I don't think there's an easy answer at this point, Abby. That sort of love can be like a river in flood. You've just got to hang on to something till the flood passes.'

'What do I hang on to?' Abby pleaded.

'Us, Abby, and the faith of the church.' She walked around the table and wrapped her arms about her daughter.

Abby nodded but somehow she didn't think her church was going to come up with any answers.

Enid and Phillip arrived home and Barney and the dogs ran down the steps to the driveway to greet them. Barney gave his mother an effusive hug, lifting her off the ground, causing Enid to gasp in surprise.

'Barney, put me down. What has come over you?'

Barney grinned and ignored the question. 'How are you, Mum? How did the tests turn out?'

Before she could reply, Phillip interrupted. 'Not quite the right moment for medical details, Barnard. A little later perhaps.' He stretched out his hand, which Barney took. 'Good to see you, son. Any problems about the place?'

'Everything is perfect, Father. Absolutely perfect,' he said with enthusiasm. Phillip gave him a quizzical look as he unloaded the suitcases from the car. Mrs Anderson appeared and she and Enid led the way indoors.

That night, after dinner, Phillip sat with Barney in the study sharing a port.

'It's not too bad, son. Your mother has a heart problem that can't be fixed. But as long as she is careful and there's no excessive stress, she should handle the condition for a long time to come.'

'Not too bad . . . but not too good either,' said Barney.

'Well, your mother is handling it very well, son, and it's up to us to give her all the support we can.' Phillip took a sip of his port. 'By the way, we took your advice and went to the Tivoli. Splendid variety show. Enid enjoyed it immensely.'

Enid was sitting in her rose garden the next day when Barney arrived with two glasses of lemon squash for their morning tea.

'It's lovely to be back home and in the garden,' sighed his mother. 'And with you,' she added fondly.

'Good to have you back, Mum. Dad tells me that the medical situation isn't all that bad,' he said, trying to mask his concern.

'No. It's nothing to get alarmed about I'm told. No point in worrying anyway.' Enid sipped her squash. 'By the way, I was talking to Mrs Pemberton after breakfast this morning.'

Barney drained his glass. Uh-oh, he thought. Here it comes. He turned towards his mother. 'I suppose she was full of news.'

'Yes. She told me Shannon was upset at you seeing so much of the McBride girl.' Enid studied his face. 'You're fond of her, I take it?'

Barney nodded.

'Your father isn't going to like this, Barney. You know he wouldn't approve of such a match. Best to end it now, dear.'

'I love her, Mum.'

Enid looked helplessly at him. 'Oh dear . . . Oh dear,' she sighed.

One afternoon Abby went for a walk before tea. She was confused about her feelings and needed to think things through. It was late afternoon; the sun was sinking, tinging the clouds pink and gold, and the first breath of evening air stirred the leaves. She walked in a world of her own, lost in thoughts of her love for Barney. She tingled as she hugged memories to herself: of Barney's arms and lips, the touch of his hands on her body, the sound of his soft laugh and gentle voice. How she loved him; he dominated her thoughts and emotions to such an extent that she could think of little else and sometimes it threatened to make her feel physically ill. She sat down and leaned against an old eucalypt and watched the day fade. Soon she would have to go back as tea would be on the table. Tripe and onions in white parsley sauce. Abby closed her eyes, not feeling at all like food.

Through her closed eyelids, a light seemed to burn like a ball of fire. In a flash she saw and felt and knew . . . she was pregnant. The little signs she had ignored, a creeping awareness that had tried to penetrate her mind but which she had pushed away, now struck her with the force of a blow. Yes, weeks had passed, more than she had realised.

Fear, shock, dread were quickly replaced by a growing feeling of joy. That within her body was a part of Barney. That their shared love had created a tangible result. The crystallisation of their love and passion would be there for the whole world to witness. She would always have Barney with her now for she had his child.

Abby put off facing the reality of her condition for a month. She longed to share the burden with her mother, but first she realised she needed medical confirmation. With great difficulty she worked up courage to ask Doctor Malone to examine her.

She stood in his office, her eyes downcast as he studied her. 'What seems to be the problem, Abby? You aren't feeling well?'

She shook her head. 'I won't go through the symptoms, they're pretty standard, I suppose. I . . . I think I might be pregnant.'

Doctor Malone tried to cover his own surprise and disappointment. He would never have picked Abby as a girl that would come to him 'in trouble'.

He confirmed her suspicions and then drew the curtain around the examination table. 'What are you going to do, Abby?' he asked, as she dressed with shaking hands.

'I don't know. I'm still adjusting to the whole idea. I wasn't sure. You won't say anything, will you, Doctor Malone?' she asked quickly.

'I'm bound by my oath, Abby. But it is a situation you are going to have to think through carefully. I would like to advise you. Have you told the father and your own family?' he asked kindly.

Abby stepped from behind the short curtain and sat down opposite his desk, shaking her head.

'You are going to tell them soon, I hope. You have a pretty serious decision to make.'

Abby looked taken aback. 'What's that?'

'What is to become of the child.'

Abby closed her eyes, suddenly feeling she might faint as confusion swept over her. 'What do you mean, *become* of the child? It's mine, I'll keep it.'

'Is the father going to marry you?' As Abby stared at him, pale-faced and silent, Doctor Malone continued. 'Be practical, Abby. If you both love each other and plan to marry, then do so in the near future. This is not such an unusual occurrence. But if you don't plan to marry, then the child must be taken care of. Naturally, as you and I are Catholics, we must see this matter through. I can put you in touch with a home in Sydney that looks after girls in your condition and finds good Catholic families for the babies.'

'I have my own family. They'll look after me. I don't need to find a home for my baby.'

'Abby, you will need medical supervision. This doesn't just affect you and your future. There is the father, your own family. It could hurt your brother and sisters at school. You know how people gossip.' He reached out and patted her hand. 'Go home and talk it through with your family. And tell them there are lots of families wanting a baby to love. You will get over this and go on to have your own family. Don't throw your life away, Abby. I've seen it happen too often.'

Abby put it off. When Barney phoned her the following week at the surgery she was evasive about meeting him. 'Abby, I really want to see you. What's wrong?' He could tell something was bothering her.

'Nothing, I'm fine.'

'Abby, you sound funny. Let me cheer you up. I want to spend all day Saturday with you. Please, Ab . . . Get out of hockey practice if you can.'

'I already have,' said Abby slowly. She'd had a hard time giving Cheryl an excuse for getting out of the team. She felt it best to do so early and had said she had to spend more time helping her mother.

'Good. Great minds think alike. I've been planning it all week. I'll pick you up at ten Saturday morning.'

Abby spent two agonising nights lying awake in her bed, rationally thinking through her predicament. She loved Barney but she knew there had always been a time limit on their love and finally it had run out. She would tell him she couldn't see him anymore. That it had gone too far, got too serious and it would be best for both of them to cut it off now. She wanted his baby, but she didn't want Barney to be forced into a situation he hadn't chosen. She could just hear his parents telling him she was using the oldest trick in the book; but even if this hadn't happened, she knew she and Barney didn't have a future together.

On Saturday morning, Abby told her mother she was going out for the day with Barney. She set off down the track to the gate and met Barney halfway.

'Couldn't wait to see me, eh?' he grinned, leaning over and opening the door for her.

Abby gave a wan smile and he kissed her on the cheek. 'So what are we doing, Barney?'

'You'll see.'

They drove for an hour and turned off the main road onto a dirt road and then onto a track. A stand of casuarinas on the bend of the river came into view.

'A magic spot, Abby, magical and beautiful, like you.'

They unpacked Mrs Anderson's picnic hamper, collected twigs and built a fire to boil the billy for a cup of tea, then they went exploring. To their surprise, they found a little fenced graveyard. Standing in the little graveyard was a headstone which recorded the loss of a baby — *Joan Alice Gilbert aged one month* — and suddenly Abby began to cry.

Barney gathered her in his arms and comforted her. 'Ab . . . why are you so upset?' He kissed her teary face.

'Normally it wouldn't...Oh Barney.' She wrenched away from him and turned and ran, stumbling blindly over the rough ground.

Barney quickly caught up to her, took her arm and spun her round. He spoke firmly, concern in his eyes. 'Abby, what is the matter? Please, what's bothering you?'

Abby closed her eyes and through her tears, whispered, 'I'm going to have a baby.'

'Our baby? A child? You and I?' Barney could hardly speak.

Abby nodded, too afraid to open her eyes.

He didn't speak for a moment and Abby slowly pulled her arm away. Fearfully, she looked up at him. Barney had a silly grin on his face and his eyes were shining. 'Oh Abby . . .' He gathered her in his arms. 'Why are you so unhappy? Don't be scared. It will be all right. I'm happy.' He rocked her in his arms and she leaned against him, great sobs escaping from her.

When she finally gathered herself together, she took a deep breath and spoke calmly. 'I know we didn't want this to happen, but it has and it's my decision as to the future. I know your position, and I'm not asking anything from you, Barney, nor expecting anything —'

'Wait a minute, Abby,' he interrupted, 'I have a say in this. It's my baby too and I say there is no question but you marry me. I *want* to marry you. I love you, Abby.'

Abby gave him a tremulous smile. 'Barney, that's a lovely thing to say. But be sensible. You know there is no way your family will allow you to marry me.'

'They can't stop me!'

Abby put a finger to his lips. 'They will, Barney, there's more than one good reason for them to object. And the future of Amba rests with you. I love you too much to let you ruin all that.'

'No, Abby, you're wrong.' Barney looked angry. 'And I don't want you to even think about any other solution . . . like, you know, getting rid of it.'

'I'm a Catholic, Barney, I can't go against my faith. Another reason your parents won't let us marry . . . my church.'

'You'd put all that before us? You obviously don't love me as much as I love you,' said Barney bitterly.

His words stung Abby and she turned away from him, starting back to the car. She loved him enough to refuse to marry him and to keep their baby. They packed up the car in silence, each absorbed in their own thoughts. Barney was still coming to terms with the news but wouldn't for one minute take back anything he'd said. He did want to marry Abby; he was falling in love with her and this just affirmed the strength of his feelings. It would not be easy, he could see that, but they'd work something out. She was proud and stubborn but he had just as much say in this situation.

He opened the car door for her and suddenly asked, 'Who else knows, Abby? Your parents?'

'Not yet,' she answered quietly.

'Do you want me to come with you when you talk to them? You can't do everything on your own.'

'It's all right, Barney. It's best if I talk to them alone. I'll tell them what you said,' she answered in a tired voice. And sensing his next thought she added, 'I'd put off telling your family for a bit. Until we've sorted things out.'

He nodded but he knew what their reaction would be.

They drove home in silence. Once, Barney reached over and stroked Abby's cheek. She felt his love in the tender gesture and her heart ached. He wasn't making this any easier for her. She was trying to be practical and, although she wanted to marry Barney more than anything else in the world, she knew it wouldn't work in the long run. But she had his child within her and that would always bond him to her no matter what. A tear rolled down her cheek, but Barney, lost in his own tumbling thoughts and churning emotions, didn't see it. By the time they'd arrived at the entrance to Anglesea, Abby had composed herself.

Barney parked away from the house and for a moment they sat in silence, watching Kevin and the girls shoo the chooks and Tom Turkey into their pen in the distance.

'Abby, I'll ask you again . . . please marry me.'

'Don't ask me again! I can't! *It won't work!*' She wrenched open the car door and stumbled out of the car and raced to the house. Miserably, Barney drove away, and Abby went to her room and shut the door.

Kevin edged in the back door with the eggs. 'Here, Mum — catch!' He bowled an egg to her.

'Kevin! How many times do I have to tell you — don't do that to me! Put the eggs in the bowl carefully,' grumbled Gwen.

'You always catch them, Mum. Just checking your reflexes. Say, what's up with Abby? She and Barney have a blue?'

'I don't know. Why?'

'She looked pretty cranky and she ran away from him.'

'I thought I heard the back door slam. Leave her be, Kev.'

Abby excused herself from having dinner and later, with Brian in bed and Bob fiddling with spark plugs spread on newspaper on the kitchen table, Gwen went to see Abby. She sat on the edge of the bed and, looking at her daughter's pale, tear-stained face, took her hand.

'What is it, darl?'

'Oh Mum.' The tears flowed and Gwen held her hand until she could speak again. 'I love Barney, I really do. But I can't see him any more...'

'Well, you knew it was always on the cards. You belong to different worlds.'

'Mum, you don't understand. Barney wants to marry me. But I won't...because I'm... pregnant.'

Gwen stared in stunned silence as Abby rushed on. 'I'm sorry. I didn't mean this to happen. It was just once...He didn't take advantage or anything like that. We both love each other...'

'Abby, if he wants to marry you and you both love each other, why not get married?'

'I don't want him to marry me because he feels he has to...it would go against us in the end.'

'But surely it's better than what people will say anyway.' Gwen hesitated. 'Will you put the baby up for adoption? What does Barney think? We'd better talk this over with Dad.'

'It's my decision, Mum.' Abby began weeping again. 'It's my baby and I want to keep it.'

'It won't be easy,' said Gwen, then added brightly, 'but still, what's another mouth to feed in this house. Abby, I don't want to lose my first grandchild, so if you want to keep the baby that's fine by me and your dad will back you up, you can be sure of that.'

Abby looked at her mother with overflowing love. 'I love you both so much. I knew you'd stick by me.'

Mother and daughter held each other in a silent embrace.

CHAPTER ELEVEN

ABBY CLOSED THE DOOR TO DOCTOR MALONE'S office and returned to her desk feeling faint. It hadn't been an easy conversation. She had broken the news to him that she had the support of her family and would keep her baby.

He had shaken his head. 'I should talk to your parents, Abby. Do you really realise what a dramatic change this will be and what hardship this is going to bring to all of you?'

Abby smiled ruefully. 'I believe so. But I have an extraordinary family, Doctor Malone. I'm very lucky. The baby will be part of that family. Mum is determined that I still make a life of my own. Although naturally I'm not just dumping the baby on her. It's still my responsibility.'

Doctor Malone shook his head in resignation and respect. 'Well, it's a shame more families aren't as supportive and caring as yours, but I still leave the option open to you that I can put that baby in a secure home with good people who cannot have a child of their own. Maybe they can give your child more opportunities than you can, Abby — a good school and so forth.'

Abby had thought of this but simply said, 'But I am its mother and no one will love it like me.'

'And the father?'

'He's upset I won't marry him. At least this way he can also have access to his child.'

'You seem to have thought it all through, Abby. I just hope you're strong enough and prepared enough for the backlash that will come your way in a small town like this. Your whole family could be ostracised.'

'My, what a furore over one small baby,' Abby smiled. 'Thank you for your kindness and advice, Doctor Malone.'

Barney rapped at the screened front door. Gwen came out, wiping damp hands on her apron. She looked surprised to see Barney standing there holding his hat.

'Morning, Mrs McBride. Could I come in and have a talk with you and Bob please.'

'Of course, Barney. Come in and make yourself at home. I'll give Bob a hoy, it's near enough to smoko time.' She banged on the sheet of metal hanging by the back door to summon Bob to the house. 'Do you mind sitting in the kitchen? I've got a couple of things on the go, a cake and bread and such.' As Barney settled himself at the table, tucking his long legs out of the way, she began kneading dough in the bowl. 'I know why you're here, Barney. Abby has told us the news.' Gwen spoke calmly without animosity or accusation.

'I love Abby and I want to marry her. I mean it, but she doesn't seem to think I do. She says she doesn't want to marry me. I thought she loved me.'

'Things aren't quite as black and white as that, Barney. It's because she loves you that she's saying no. Look, wait till Bob is here before we get into this.' She kneaded the dough one more time and put it to one side. Taking a French-knitted potholder off a hook, she opened the door of the Kooka gas stove and pulled out two cake tins filled with golden sponge halves. The warm smell of just-baked cake wafted around the room.

'Is that for me?' asked Bob, sniffing appreciatively as he stepped out of his boots at the back door. Barney stood and they shook hands. As Bob sat down he asked, 'Abby know you're here?'

Barney shook his head. 'I wanted you to hear my side of it. I want you both to know I love Abby and I truly want to marry her. And not just because of . . . the baby.' He drew a breath. 'I've never felt like this before and I don't think I will again. It seems you just sort of know when two people are right together.'

'What do your parents say?' persisted Bob.

Barney looked down. 'I haven't told them yet. I wanted to straighten things out with Abby first.'

Gwen sat beside Bob. 'They're not going to agree to this, Barney,' she said gently.

'But this is my decision,' he answered hotly.

'You can't go against your father's wishes, son,' said Bob. 'I think they might have someone a bit different in mind for a daughter-in-law. Not that we're criticising our Abby — we all know what a lovely girl she is — but there is no getting round the fact we come from opposite sides of the tracks . . . and then there's the religious side of things.'

Barney rubbed his eyes and didn't answer.

'Look, Barney,' said Gwen, 'talk to your parents and then see where things stand. Abby is very determined to keep the baby.'

'She is?' Barney looked at them, hope and

happiness lighting up his eyes. 'How is she going to manage that if she doesn't marry me?'

'You know us, always room for one more round the table. We can manage another little mite. The doc advised her to have it in Sydney and put it up for adoption, but she won't hear of it.'

'No, I don't want that either,' said Barney firmly.

'Well, you can't raise it, mate,' said Bob. 'This is going to put a bit of a strain on us, there's no escaping that. But we want Abby to try and make a life for herself... as best she can under the circumstances.'

'We thought of moving somewhere else so Abby could start over, but... well, you know how gossip travels. And Bob has a good job here. We have to take that into account.'

Barney suddenly saw the financial strain this would put on the McBrides and he wondered how the Pembertons — especially Shannon — would take this news. The McBrides might not be as secure as they thought. 'Why won't she marry me? She says it wouldn't work. I just don't understand.'

Barney's bewildered face touched Gwen's heart, she could see he genuinely loved Abby. 'She loves you more than you realise. She doesn't want to see you lose everything that should be yours,

Barney. Nor does she want to come between you and your family. Family is important to Abby. There can be times in a marriage where things get rocky, and if you have to give up Amba you might blame Abby later on for holding you back. She can see that.'

The realisation of what Gwen said hit Barney hard. *Give up Amba.* Surely it wouldn't come to that. 'I'll get my parents to come round.' He stood, suddenly resolute. 'I won't give Abby up. Once I sort everything out, she'll have no excuse not to marry me. You'll see.' When he reached the door he turned. 'I think you are really exceptional people. Abby is very lucky.'

The meeting between Barney and his father was in stark contrast. He asked to speak to Phillip privately in the library after dinner. He stood and made the small speech he'd prepared and waited for Phillip's inevitable reaction.

'Barnard, I'm shocked and horrified that you find yourself in this predicament. Surely you have been taught about these matters . . . I understand a young man has to sow his wild oats, but . . . You will have to get the matter taken care of. They'll want money of course.'

'Dad! I want to marry her. I love Abby!'

'Don't be ridiculous. It's out of the question.'

Then, seeing the expression on Barney's face, he added, ' You can't be serious. I knew that girl was trouble,' he fumed. 'Just settle the matter as quickly and quietly as possible so your mother doesn't get wind of it. Think what this will do to her.'

'Dad, listen to me. You're not hearing what I'm saying. Abby is having my baby. I intend to marry her.'

'I hear you but I'm not listening. Now you get this clear, Barnard — there is no way I shall permit you to consider this wild idea, let alone go through with it. I will cut you off without a penny before I see you with that girl. *Do you understand*?' His voice had risen and father and son glared at each other.

Barney was shaking with anger. 'Well, you might as well know, I've asked her to marry me but she refused. But I'm going to make her change her mind. You can't bully both of us.'

Phillip was momentarily taken aback at the news of Abby's refusal, then put it down to a clever ploy. 'You have till the end of the week. I expect you to settle everything by then. And the matter is not to be mentioned again.' He turned away and opened his book. Barney sighed. It was pointless arguing further. He certainly would have the matter sorted out by the end of the week. But not the way his father expected.

Abby was tired and her head ached. How she wished she could share this burden. For a moment she wondered if she was doing the right thing. She suddenly remembered a past girlfriend talking about abortion, how a girl she knew had sat in a hot bath drinking warm gin laced with caraway seeds, swearing it brought on a miscarriage. Would that be the answer? Never! She wouldn't give up on this tiny speck she and Barney had created. A feeling of warmth spread through her as she thought of the gift Barney had given her and for the first time she wondered if 'it' was a boy or a girl. She dragged her mind back to the present, realising her mother was speaking to her.

'You feeling all right, luv? I was just wondering how long do you think you'll be able to keep working?'

'I spoke to Doctor Malone today. He said that was up to me. I could stay until I got too cumbersome to work comfortably. He said if I was strong enough to walk around town with everyone knowing, then he wasn't going to be seen to be throwing me out. He's still trying to get me to go to Sydney though.'

'And you haven't changed your mind?'

'No.'

'So what's next, Abby? Barney seems determined to get you to change your mind.'

'Well I won't.'

Bob and Gwen exchanged a glance and a shrug. But Abby's heart twisted with a pang. She would love to be married to Barney and she loved him dearly for being so staunch, but she knew one of them had to be strong and stand firm.

That night, after dinner, Abby asked Kevin to make himself scarce while she talked to her parents. Kevin scooped up the Meccano set he'd been building with Brian and glared at the three of them sitting in the little lounge room.

'When am I going to be told what's going on?' he demanded.

'In good time, mate,' answered his father.

'Secrets. I hate secrets,' muttered the boy as he headed for the kitchen table where the girls were playing tiddlywinks.

'Poor Kev, the girls are always whispering secrets they won't share with him. He feels quite left out at times,' said Gwen. 'We'll tell them your news when it's a bit more obvious, eh, Abby?'

Abby nodded, suddenly feeling shy at explaining her situation. 'They're going to wonder where the baby came from when I'm not married.'

'Don't worry, pet, they'll be so excited at the idea of a baby they won't even ask about it,' said Gwen, hoping to mollify Abby.

'Want to bet?' commented Bob.

A week later, Barney broke the news to his father that Abby intended keeping the baby and she wouldn't marry him, but he was determined to change her mind and wanted their support.

Phillip Holten exploded in anger. 'You are being very foolish, Barney. How do you even know it's your child? Are you sure? Maybe she wants money.'

'Dad! You apologise for that remark!' shouted Barney.

'You are the one who should be apologising. You are bringing shame on all that I have worked for. I have a good mind to ask you to leave this house until you have come to your senses.'

'Don't bother. I'll go of my own accord.' Barney turned angrily towards the library door.

'I'll make sure you don't have access to one penny. Not one sou until you swear to have nothing more to do with that girl or her child,' shouted Phillip Holten.

'Keep your damn money!' Barney slammed the door behind him and stomped down the hallway.

Enid appeared at the doorway to her sitting room, fearfully clutching the two dogs. 'What's going on, dear? I heard raised voices.'

'You heard shouting, Mother. Dad is being totally unreasonable . . .' He stopped and drew a deep breath. 'I'd better tell you.' He took her arm, ignoring Tucker's low growl, and led her back to her settee. Sitting beside her, he told her as gently as he could how much he loved Abby and that she was pregnant and that he wanted to get married but she didn't.

'Why not, dear? Doesn't she love you? That seems strange.'

'She says it's because she's just a shearer's daughter and she's Catholic — she thinks that would stop us being happy. I disagree. Dad doesn't want me to see her again. I can't agree to that. So I'm going to leave the house for a little while. Just till matters cool down. I'm still hoping I will be able to persuade Abby to marry me. They're a good decent family. You'd like them.'

Enid didn't speak for a moment, trying to take it all in. She reached out and patted his hand. 'But where will you go, dear? Not far, I hope.'

'No, mother. I'll stay in town for a bit. I want to keep near to Abby.'

'I suppose people will talk. Your father will hate that.'

'I suppose so. It's going to be harder for her.'

'You really love her and want to marry her?'

'Yes, I do. I know you probably wanted me to marry some nice grazier's daughter with money and position and class, but well, it just hasn't turned out that way. I'm sorry.'

'Don't be sorry. Love rarely turns out the way you expect,' said Enid enigmatically.

Barney gave her a strange look. He hadn't expected this reaction from his mother. 'Dad was afraid the news might upset you. I hope it hasn't. Please don't fret about things. I'll work something out.'

Enid nodded, gave Barney's hand another pat and turned her attention to the dogs, fondling their ears, lost in thought.

'Would you like anything, Mother?' asked Barney gently.

'I would like for you to be happy,' she said simply.

Touched, Barney leaned over and kissed her cheek, then quietly left the room. He went to the kitchen looking for Mrs Anderson, who was tidying away the dinner dishes.

'I'm toddling off to bed in a minute. Jim's already gone. You want anything?' she asked. Then, seeing his face and having heard the distant shouts, she added, 'Maybe a shoulder?'

'Oh, Mrs A, I do.' Barney slumped into the rocking chair by the fuel stove and poured out his story.

'Why didn't you come to me at the start? This is a terrible burden for you to carry around.'

'I suppose you heard the ructions. I'm going to move into town for a bit. Till we decide what to do. I just wish Abby would marry me. I've told Mum; she took it surprisingly well.'

'It's all very well saying you want to marry her, but maybe you have to show her how serious you are. It's a choice, Barney — Amba or Abby.'

'It'd break Dad's heart if I walked away from this. It's what I've been expected to do all my life, take over Amba. God, I wish I had a brother.'

'You've never had to make a choice, all the decisions about your life have been made for you. Maybe it's time you took control and decided what *you* want.'

'You can't always do what you want yourself, Mrs A. One has obligations and moral responsibilities to family.'

'And sometimes you only get one chance at happiness.'

They stared at each other across the room.

'A terrible choice, isn't it?' said Barney miserably. 'Damned if I do, damned if I don't. I was hoping that if Abby won't marry me I could work things out so I could still see her and the baby.'

'Sounds like half a life to me. They'd move at some stage, believe me, Barney, and you'll lose them anyway. Best to make the decision now.'

She rose and patted him on the shoulder, her heart aching for him. 'Think about your life, Barney, and what sort of a life your child will have as it gets older. I didn't have kids, and I'd hate the idea of losing one I did have. Goodnight, luv.'

Barney prowled through the large silent house, knowing sleep wouldn't come easily. A thin slice of light shone beneath his father's study door. His mother had retired to her bedroom, having seen Diet and Tucker bedded down for the night. The rest of the house was cold and dark.

He opened the door to his childhood bedroom, flicking on the light, and stared around at the memorabilia of school and growing-up days. All at once he was swamped with long-buried feelings of aching loneliness. The nights at boarding school where he had cried himself to sleep, his sobs muffled by a pillow. And nights and days here in this room where he had longed for laughter and the companionship of a family . . . a family like the McBrides.

He had a father he couldn't talk to who would never think him good enough, a mother whose affection had been transferred to the dogs who loved her devotedly and never demanded anything from her. No, there had to be a better way. Money, security, position, they weren't the answer. But nor was struggling in poverty.

Barney switched off the light and strode from the room. He was not going to condemn his child to a confused and lonely childhood like his. He and Abby would give their child the joy of a family. Somehow.

CHAPTER TWELVE

MRS DOHERTY, STALWART MEMBER OF THE Country Women's Association, shopping basket over her arm, strode quickly in sensible shoes towards the haberdashers. Her stout figure was accentuated by a belted, full-skirted flowered frock with cap sleeves and pearl buttons. The plastic cherries on her straw hat bounced energetically as she hurried on, determined to be first to break the news about Barney Holten.

Gaining the shop owner's rapt attention, she launched into details. 'That's right. Into town. Moved two days ago. Into the house the Undersides lived in till old George died. He's only renting, very temporary I was told. It must have been a lulu of an argument for him to move out of Amba.'

The lady on the other side of the cedar counter was agog. 'Wonder what it was about.'

'A girl I should say. And I think I know who,' said Mrs Doherty with an air of superior knowledge.

'Barney, I can't believe you've done this,' whispered Abby into the telephone.

'Shall I come round and see you at lunchtime? Seeing as I'm now living in town,' he said, trying to sound cheerful.

'Do you think that's wise? Maybe we'd better not be seen together for a bit. It must already be all over town you've moved out of your parents' house.'

'People are going to find out about us soon enough, Abby.'

'What are your plans, Barney?'

'I'll tell you when I see you. I'm meeting my mother for morning tea, she had to come in to the hospital for a checkup.'

'Barney, I don't know about lunchtime today, Doctor Malone is busy . . . maybe tomorrow . . .'

Barney heard the hesitancy in her voice and was momentarily stung, but then he softened. 'A lot has happened all at once, hasn't it? I'll see you tomorrow. Do you feel okay?'

'Yes, Barney, I'm just a bit dazed. I feel so responsible for everything that's happening to you.'

'I'm just as responsible, Abby,' he said gently. 'And for the first time I'm taking control of my life and responsibility for my own actions. I'll talk to you tomorrow. I love you, Abby.'

At lunchtime, Abby walked slowly down the street in the blazing sunshine, deep in thought. She was feeling confused and overwhelmed by the emotional currents swirling around her. Everything had seemed so straightforward. Now, like the flooded river her mother had talked about, her life was in turmoil. She was hoping the walk would help clear her head but Barney dominated her thoughts, as he always did. However, now it wasn't just the great love she felt for him that occupied her mind, but the concern as well. It was hard seeing him all the time, having him so close. She wished she could find the strength to keep him at bay. Suddenly she realised that one day she would have to move away with the baby to make a new life for herself and allow Barney to return to Amba and continue his life as it had been mapped out for him. The thought of leaving him filled her with pain.

Abby found herself across the street from her church. The door stood open and Abby slowly walked up the steps into its cool and peaceful interior. Her fingers lightly touched the holy water in the font and she crossed herself. As she genuflected, she noticed another person in a pew close by. A woman, in a neat hat, sat with her head bowed.

Abby adjusted the scarf knotted under her chin and slipped into a rear pew. She hadn't been to confession since discovering she was pregnant. Was it guilt that had kept her away, not wanting Father O'Leary to know what had happened and offer his advice as well as possible condemnation? Although Abby chose not to go to the confessional, she drew strength from the sanctity of the church and felt that despite her transgression, she was nonetheless loved and accepted. She assumed she'd abide by the church's dictum and raise her baby in the same faith, even though Barney was Presbyterian. She wondered if she should discuss it with him, then decided that as she was taking responsibility for the baby, it was her choice.

Again it came to her what a chasm separated her from Barney, despite their deep love. The knowledge stabbed at her heart and tears came to her eyes. How unfair life was, she told herself as she buried her head in her hands and tried to pray.

She didn't notice the other woman walk slowly down the aisle and pause beside her, then slip into the pew and sit next to her.

'Hello, Abigail.'

Abby looked up in shock. 'Mrs Holten... Hello. I didn't expect...' Abby hesitated and Mrs Holten completed the thought.

'To see me here.' She offered no explanation but clearly wanted to talk to Abby. 'Since we've happened to meet, I want you to know that I really feel for your predicament. Barney has told me how he loves you.'

Abby was astonished. 'Thank you, Mrs Holten. I really hadn't expected any sympathy from you or your husband.'

'Phillip is a proud man. He sets great store by certain things. How one lives one's life. But you know... Abby... sometimes things aren't what they seem. There can sometimes be a way through... problems.' Enid was breathless, speaking faster now as if she only had a few minutes to pass on a secret message. 'It just takes one person to make that leap of faith, or compromise, I suppose. But you only get one chance when you come to the fork in the road, to decide which way to go. I cannot advise you and Barney. I don't want to see my husband hurt, but nor do I want to see my son lose his chance at happiness.

Think carefully about the decision you've made...'

'I'm not going to give up my baby, Mrs Holten,' said Abby quickly and firmly.

'I didn't mean that. I meant about you and Barney. Differences can be overlooked, ignored...People have done it you know.'

'What sort of differences? You mean class and background and religion? They're big differences in this society,' said Abby with a tinge of bitterness.

Enid Holten stood and briefly touched Abby's shoulder. 'Please don't tell Barney we've spoken. In my generation a woman doesn't challenge her husband, but if I had my life over...maybe it would be...different. Barney was a gift. I want his happiness more than anything.'

'Me too,' said Abby tearfully.

'Then don't deprive him of his child. Think carefully, Abby.' She drifted quietly away and was gone.

Abby sat and stared at the flickering candle Enid had lit at the altar. Was she obliquely asking Abby to give up the baby and hand it over to Barney? Surely not. Abby strode from the church and in the bright daylight blinked as she pulled her scarf from her head. She was halfway down the street before she'd started to calm down and then the questions came. What was Enid Holten doing in the Catholic church? She couldn't have known Abby would go in on an impulse. What did she mean? She'd been telling her something but Abby didn't understand what. Should she mention it to Barney? She decided not to.

Barney waited for Abby when she got off the school bus with the children.

He opened the car door for her and she slipped onto the front seat. He got in and drove the car along the track a short distance, stopping by a gumtree. Then he turned and kissed her lightly.

She stared back at him with sorrowful eyes. 'I can't believe you've moved into town. What happened? Now everyone will start talking.'

'Can't be helped. The break with the family was inevitable. I've made my choice, Abby.'

'It needn't have come to this. I'm not going to marry you...This is just what I was trying to avoid,' said Abby brokenly.

'Abby, I love you — I don't know how else to prove it to you. But this is what I'm going to do. I'm going north to look for work. Then I'll send for you. We can start afresh, make a new life for ourselves. I swear to you, Abby, we'll make it work. I want it more than anything.' He spoke with passion and conviction.

Abby was overcome, close to tears. 'You love me that much?'

'I do, I do. Oh Abby.' He reached over and embraced her. Suddenly Abby felt herself melting, her resolve quavering in the security and warmth of Barney's arms. Barney sensed it, and relief flooded through him. 'I'll send for you just as soon as I can, Ab. You'll see, everything will work out; we're meant to be together, no matter what.'

He kissed her and she returned his kiss with passion and surrender, but then she pulled back, brushed the tears from her eyes and drew a deep breath. 'Barney, you're being rash, carried away, I don't know . . .'

He touched her mouth with a finger, stemming her words. 'Yes, we're being rash and wild and impetuous and all those things, because it's the only way. The only way we can be together, Abby. And we'll never regret it. I'll see you Sunday and say goodbye.'

'So soon?'

'The sooner I get work and a place for us, the sooner we can be together. I'll drive you up to the house.'

'No, I'll walk. I enjoy it after sitting in an office all day.'

He kissed her again, hope and love shining in his eyes.

Abby was thoughtful as she went through the homestead gate. She turned at the sound of a horse and lifted a hand in greeting as Shannon rode up. She dismounted and walked beside Abby.

'Hi, what's new? I've been wanting to talk to you.' Their steps slowed and Shannon took a deep breath. 'I've heard Barney's moved into town. That's pretty sad.'

'It wasn't my idea.'

'No, but it's a pretty drastic move. His family must be devastated. What's going on, Abby? I didn't think it would come to this.'

Abby stopped and studied Shannon.

'Didn't think *what* would come to this?' She didn't like Shannon's accusing tone.

'Well it's no secret he's been seeing you. Naturally we all let him get on with playing around before he settled down.' Shannon tossed her blonde hair. 'But we certainly didn't think he'd get this carried away and be so stupid.'

Abby went cold and she spoke in a steady voice. 'It's his decision. I certainly don't agree with it either.'

'Then why has he moved out? I mean it must have been some fight with his family and everyone thinks it must be because of you.'

Abby clenched her fists and decided not to beat about the bush. 'I'll tell you the reason, Shannon.

Barney asked me to marry him. I said no but he won't accept that. He spoke to his father, they had a big disagreement and Barney stormed out. He says he's going north to find work and then he'll send for me.'

Shannon had listened in increasing shock to this explanation. Quickly she turned the facts around. 'Oh for goodness' sake, surely you don't believe that for one minute! That he'll send for you. Poor thing, he's using that as an excuse to get away from you. You must have really frightened him off!' She gave a mean small laugh. 'What did you do, tell him you were pregnant?' It was a throw-away remark, meant to wound Abby. No matter how serious Barney might have thought he was about Abby, he wouldn't have slept with her.

Abby was obviously hurt. 'I wasn't doing the chasing, Shannon. Despite what I feel for him, I don't want to see him lose his family and Amba, baby or no baby. That's why I won't marry him.'

There. It was out in the open. Now Shannon was reeling with hurt and shock. 'What do you mean, baby or no baby, are you . . . you mean . . .' Her gaze fell to Abby's belly where her hands were protectively crossed. A small smile played at Abby's mouth.

'You slut!' hissed Shannon. 'All the time pre-tending to be the good Catholic girl. Well your tricks won't work. He'll never marry you. No one will. You and your family's name will be mud around here, just you wait. When you're gone, Barney will come crawling back to me, but I won't take him back. Not now!' She swung onto her horse and glared down at Abby. 'I should feel sorry for you, but I don't.' She kicked her horse and galloped off, her temper raging and hurt tears stinging her eyes. She knew Barney was lost to her.

It was Sunday and the McBrides were preparing to go to church. Abby asked to be excused, pleading she was feeling unwell. She did feel sick to her stomach, knowing in a short time she would be saying goodbye to Barney. She would make one last attempt to get him to change his mind and give her up and go back to Amba. She brushed her hair, pushing a simple alice band on top of her head. Tying the bow at the back of her skirt she noticed how her waist was thickening and her breasts, now fuller, pushed at the bodice of her pale blue blouse.

After Betsy had headed down the track with the twins waving from the windows, Abby closed the gate and perched on the fence, waiting for Barney's car. But he surprised her by cantering towards her on his stockhorse. He slid down and gave her a big happy hug. Abby hugged him tightly then pushed him from her. As he looped the reins over the fence she studied him closely, drinking in every feature: the way his hair curled into the nape of his neck, the laugh lines around his eyes, the sprinkle of golden hairs along his arms.

'So, my darling, I'm all set. It won't be for long, I promise.' He smiled reassuringly at her.

'Barney, this is wrong. You must go back to your family.'

His ebullient mood faded. 'Abby, I thought after yesterday we had this settled. I won't go back to Amba without you. Please, oh please, darling, don't think I'm running away from you. I will send for you, I swear, wherever I am.'

Abby began to cry and turned away from him, walking swiftly down the track, her arms wrapped tightly around herself.

Barney hurried after her. 'For goodness' sake, Abby, what now? What's wrong?'

She spun around, her face contorted in anguish. 'Barney, I can't marry you. How can we live happily knowing what you've given up, what you've lost. The guilt and resentment would start to eat away at us.'

'It doesn't matter! I love you, and you love me no matter how much you try to stop yourself. We'll make it work. It has to, Abby. It's too late to go back now.' Barney grabbed her and swept her tightly to him. 'I won't give you up. You're everything to me! Tell me you don't love me, Abby. Tell me that.' He took her face between his hands, his eyes burning into hers. She wrenched her face away, tears running down her cheeks. 'You can't, you can't say it. Then for God's sake tell me you'll join me, please, Abby.'

'It's because I love you so much that I can't marry you. Think ahead, Barney — we'll always be struggling and you'll blame me and the child for taking away the life you should have had. Please try to understand this is best for all of us.'

'No!' Barney shouted. Then a sudden image of his parents flashed into his mind. He recalled the unfathomable guilt he'd suffered as a child because he felt responsible for the tensions between his parents. Is that what his mother had meant when he'd said goodbye and she'd whispered, 'Don't let history repeat itself'?

Barney's face settled into a stubborn expression, but his voice was tender. 'I will not give up on you, Abby, or our baby, no matter what you say. I'll send for you and I'll expect you to join me and we'll get married. That's all there is to it.'

'And live happily ever after?' Abby gave a sad smile.

'Yes. I won't consider any other alternative. When we're settled, married and have children,

Mum and Dad will come round. Otherwise, if you don't marry me, we'll all be left alone. Come on, don't make this any harder for us.' He gathered her to him again and rained kisses on her face, her neck and her hair, murmuring in her ear, 'I love you, Abby. I always, always will. Never forget that in the days ahead.'

His voice was choked and he couldn't look at her any more. He swung onto his horse, turned around and kicked it into a fast canter. Abby clutched the gatepost, one arm curled protectively across her belly as great thudding sobs were torn from her body. And with the realisation she hadn't said what was uppermost in her heart, she screamed into the trees, 'I love you, Barney.' But he was gone.

She lowered her head onto the splintery wood and cried as if her heart were truly broken.

Abby didn't know how long she crouched, huddled miserably by the gate, but at the sound of a car motor, she struggled to her feet, wiping a dusty hand across her eyes leaving muddy streaks on her cheeks.

She peered down the track expecting to see Betsy, but instead a very battered utility truck, trailing smoke from its exhaust and churning up a column of dust, chugged towards her and stopped at the gate to Anglesea. The driver got out and took off his very worn hat. He was an older man, but straight-backed and broad-shouldered with a thick beard and very clear light blue eyes that Abby noticed immediately. He radiated enormous strength, and seemed to bristle with energy. He was dressed in overalls that had seen better days, a work shirt, and worn but solid boots.

Holding his hat, he came to her and stood looking down at her. 'Hello, Abby,' he said.

She stared at him. 'Do I know you? I'm sorry.' Abby brushed at her face again, trying to compose herself.

'No, we haven't met before. I'm Mr Richards. Here...' He reached into his back pocket and pulled out a neatly folded clean handkerchief.

Abby wiped her tear-stained face and stared at his gently smiling face. She began to feel strangely calm and managed a brief smile in return as she handed him back his handkerchief.

'Thank you, Mr Richards.'

'Things are never as bad as they sometimes seem, you know.' He leaned back against the fence, perfectly at ease.

'I hope you're right. Well, where are you off to, Mr Richards?'

'Anglesea. I'm looking for work round here for a bit. I figured I might be needed here or there.'

'I'm afraid I can't help you there. But here comes my dad. He'll know.'

'Right then.' Mr Richards helped Abby open the gate for Betsy.

Bob McBride leaned out of the window. 'Thanks, mate. How you doing, Abby?'

'All right thanks, Dad. This is Mr Richards, he's looking for work.' Mr Richards stepped forward and shook Bob's hand. Bob felt the calluses on the older man's hand, earned from fencing and dingo and rabbit trapping. He looked into the clear cheerful eyes of Mr Richards. 'You been travelling a bit, have you?'

'I have. But here I am,' said Mr Richards.

'Well, follow us up to the house and join us for Sunday lunch. That okay by you, luv?' Bob turned to Gwen, who smiled and nodded.

'Want to ride with me, Abby?' suggested Mr Richards.

As he helped Abby into the cabin of the ute, Colleen nudged Shirley. 'He looks like Santa Claus.'

As the ute followed Betsy's plump rear end, Mr Richards asked, 'How far up to the homestead?'

'Just a mile.'

Mr Richards nodded and murmured, 'The last mile home, it often seems the longest, doesn't it?'

Abby twisted away and looked out the window, suddenly overcome by tears again as she wondered where her own track was taking her and her child.

CHAPTER THIRTEEN

THE DAY WAS DRAWING TO A CLOSE; A LINGERING
lavender light hovered above the hills, reluctant
to give way to the soft fringes of the night
claiming the sky.

Leaning on a fence post, Mr Richards lit his
pipe and puffed contentedly, the wisp of exhaled
smoke dissipating in the twilight.

He had finished the week's fencing work
around Anglesea. Keith Pemberton had
been glad of the extra hand and Mr Richards
had gratefully accepted the invitation from
Bob and Gwen to stay in the verandah sleepout and join them for meals. From the

moment he arrived it seemed he was one of the family.

The children loved him. Each evening after work he would help with their homework or join them in games and would round off the evening with stories of his travels and adventures, which enraptured the whole family. He was a good storyteller, just as he was a good worker.

Abby found that during the evenings she'd often catch him watching her, and he would give her a brief smile and wink which made her feel they shared some secret bond.

With the fencing done, Mr Richards went over to Amba to see if work was available there. He spotted Enid's straw hat bobbing in the rose bushes and walked towards her. Two fluffy white bundles hurled themselves at him.

Enid straightened up, ready to call the dogs, but she hesitated when she didn't recognise the visitor. Then, to her amazement, she realised that the dogs were not barking in warning or taking up their familiar aggressive position. Instead they were braying in delighted welcome — puff-ball tails wagging, tongues licking Mr Richards's boots — and leaping up to be petted. He bent down with a smile and fondled their ears as they rubbed happily against him.

Enid came closer. 'Well, I've never seen my

dogs give anyone such a welcome, especially someone they don't know.'

'They know me, don't you now?' He straightened up and pulled his hat from his head, revealing thick salt and pepper curls that matched his beard. 'My name is Richards. I was told there might be some work going here for a time.' He smiled and Enid, who was normally timid with strangers, gave him a friendly smile in return.

'Well, you'll have to speak to my husband of course. I'm Enid Holten. My husband, Phillip, is down at the woolshed, I think.' Enid turned back to her pruning.

'Can I help you there?' offered Mr Richards. 'Some of those branches are very thick to cut through.'

'Well, that's kind of you, I was having a bit of struggle with my Celeste here.' She handed over the shears and he expertly snapped through the branches at the correct position and angle.

'We have to get rid of the dead wood before new growth can flourish, is that not so?' Mr Richards tipped his hat to her and headed towards the woolshed, leaving Enid wondering whether it was roses or life he was referring to.

Phillip Holten's normal suspicion of itinerants was restrained as he talked to Mr Richards. He knew he had only to phone the Pembertons to check on the man but there was no doubting with Barney gone an extra pair of hands would be useful. The man looked like a hard worker too. They shook hands and Mr Richards offered to start straightaway.

On leaving at the end of the day, he called by the house to thank Mrs Holten for the lunch she had sent down to the shed for him. She was sitting on the side verandah in a favourite rocking chair, eyes closed. When she opened her eyes, he was standing at the steps, hat in hand and smiling. She had no idea how long he'd been there.

'It's a lovely time of day for thinking, isn't it?' he said quietly.

'Yes it is,' said Enid, a little puzzled by his sudden appearance, yet pleased that he was talking to her. 'Do you have family, Mr Richards?' she asked.

'Ah yes, I have a family, of sorts. 'Tis one of the greatest gifts of all, don't you think...family, that is.'

Enid felt a little flustered but gathered her composure. 'Indeed. But sometimes some of us are deprived of the gift. It's like...' Enid paused struggling for words. 'Like unwrapping the gift and finding nothing in the package. Do you understand?'

'Oh, yes,' he acknowledged warmly. 'It's as if something got lost on the journey.'

'That's it,' said Enid with enthusiasm. 'You've put your finger on it, Mr Richards.'

'Well, I must be going, Mrs Holten. Thank you very much for the lunch. See you tomorrow perhaps.'

He had turned to walk back to his ute when Enid asked, 'Mr Richards, what do you think was lost . . . on the journey?'

The tall bushman turned and stood silhouetted against the glory of the setting sun. After a minute, he spoke. 'Love, Mrs Holten. It's the only reality.'

Enid was still puzzling over this reply when the dust trail of the ute disappeared over the ridge. She stepped off the verandah and, flanked by the two small dogs, wandered, a lonely figure, in the darkening garden.

As she walked, Mr Richards's words echoed through her mind. She felt a quiet and rare confidence and decided to talk to her husband.

'Phillip,' she said when she found him, 'I've come to the conclusion we must reconsider Barney's wishes.'

Phillip looked up from his stamp album in astonishment and removed his glasses. 'I beg your pardon, Enid?'

'I believe we must accept the girl and the baby. It is the only way Barney will come back to us.'

'Don't be ridiculous, Enid.'

'I don't want to lose my son.'

'Give him time. He'll come to his senses. He simply can't marry that girl, baby or no baby, and that's that.'

'He loves her, Phillip.'

'He'll have to learn to love someone more appropriate. The girl is not suitable — she's from a different class and she's a Catholic.'

'I was a Catholic when I married you, Phillip. Even if I wasn't a practising one.'

Enid spoke quietly but her statement hit Phillip hard. 'Enid,' he gasped, 'how could you bring that up again? We agreed before we married that this matter was in the past, finished.'

Enid's mind was a whirl of images as she recalled the long and agonising talks she had had with Phillip when they were courting. As she battled with the agony of the loss of her first love, she questioned her belief in God and the infallibility of the Catholic church. Her faith had almost been destroyed and, under Phillip's pressure, she had renounced it, seeing that as a way of showing him how much she cared. She had abandoned the Catholic church and agreed to raise as Presbyterians any children she and her husband might have. At the time, Phillip had made her promise never to refer to it again, and she hadn't, until now.

'We only thought it was finished, Phillip.'

'Only thought . . . what do you mean?' snapped Phillip.

Enid leaned back and closed her eyes. This was not how she had expected the confrontation with Phillip would go. She was grateful that Phillip did not demand an immediate answer but sat silently waiting while she regained her composure.

'I'm sorry to upset you like this, Phillip, but in recent years I have felt a great yearning to return to the Catholic faith. I can't explain it too well, and you'll have to bear with me,' she pleaded, her face showing the agony of her predicament.

'Why? Whatever for? Why bring unwanted tensions into our life?'

Enid took a deep breath. 'What do differences really matter, Phillip? Marriages should be based on love, understanding and compromise. Not sacrifice. Real love should override all differences. Can't you see that?'

'What are you really saying, Enid?' Phillip felt uncomfortable, vulnerable, as if the defences he had built up over a lifetime were crumbling.

'Why shouldn't Barney and Abby marry if they are so much in love? You're turning your son away. What little we had to call family will be reduced to nothing, Phillip. You will regret this, but at least I tried and it gives me some comfort to know at least I was prepared to accept Abigail.' Enid slumped back in her chair, exhausted, one hand resting on her heart.

'You're being melodramatic, Enid,' said Phillip gently, suddenly feeling concern for his wife's condition. 'You know I cannot approve of what Barney has done. He'll come to his senses. Amba means too much to him. Now let me help you to bed.'

That evening, as Bob McBride and Mr Richards entered the usually bustling and noisy kitchen, they found everything very quiet.

'What's up? Someone drop a bomb in here?' asked Bob, giving Gwen a kiss on the cheek.

She finished peeling the vegetables, rolling the skins into the spread newspaper. 'You might say that.' Then in a low voice she explained, 'Kevin heard about Abby. We'll have to tell them all now.'

'How'd he take it?'

'He's upset. He's out doing the chooks. The girls are in their room with Brian.'

'And Abby?'

'Back steps. She got her first letter from Barney today. She misses him so much, the poor luv.'

'Better have a family conference after dinner, eh?'

Mr Richards went around the verandah to his sleepout and put on a clean shirt. He spotted Abby on the steps and sat down beside her. 'Mind if I join you? Um, good place for star-gazing. And thinking through things too, I suppose.' He noticed Abby was holding a letter.

'Mmm. Thinking is one thing, finding answers is another thing altogether.'

'Perhaps. You have to know where to look. People travel here and there, all looking for something, when it's right under their nose all the time.'

'How do you mean, Mr Richards?'

'I take it you have a decision to make?'

'I've already made it.'

'And is it the right one, Abby? Before you answer that, look to the place where answers are found.'

'And where's that?'

He smiled at her sceptical face. 'Life is a journey and you can travel a long way looking for answers and meanings . . . The answer could be at the end of a journey as long as the light of the stars.' He paused as they both looked into the early evening sky. 'Or it could be found at the end of a single mile track that leads from the gate to your home. Or the answer could be right here.' He pointed to her heart. 'Take the inner journey and look into your heart. That is where your true spirit rests and that is where you'll find your answer, Abby. In your heart. Nowhere else.' He touched her hands clasping Barney's letter, and stood and went inside.

After dinner, Gwen and Bob quietly and calmly talked to the children and Abby told them of the baby. While the girls clapped their hands in excitement and Brian copied them, Kevin sat stony-faced.

Abby reached over and touched his shoulder. 'Don't look at me like that, Kev. Don't be angry. I want you to understand. Please don't think I've let you all down. I love Barney and he loves me and that's all that matters for the moment.'

'Sometimes things happen that aren't planned, and although we mightn't see it at the time, it's all part of God's plan,' said Gwen gently.

'But people are saying horrible things about us. About Abby,' he burst out. 'Kids at school and ladies in the shops.'

'That's life, son. People talk, and they like to talk about the bad things, never the good,' said Bob. 'Just about everyone's got a chip on their shoulder or some sort of bias against people or someone else's ways.'

'We know Abby; we know ourselves, and we know what we believe. We have each other and that will protect us,' added Gwen.

'I need you to stand by me, Kev,' said Abby to her brother. 'It won't be easy. You'll get a bad time from some of the kids at school.'

'If anyone says anything about you, I'll thump them,' said Kevin defiantly. 'Don't you worry, Ab. We'll look after you.'

'Thanks, Kev.' She smiled at him and he looked at his beautiful big sister with eyes full of fierce love.

'That's the spirit,' said Bob.

'But don't you get into any fights; just ignore them, Kev,' said Gwen. 'Don't go down to their level. Now, how about a bedtime snack?' She reached for the large square tin of Arnotts mixed biscuits she kept on the top of the pantry shelf.

Before she went to bed, Abby went into the garden and looked up at her special star. 'Oh Barney, are you looking at these same stars and thinking of me?' His letter had been so full of hope and love. He was leaving Charleville and following up a real possibility for a job. *So we can be together soon. I miss you so much, Abby. I'm doing this for us, for our future. And I know things will work out. Have faith in me Abby and come to me. I should have good news soon. I love you.*

She patted the folded letter in the pocket of her skirt. Come Christmas she would be holding her child and facing an unknown future. Abby didn't know what the new year would bring — the path she'd chosen would not be an easy one — but for the first time in many weeks she felt sure of her own strength.

She patted her womb and whispered to the child within, 'We're going to be all right. I know it.'

CHAPTER FOURTEEN

ABBY STEPPED FROM THE SCHOOL BUS, GAVE THE driver a wave and slowly followed the skipping, singing threesome ahead of her. Kevin and the twins were delighted it was Friday and a weekend awaited them. But for Abby a longer break stretched ahead. This had been her last day working for Doctor Malone. While she still had several months to go before the baby arrived, the strain of sidelong glances, sudden silences when she went into a shop or tea room, the gossip she knew was being whispered behind her back, had proved too much.

When they reached the homestead gate, Shirley

climbed over — they all did, rather than drag it open — and called over her shoulder, 'We gotta visitor.'

Kevin peered at the small black Austin. 'That's Father O'Leary. Wonder what he wants.'

'Collecting money and stuff for the poor,' suggested Colleen. Abby's heart sank. She didn't fancy facing the priest but knew there was no escape. She had been expecting him for a while.

Gwen had served Father O'Leary tea and biscuits in the lounge room and the children dutifully filed in to greet him. He asked each in turn for their news, how they were doing at school, and said he looked forward to seeing them at mass on Sunday. The children nodded and, at a word from Gwen, made their escape to wash hands, do chores and start homework. Father O'Leary turned his attention to Abby.

'Now, Abigail, I've missed you in church these many weeks.'

'Yes, Father,' she said meekly, offering no reason for her absence.

The priest put his cup back in its saucer. 'I am aware of the situation you find yourself in, my dear. Very unfortunate. Very sad indeed.'

'I don't consider my situation sad, Father. Some may consider it unfortunate, but a child is a gift.'

'Ah yes, my dear. But a child is a gift when

sanctioned by the state of holy matrimony. Surely in this case it is more of a burden. However, I am prepared to offer a helping hand. There are so many good families who have not been so blessed, who would dearly love to give your child a good and decent Christian home.'

'My child has one. Right here,' said Abby curtly. She sat and listened with a stubborn expression as the good-hearted man tried his best to find a better path for this member of his flock who'd strayed. He urged her to put the baby up for adoption, to think of the strain it was putting on her family, the handicap to her own life.

'Father, you always preach the virtues of family life. This is my family, they accept me, they are sticking by me and my child. I think they are truly Christian and there is really no more to be said.'

The priest was not about to give in. 'What about the father? Is he sticking by you? Is it fair that this child begin life with the stigma of illegitimacy?'

'I don't see that it has anything to do with the father as I am bringing up the child myself.'

'Surely, my dear, if he isn't willing to face his obligations it is another reason for considering placing the child in a secure and stable home.'

Abby rose to her feet. 'Mum, I think I'd better

go check on Brian out there. Nice to see you again, Father.' Abby shook the surprised priest's hand and hurriedly left the room.

'She's a very determined young woman,' said Gwen, privately cheering her daughter's stand. 'This child is going to be brought up in a secure, stable and loving home. I appreciate you coming, Father, but nothing will change her mind.'

Mr Richards, driving back to Anglesea from Amba, passed the priest on the road. When he reached the gate, he spotted Abby trudging along the track. She hurried to the gate and swung it open for him. He drove through, got out and leaned against the fence, gazing around at the bush tinged with the last of the day's sunlight.

'Nice time of day this . . . How's your day been? Not too good by the look on your face,' he smiled.

'It shows, does it? This was my last day at work.'

'Ah. You're moving on. Moving forward though, I hope.'

'Well, definitely in a new direction. I'm going to be a mother,' said Abby somewhat ruefully.

'Ah, I see.' Mr Richards didn't show any surprise. 'You chose to leave your job before you really needed to, I take it.'

'Yes. It's been difficult. Maybe I'm a coward

but I couldn't take the whispers and looks I got everywhere I went. I think I'm regarded as the town's scarlet woman.'

Mr Richards laughed. 'Do you feel like a wicked woman?'

Abby shook her head. 'I can't say I do. I don't feel I've done anything wrong, but people, they make me feel grubby and that I should be ashamed, when I feel lucky. So very lucky.'

'And does the father feel lucky too?'

'I believe so. He wants to marry me but I've said no.'

'He loves you and you love him?'

'Yes.'

'Is he asking you to marry him because of the child?'

Abby was swift to answer. 'There are other reasons. He is prepared to give up everything — his family, his inheritance, his future — and I can't agree to that.'

'Then he loves you indeed. As you obviously do him. And where there is love there is pain. So you believe like the knights of old that one's love has to be tested? And whether he or you fail or succeed in proving your love to the other, you are going to keep your baby, bring it up alone, and exclude the father from what he wants most?'

Abby looked distressed. 'I think that is the best

thing to do. Though the more I think about it all, the more confused I become.'

Mr Richards gazed into the distance. 'The other night when we were having a yarn I told you maybe you should follow your heart and not your head. There are times when one should listen to the other, but in matters of love, the heart rules. You see your love as being in conflict with your life and your beliefs, when you should see it as a spiritual flowering that heightens the joy of your life.'

'How I feel doesn't matter when almost everyone else sees it differently and behaves accordingly.'

'Of course it matters how you feel.'

Abby expected him to go on, but found instead that he was concentrating on the ritual of lighting his pipe. She said nothing but contemplated what he had just said: 'a spiritual flowering that heightens the joy of your life.' She looked at him again as he struck a match and worked the pipe. They were beautiful words. You're a strange man, Mr Richards, she thought, but said nothing.

'I suppose you think it's strange to hear words like that from an old codger like me?'

Abby was too stunned to say anything. It was if he had read her mind. She merely let a half-smile speak for itself.

'Yes, well, it's not every day that a bloke gets a chance to sound off on things he's thought about over a thousand campfires. Now, the way I see it goes something like this. Our mob is made up of individuals and each must follow his or her own path, always listening to the heart and being guided by the head.' He puffed on his pipe. 'It's the head that puts on the hobbles of restraint and judgement as each of us goes through life. Then comes the time, if you are lucky, when you meet your other half . . . your partner. Each fulfils the other, and together you make a new whole and life has a new meaning. Now, how's that for a sunset sermon?'

They both laughed and for a moment leaned on the fence together, taking in the artwork in the western sky. Eventually Mr Richards broke the silence. 'Sometimes things work themselves out in an unexpected way. If you let the reins go the horse will find its own way home. Right?'

As they drove up the track, Mr Richards told Abby that he planned to move on. The announcement was a surprise and a disappointment and it showed in Abby's face. She really valued the talks she had with him and appreciated the extra warmth he brought to family evenings.

'I'll miss you, Mr Richards. We all will.'

'Well, you never know when I'll turn up again. Thanks, Abby.'

That night Gwen turned on a special roast dinner and the children were allowed to stay up late to join the sing-song and charades with Mr Richards. The evening wound up with Gwen, Bob and Mr Richards having a beer on the dark verandah, taking in the symphony of night noises and looking at the stars.

'I'll be off before sun-up,' said Mr Richards. 'Thanks for the helping hand and hospitality. Nice to be one of the family for a while. I'll repay you one day.'

'No need for that. We've really enjoyed having you,' said Gwen gently.

'Been good having a mate around the place,' said Bob.

True to his word, Mr Richards was gone when Bob got up at sunrise. Odd chap, thought Bob as he stirred the ashes and put some kindling on the fire. We accepted him as if we had known him all our lives, yet we know practically nothing about him. He opened the back door and saw a small box on the back step. He put it on the kitchen table and found inside a beautifully made wooden train. Scrawled on the flap of the carton Mr Richards had written, *For Abby's baby*.

Mr Richards didn't go far. He drove to Amba and waited in the bush, reading and having a pipe or two until the sun was high enough for breakfast to be over at the homestead.

Phillip was surprised to find him standing on the back steps when he wandered out with his coffee, listening to a record on the radiogram.

'Elgar. *Enigma variations*,' observed Mr Richards. 'Good morning.'

'Yes, it is. You know your music then?' said Phillip.

'I've been to a concert or two.'

'Join me for a coffee,' said Phillip, conscious of bush etiquette.

In the library Mr Richards picked up the book lying on the chair and flicked through its pages while Phillip poured the coffee. 'Proust. *Remembrance of Things Past*. A hefty read, Mr Holten.'

'Indeed.'

'Interesting how the past influences the present. Thanks,' said Mr Richards, accepting the cup. 'In youth we want to change the world. With age comes nostalgia. And then some of us want to cling to the past, especially if the present isn't to our liking. We forget that life isn't a straightforward track. We get pushed and shoved around, sometimes get lost, wandering all over the place. But we can also take control and change things, change the way our life is going. Trouble is, we sometimes forget we can do that.'

Phillip was perplexed and covered his discomfort by sipping his coffee. His guest continued, intent on his own train of thought.

'Can't keep living in the past. Blinkers are only good for the carthorse ... but then as a man of the land, Mr Holten, that's hardly news to you.'

Phillip half smiled. 'Rather heavy talk for breakfast, but I take your point.'

'What would you like to change about your life, Mr Holten?'

The question came as a shock to Phillip and the cup rattled on the saucer as he put it down. He wanted to say he did not consider it appropriate to continue the conversation and to dismiss his visitor, but something he couldn't immediately understand forced him to take up the question. 'Well, I'm afraid that in my case the matter really isn't quite that simple.'

Phillip paused, but the other man simply raised his cup again, looking over the rim with expectation.

'Well, I live with a wife who spends more time in the past than in the present. It is hard to look forward when someone beside you keeps looking back. Of course, she has a heart condition which puts a cloud over her future. It all makes life very difficult. There must have been a crossroads somewhere, and I think I missed the signpost.

Now I feel like I am in limbo. I'm estranged from my son and neither of us has much to look forward to . . .' Phillip was astonished at his confession but felt a huge relief at having unburdened himself by saying it out loud.

'You make it sound like a paddock that's been through a five-year drought,' said Mr Richards, pulling his pipe out of his waistcoat pocket. 'Do you mind?'

'Not at all,' replied Phillip calmly. He studied the suntanned leathery face of the man opposite; his impressive white beard slightly nicotine stained, his high broad forehead and warm friendly eyes. It suddenly occurred to Phillip that the visitor was totally at home in his own living room, as if he belonged there.

Mr Richards's pipe was alight and he picked up where he left off. 'Now, the thing about a paddock that's been in drought is that it doesn't die, it's more like asleep. Bounces right back the moment it rains. People can be like that. They reckon the drought in their lives is never going to break, but it always does. People don't necessarily have to sit around and wait for rain. Sometimes they can make it happen. I was yarning to someone only the other day on similar lines, about the head and heart.'

'The head and the heart?' repeated Phillip.

'Yes, about when to listen to the head and when to listen to the heart.' He paused, then reached decisively for his hat. 'Well, we're not going to make a quid sitting round philosophising all day,' he said with a chuckle. 'Must be on my way. Thanks for the coffee and the yarn.'

Phillip went to his desk and got his pay packet and handed it over. 'I've enjoyed our chat too. Thanks for your help, you came at just the right time.'

Mr Richards merely smiled. 'Give my regards to Mrs Holten.'

At the McBrides', breakfast was under way, orchestrated by Gwen's fine sense of timing and skill. Porridge was served, as toast, eggs, bacon and bubble and squeak were readied for the second course.

'Where's Colleen?' asked Abby, taking away Brian's empty bowl and handing him a piece of Vegemite toast.

'She went to get a fresh egg for herself,' said Gwen, putting Bob's loaded plate in front of him. 'Yesterday's eggs wouldn't do.'

'Well tell her she can boil it herself. Sit down, luv, your porridge is getting cold,' said Bob, shaking tomato sauce over his eggs and fried leftover vegetables.

The door banged as Colleen rushed in, her eyes wide. 'Lookit *this*!' she exclaimed, showing them a very large egg. 'Tom Turkey laid an egg!'

They all burst out laughing.

'I told you it was a hen. It didn't have the dangly bits on its face,' said Kevin in a know-it-all voice.

'Better call her Tomasina,' said Gwen. 'Pop the egg in the saucepan, Col.'

'I want a big egg too,' wailed Brian.

'And me,' added Shirley.

'Tomorrow. Tomorrow,' said Gwen, restoring order. 'Who knows what tomorrow will bring.'

'That's the motto for today. Make every day an adventure,' declared Bob.

Gwen grinned at Abby. 'I don't know that I can stand the excitement.'

Abby chuckled and tucked into a hearty breakfast, now understanding the expression 'eating for two'. But in her heart she was thinking about the things Mr Richards had said to her over the weeks he'd been with them. Would she be missing out on life's little adventures, tied down with a baby and the responsibilities being a mother involved? She wished for a second she was free as a bird and could simply take to the sky and fly where the winds took her, and alight in some magical land. A land where dreams came true and life was as you wanted. Was there such a place?

'What are you thinking, Ab?' asked her father, seeing the faraway look in her eyes.

'I was wishing I could fly away to some magical land where there aren't any problems, but I don't suppose there is such a place.' She gave a small laugh.

Gwen, carrying plates to the sink, dropped a kiss on top of Abby's head. 'Yes there is, luv,' she said. 'It's right here, here at home.'

Bob lifted his arms, holding knife and fork aloft. '*Somewhere over the rainbow, way up high, there's a land that I heard of . . .*' He got no further as Gwen stuffed a piece of toast in his mouth and the children took up the chorus, drowning him out.

Abby and Kevin took up their stations for washing and drying up duty. 'Meal times are never dull round here, are they, Ab?' he commented drily.

'Family life at the McBrides'. Wouldn't miss it for squillions,' she laughed. 'I wonder if other families are as daffy as us?'

CHAPTER FIFTEEN

ABBY AND HER BROTHERS AND SISTERS WERE
playing in the swimming hole. Abby floated in the
cool brackish water, watching Kevin and the girls
take turns swinging on the old tyre. Brian sat at
the edge of the creek making pies, his body, face
and hair caked in the dark yellow mud.

Abby found the water a refreshing relief from
the heat. She also liked the feeling of lightness and
buoyancy it gave her, for now she was only a few
weeks off giving birth and her bulky shape was
cumbersome. Drifting in the water, swathed in
one of her father's old shirts, she felt comfortable.

The delighted shouts, dares and laughter of the

youngsters were infectious. Abby closed her eyes, feeling the baby turn and kick inside her womb. It seemed impossible to believe that she would soon hold a small human being in her arms. A living symbol of her and Barney's love. How she ached for him. She longed to be able to rest her head against his shoulder, feel his arms about her, to feel his strength, his warmth and to hear his comforting words of love.

She tried yet again to push the fears and concern about him from her mind. Three weeks had passed without word, which was so unlike Barney for he had been devoted in sending her notes, postcards and long passionate letters whenever he could. He'd phoned a few times, but the calls had been unsatisfactory, lacking in privacy as well as being bad outback connections. But how she treasured his letters. So full of love, and of interesting details about the places he'd been, the people he'd met; always full of the hope they would be together, that'd he'd find just the right job.

This silence was worrying. Doubts crept into her mind. Had he given up on her, and decided he liked his life of freedom? Had he met someone else, or had it all become an impossible dream? She knew she had to hang on as she had been doing all these months, drifting in limbo, only thinking of one day at a time. She sighed and opened her eyes, the day of reckoning would soon arrive.

She dragged herself from the water and asked Kevin to take Brian into the water to rinse off at least some of the mud.

'I'm not having a bath with him tonight,' declared Colleen.

The wet group trudged towards home.

'Wish I had a bike,' sighed Kevin. 'I'd be home by now.'

'Ask Santa,' said Shirley.

'Oh sure,' muttered Kevin. 'I think Santa Claus is going to bring baby stuff this year,' he said, giving Abby a wink.

'Santa doesn't bring babies, that's the stork,' said Colleen.

'What do you want for Christmas, Ab?' asked Kevin.

'A healthy little baby.'

This set the girls off on their favourite game — would it be a girl or boy and what would 'it' be called.

When the letter finally came, Abby turned it over in her hands, smoothing it, looking at his handwriting and the postmark, Katherine. For a moment her heart flipped, then a warm feeling came over her. This had passed from Barney's hand to hers. She read it slowly.

My darling Abby,
This is the big *letter. I've been crazy these past few weeks, for various reasons. I was put in touch with a fellow who works for a pastoral company that owns a big station up here — a thousand square miles with roughly six thousand head, they reckon — no one's mustered for some time and, are you sitting down Ab? I've got the job as manager! I've been over the place. Decent sort of a house, some Aboriginal hands, and a lot of opportunity. They want to sink a lot of money into the property and they reckon I'm the chap to get it up and running at a profit.*

So Abby, this is our chance. I'm doing this for you and for our baby. I want you to come up and be my wife and start this new life with me. I hope one day my father will come round but right now all I can think of is us being together, being a family. A family like yours. You have made your stand, but things are different, now we have a future. Please, marry me, Abby. With this job we are both starting on an equal footing and together we can make each other happy. Tell me yes, my darling, and I will be there for the birth of the baby and our wedding — just name the day. I love you, and I always will.'
Barney

Abby handed the letter to her parents after dinner. Gwen read it first, pausing a couple of times to look briefly at Abby and give a hint of a smile. She handed the letter to Bob, who read without lifting his eyes, then handed it back to Abby.

'I get the impression the bloke's in love with you, Abby,' said Bob, leaning back in his chair, and the ice was broken. The three of them laughed, but for Abby the laugh only masked the internal conflict that the letter refuelled.

'Katherine? That's a long way from here,' observed Gwen, sensing how Abby felt and trying to get her talking. 'Way up in Never Never Land . . . Well, that's what we learned to call it in school. Remember reading *We of the Never Never*, Abby?'

'Yes, Mum. You don't forget books like that. Never thought it would come into my life though.'

'Has it?' asked Bob quietly. 'Has it really come into your life in the way Barney wants it to?'

Abby turned the letter over and over in her hands and looked from one parent to the other, her eyes filling with tears. 'I don't know . . . I don't know.' She stood, pushing the letter into her pocket. 'Mum . . . Dad . . . I do love him . . . so much . . . but I just don't know. I'm going out for a walk for a little while.'

Gwen and Bob watched her go. 'Poor girl,' said

Gwen, reaching out for Bob's hand, 'it must be torture for her.'

It was a clear summer night. The smallest of breezes danced lightly around the garden and Abby felt it with surprise because it was unusual. There were no clouds. Oh Barney, how I wish you were here, she thought as the breeze lifted a strand of her hair.

She walked down the track to a small rock that was a favourite spot for all the children to sit and yarn and hatch mischief. She climbed up and sat hugging her knees, trying to sort out the churning emotions that had her head in a whirl.

She wasn't sure how long she had been sitting there when she again became conscious of a little breeze, the slightest surge of air that died away almost at once, but it was enough to stir her. She stretched out her legs, leaned back and looked up at the sky.

The Southern Cross constellation came into focus. She smiled in recognition, and found the star that she and Barney had made their special star that wonderful night on the ridge nearly nine months ago.

'Hello, star,' she said softly. 'Have you got the answer?'

An hour later, as Gwen and Bob were settling down to listen to the wireless, Abby came inside and stood at the door of the living room. They looked at her and she at them. No one spoke. Bob turned down the radio play.

'I'm going to marry Barney,' announced Abby quietly.

Gwen rushed to her daughter and they hugged each other. 'Oh, Abby, my darling. Oh Abby.'

Bob came over. 'Might as well make it a family hug to mark the occasion,' he said, and kissed both of them.

Gwen and Abby sat on the lounge holding hands. 'What decided you?' asked Gwen.

Abby smiled at her mother. 'I suppose you could say I had guidance from the stars. I was looking up at them and I suddenly remembered a chat I had with Mr Richards. It was about listening to the heart, the importance of love and things like that. Every detail of that talk came back to me and suddenly I felt very calm, and everything was very clear.'

'Well, Barney said he'd put you first and he'd get a job so you could be together and independent. The letter proves he means what he said. He'll make a good husband, Abby. You're a lucky girl,' said Bob.

'And he's a lucky man,' countered Gwen.

Bob went to the Silent Knight refrigerator and took out a bottle of beer. 'I reckon a couple of toasts would be in order.' He raised his glass. 'To Barney.'

'To Barney and Abby,' added Gwen. 'All the happiness in the world to both of you.'

Long after Gwen and Bob had turned out their bedroom light Abby was still at the table in the kitchen writing to Barney. She told him everything about the day and the evening, from the moment his letter arrived to finding their star and how Mr Richards' 'sermon' had come back to her.

The strange thing about it, Barney darling, she wrote, *was that I had this feeling he was really there with me.*

The crackling, tenuous thread of the phone connection finally brought Barney and Abby together. They both cried and promised to love each other forever.

Abby held the bulky black handset in both hands, cradling it to her lips as she listened to Barney confess how painful the waiting had been, not knowing if Abby would change her mind and agree to marry him.

'Perhaps it happened this way for a reason, Barney darling.'

'Maybe it has been for the best,' he agreed. 'We've certainly been tested and we were both prepared to make sacrifices for each other, but it's been hard. I've missed you so much, Abby . . .'

'Me too. Oh Barney, if you only knew how much.' She started to cry again.

'Abby, that's all in the past now, let's think about the future. Start making wedding plans. I should be there just before Christmas Eve and, Abby, don't make me wait. I want to marry you straightaway. I'm not letting you escape this time.'

The line buzzed and faded and Abby spoke quickly, afraid the poor outback connection would be broken. 'Barney, it will be just a simple ceremony . . . I'm not sure where, we're going to have problems with the church . . . but don't worry, we'll sort something out.'

'As long as it happens, I don't care if we get married in a tree wearing gumboots!' The line dropped out for a second and Barney found himself shouting, 'I love you, Abby,' as if she could hear him directly across the miles that separated them.

'I love you too, Barn . . . forever!' the line hummed and neither could hear the other, but at the far ends of the phone line both were reluctant to let go of the handpiece that had, for a few brief minutes, linked them. Abby closed her eyes, seeing the man she loved and longing to feel his firm strong body wrapped around hers.

In the hurly-burly of plans and organisation, Abby, who'd been feeling weary, decided to take some time out for herself. So she packed a picnic, threw a blanket and a Thermos into Betsy and, kissing her mother goodbye, set out.

'I might be gone all day, Mum, don't worry. I'm going back to a place Barney and I went once for a picnic. I need to do some quiet thinking and planning.'

Gwen was unsure about this idea but could see Abby needed time alone and she was a sensible girl.

It took more than a hour to reach the remote spot that she and Barney had found on one of their Sunday drives. It was down a fire trail made by the local bushfire brigade, in the shade of a cool grove of river oaks. Abby settled down with her picnic and a writing pad on which to make lists. After a while she felt drowsy and she stretched out to nap and dream of Barney.

Abby had no idea how long she had been asleep when she was woken by a sudden tightness across her belly. She felt as if her skin would burst open. Wide-eyed she lay there, hands clasped on her bulging stomach, staring unseeing into the treetops.

'Oh God,' she whispered.

The spasm passed. She sat up and reached for

the bottle of water in the basket, drank, and leaned back thinking, It's not due for a fortnight. I must get home. Don't panic. That's the worst thing — panic. Stay calm. She began packing up and was leaning over when she became aware of rippling sensations across her abdomen. Oh, oh. Here we go again. Don't panic, girl. Deep breaths.

She somehow packed the car and began driving up the fire trail, aware that she was sweating profusely.

'Where's the nearest farmhouse?' she said out loud. 'Can't remember. Thought there was that old pioneer place round here.'

The sensations grew stronger and time seemed suspended. She didn't dare speed and every bump on the trail was frightening. She felt like she was looking at the world through wet blurred glasses. A sudden cramp made her gasp and the car swerved off the track. She braked hard, skidding into a steep ditch. The motor stalled. Breathing heavily and holding her now painful belly, she got out and walked to a little rise and looked over the open country. She could see a small cottage, just a shack really, its corrugated-iron chimney topped by a thin wisp of smoke.

'Thank you, God, thank you,' she gasped.

She knew before she turned the key that the car

wasn't going to start. When she did turn the key and nothing happened, she was hit by another spasm, as if it had somehow been triggered by the key. She collapsed over the steering wheel until it passed. Then she put the key in her pocket and set out for the shack, which looked about a mile away.

In a trance, Abby plodded along the track, trying hard to take her mind off the pain. 'Funny, I never noticed the shack when we were here before. Doesn't matter, so long as they can help me get to hospital. Not much shade now. Keep going. Ignore the heat. Think snow. Snow... that's crazy.'

She was about halfway there when her waters broke. She stumbled to the shade of a lonely tree and sat propped up against its trunk till her strength returned. Then she set off again, frightened and breathing rapidly.

Through misty eyes, Abby became aware that the hut was made of crude slabs, wattle-and-daub style. It had verandahs front and back and, despite the smoke, didn't look as if it was normally lived in. She could hear the sound of an axe splitting wood as she stepped onto the verandah. The front door was open and revealed a single room with open fire, plain table, several chairs, a cupboard made of old boxes and a bed. She was leaning on the door frame fighting back the feeling that she was about to collapse, when a man carrying wood came to the back door opposite. He was silhouetted against the glare of the summer sun and Abby couldn't make out his features.

'Abby!' The voice was unmistakable.

'Mr Richards! What are you...I'm...' She slipped to the floor unconscious.

When she came to, she realised she was in the bed and Mr Richards was sitting beside her. She smiled weakly at him and lay there holding her stomach, feeling the surges of giddying waves that threatened to overwhelm her.

'Please get me to the hospital, Mr Richards, or get a doctor.' She grimaced, then shouted, 'Please!' and pulled her knees up to her stomach to help ease the pain.

He held her hand while she relaxed a little. 'Can't go anywhere now, even if I did have the old truck. We're a long way from anywhere. You can't be left alone, Abby, we'll have to sit it out for a while. Apart from that, it's lovely to see you again. How have things been? What's all the news?'

Abby felt a momentary calm, and tried to respond to his efforts to reduce her tension. 'We're getting married, Barney and me. Only decided the other day. He's up at Katherine, managing a big station.'

'Well, how about that! Congratulations.' He leaned over and kissed her forehead.

'Thanks,' she said softly, then looked him squarely in the eye. 'Mr Richards, what are we going to do?'

'We'll have a baby. Simple as that. Don't worry now. I've done this sort of thing before, believe it or not.' He smiled and patted her hand. 'I'll put some more water on the fire.'

By the time he returned with water from the tank outside, Abby was in the agony of a severe contraction. Then suddenly they started coming faster and stronger. She lay back groaning slightly as Mr Richards rolled a blanket and placed it under her back and helped her establish a breathing pattern.

Now all Abby could focus on was Mr Richards' kindly blue eyes and his mouth inhaling and exhaling in time with her. She lost track of time. Mr Richards stayed beside her, talking softly until it was time for the baby's birth. With sure hands he settled Abby, folding a sheet across her and then, with firmness and some insistence, directed her to push out the baby. Abby thrust and panted and pushed, crying out as her body finally gave up the child it had sheltered. Deftly Mr Richards eased the child out, wrapping it in a clean towel and laying it on Abby's breast as he took the knife he'd sterilised and cut the cord.

'You have a fine son, Abby.' He lifted her into a sitting position as she stared down at the miracle she held in her arms. 'Check him over,' grinned Mr Richards.

She unfolded the towel and looked at his little body, tentatively touching his toes and his fingers. 'Oh, he's perfect,' she breathed. At that instant the baby cried lustily and she hugged him to her, tears rolling down her face. 'Oh, Mr Richards, thank you . . . thank you. You said you always turn up when you're needed.'

He threw back his head and laughed. Abby felt the baby react to the sudden noise. 'Just a happy coincidence. I was going to call in on you in a couple of days anyway,' he said, then quickly changed the subject. 'The most important thing to do now is to get you home as fast as possible. Everyone will be at panic stations by now, I reckon. I'll go up to your car and see if I can get it started.' He lit a kerosene lamp and put it on a box beside the bed. Taking a torch off the crude mantelshelf over the fire, he put on his hat, smiled, nodded and strode off.

The story of the birth was the hottest item on the district party lines well into the night. From the moment Mr Richards telephoned the McBrides from the first farm they found on reaching the main road, the telephone lines hummed with amazing versions of events. The McBrides, Sarah and Keith Pemberton and one of the local policemen were all waiting on the verandah when Betsy spluttered up the track and coughed to a stop at the gate.

Gwen ran to the car and pulled open the door. 'Oh Abby,' she cried. 'We were so worried. We had half the district out looking for you.' She leaned in and kissed her daughter then carefully took the baby from her. 'Bob, help Abby. Dear Lord, look at this precious darling,' she cooed.

Bob helped Abby from the car, nodded across the seat to Mr Richards. 'Thanks, mate,' he said softly.

Two days later, Abby, who'd been resting in a canvas deck chair on the verandah, suddenly felt a surge of energy and happiness. Trembling with joy, she called to her mother to watch the baby while she went for a walk.

She headed down the track, knowing in every fibre of her body that her love was soon to be with her. Walking slowly, still recovering from the birth of the baby, she headed doggedly towards the road. She was at the half-mile point when she heard the engine. She leaned against a gumtree, and flagged the car as it came into sight.

Barney raced from the car and swept her into his arms. Holding her tightly against him, he rocked her gently, smoothing her hair, not speaking, totally overcome by his feelings of love and longing.

Finally they drew apart and Barney kissed her passionately. 'Oh Abby, my darling. I've missed you so much...What you must have been through. God, I wish I'd been here...Are you all right? And the baby...? I've been so worried since I heard.'

'Hush, it's all right, my sweet. We're doing just fine. Thanks to Mr Richards. Oh Barney, the baby is so beautiful...'

'What are you doing so far from home? Come on, get in. I can't wait to see him.' Tenderly he helped her into the car and as he went to put it into gear he gave her a shrewd glance. 'You knew I was coming, didn't you?' And as she nodded, he shook his head. 'I don't know why, but I've stopped wondering about some things. I'm leaving my life to the fates...so far they're doing a pretty good job.'

After the excitement of his arrival, Abby lifted their baby from the cradle and placed him in Barney's arms. Barney held his tiny son awkwardly, as if he could shatter like crystal eggs, and stared at him in wonderment.

'He's a bit on the small side, but Doctor Malone says he's not really premature, just a bit early. He was ready to arrive, so he did,' smiled Abby, hugging Barney's arm affectionately.

'What are we going to call him, Ab?' asked Barney, his eyes full of love for her.

'I thought Richie, after Mr Richards.'

Barney stared into the blue eyes of his son. 'Sounds good to me.'

CHAPTER SIXTEEN

THE MCBRIDES' LITTLE HOUSE OVERFLOWED WITH people and laughter, Christmas preparations and wedding plans. Abby, Barney and baby Richie were ensconced in the sleepout, the girls in constant attendance.

Barney, his face alight with love and wonder, watched Abby sitting in the rocker breastfeeding the baby, but gradually a concerned and sad expression took its place.

'I know what you're thinking, Barn,' said Abby. 'It's your parents, isn't it?'

He nodded.

'Do you think we should go and see them? Let

them see Richie. It might change your father's mind,' suggested Abby.

'No! I know my father. Until he accepts you and the decision I've made, I'm not going to see him.'

'I feel so sad about it all, that you are giving up your family.'

Barney leaned over and touched her hands holding their baby. 'You're my family now, Abby. You and Richie. We have our own life now.' He sighed. 'Give it time.'

At Amba, Enid approached Phillip and quietly asked, 'Phillip, can we see the child? Barney's child.'

'Absolutely not! Until he comes to his senses, he is not welcome here.'

'But this is his home, Phillip. At least allow me to go to them.'

'Don't even consider it, Enid. It's out of the question. He chose to defy us, he must live with the consequences.'

Enid turned away; both men were being stubborn and everyone was suffering. She went slowly to her bedroom and lay on her bed, her energy and the small hope she had cherished, draining from her. The dogs jumped on the bed and lay by her feet but she ignored them as she closed her eyes and wondered what was to become of her son and her grandchild.

Mr Richards became a regular visitor again now he had his old ute back from being repaired. Barney thanked him profusely for being around when Abby needed help.

'You're Richie's fairy godfather,' declared Abby. And so it was to Mr Richards they turned for advice on who should marry them.

'You understand the problem, seeing as we're both different religions,' said Abby. 'We've decided we want to be married in the open air — Mum and Dad have never heard of such an idea, of course!'

'Do you know the common, down by the river?' asked Barney. 'There's a small community hall there and it's very pretty. It gets used for all sorts of local events. Abby has chosen Christmas Eve, she thought it was the best gift we could give each other.'

Mr Richards smiled at the couple, so much in love, so contented with their baby, so looking forward to their new life. 'Leave it with me, I know just the bloke,' he smiled.

The children were so excited even Brian decided the new little baby hadn't usurped his place.

Everyone was busy making gifts in secret, making Christmas decorations and helping with the food preparations. Gwen baked fruitcakes, puddings and biscuits, and promised Brian there'd be a rainbow cake. She knitted Richie his own Christmas stocking to hang out for Santa. Late into the night she and Abby took turns at the old treadle Singer sewing machine, making the wedding dress and new dresses for Colleen and Shirley. No one could talk of anything but that this would be a Christmas to remember.

'We must be mad — a wedding, christening *and* a big family Christmas,' Gwen sighed to Bob as she fell into bed.

'Go on, you're loving every minute of it,' he teased. 'But don't overdo it, luv.'

'I'll miss them when they've gone north,' Gwen sighed. 'I don't mind the work. I just want everything to be nice for them.'

Two days before the big event, just when Barney was getting nervous about who would perform the ceremony, Kevin rushed inside to announce someone was coming up the track.

The visitor arrived on an old Norton motorcycle with a sidecar. As he drew up, shutting off the engine, the group gathered in front of the house saw he was a member of the Bush Brotherhood. He was a chubby man in his thirties, dressed in the simple brown hassock of the men dedicated to spreading God's word through the outback. He had a round ruddy face and short sandy hair.

'He looks like the jolly monk in the brandy ads,' whispered Bob.

'I'm Brother John, Mr Richards sent me,' the man said, shaking Bob's hand. 'I'm heading north, visiting my flock.'

Over sandwiches and tea, the ebullient Brother John had everyone laughing with his stories of evangelising in remote areas where men and women could go months without seeing another soul.

'How did you get to know Mr Richards?' asked Gwen.

'Strange bloke, Mr Richards. Keeps popping up all over the place, and usually when he's needed.' Brother John paused to chuckle. 'He jokes with me that he has the power to become invisible and actually travels on the pillion seat of the Norton.' They all laughed and Brother John slapped his thigh, laughing loudest of all.

There was a short spell when everyone became serious and discussed details of the wedding, giving Brother John a briefing on the circumstances. Nothing was held back and he listened with compassion and warmth. When the arrangements were completed for the wedding and the baby's baptism, the churchman smiled. 'Well, this is going to be quite an ecumenical event, isn't it? Catholic, Presbyterian and Church of England.' His smile got even larger. 'The Methodists will be furious at missing out.' And again he threw back his head and roared with laughter.

As the sun set on the hot Christmas Eve, the small wedding party assembled on the common. It was a flat pocket of lush green grass with a fringe of weeping willows and casuarinas lining the creek bank, which curved around the river. On a slight rise above the flood line sat the small white-painted and red-roofed wooden community hall.

Gwen held Richie in the crocheted shawl that all the McBride children had worn for their baptisms. Mrs Anderson and Jim stood behind her and Mrs Anderson peered over Gwen's shoulder to coo at the sleeping baby. Sarah and Keith Pemberton joined them. Shannon had unexpectedly taken off on another trip, so wasn't there to sour the day's joy.

A distant toot announced the arrival of the bridal party in Betsy, which Kevin had polished and tied Christmas bush to the bonnet. Brother John took his place and signalled Barney to stand beside him. Bob McBride opened the door for Colleen and Shirley, who stepped proudly out in their white muslin dresses sashed with yellow ribbons, carrying posies of small daisies.

Abby followed and took her father's arm. 'Righto, Ab,' whispered Bob, 'shoulders back, right foot forward, here we go.'

Barney's eyes misted as he looked at Abby, dressed in a loose cream ankle-length dress. She wore a small hat with a short veil covering her face and carried a bouquet of cream and yellow rosebuds.

They stood together, a small cluster of people beneath the canopy of rose-gold light as if the sun itself was joining in the celebration. Brother John began by welcoming everyone and remarking on the beautiful setting. 'As some of you may know, we of the Bush Brotherhood spend a lot of time in the bush and worshipping outdoors is not unusual for us, for in a beautiful setting like this it is just as easy, perhaps easier, to acknowledge the gift and presence of God as it is in a church or a cathedral. Just as He is everywhere, so too is His gift of love, and it is in recognition of the love between Abigail and Barnard that we are gathered together here today. Love is what starts a family, love is what holds a family together and gives it strength. Love is the essence of living and, without it, without sharing it, we are nothing.' He paused, smiled broadly and clapped his hands together. 'Right, enough of the preaching, let's get down to the business of the day.'

The simple words of the ceremony were punctuated by the calls of birds working the willows and the creek for their evening meal. But neither Abby nor Barney heard their singing — the solemn yet joyous tone of the Bush Brother made them aware only of the words of the ceremony.

When he pronounced them man and wife, they turned to each other with love in their eyes, and kissed. It was only then they heard the birds singing and they both looked to the trees and smiled.

'I'll now baptise the baby,' announced Brother John. When it was over, Bob shouted, 'Three cheers for the bride and groom', and as the cheers echoed up and down the creek, everyone moved forward to embrace and wish them well.

Mrs Anderson took Barney aside and gave him a small parcel. 'Your mother sends her love and this . . . it's your silver christening cup. It's for Richie. And she thought you might want to give this to Abby.' She handed over a small blue box.

Barney put it in his pocket and bit his lip. He knew it was the gift that Enid had always promised his bride.

'Your mother wanted to come very much. But she won't go against your father's wishes. He'll come round in time,' said Mrs Anderson comfortingly. 'You get along and enjoy your life. I'm sure it's going to be tough going up there and starting out with so little, but well, that's how most of us have to do it, Barney.'

'I don't care, so long as I have Abby and the baby with me, that's all that matters.'

It was a merry Christmas Eve at the McBrides' with a splendid dinner of cold meats, salad and Christmas pudding eaten in the garden lit by hurricane lamps. The Pembertons and the Andersons left early and Mr Richards put his swag in the ute.

Before leaving he had a quiet yarn to Abby and Barney. 'Well, we're always off on journeys it seems. I just want to wish you well. Who knows, I might drop in one day.'

'Oh, I wish you would,' enthused Abby. 'You've become very special to us, Mr Richards, and we owe you so much.'

'You owe me nothing, lass,' he said. 'The reward for an old fella like me is to see the love you both have for each other. It's a precious gift, and some people spend a lifetime searching and never find it. A thinking bloke I knew once wrote that love is the only reality. What I reckon he was saying is that love is the only real thing that matters in life when all is said and done. So I reckon you have a lot going for you.'

He reached out his hand to Barney and Abby kissed him on the cheek and hugged him.

'God bless you, Mr Richards,' she said softly.

He said his farewells to the children, kissed his fingers and put them lightly on the forehead of a sleeping Richie and was walked to the battered old utility by the rest of the family. There were more handshakes, a kiss from Gwen and with an exchange of wishes for a Merry Christmas, he was on his way.

When the table was cleared, the dishes done and the children in bed, Barney and Abby went for a walk.

'There's our star,' said Abby looking up to the Southern Cross. 'We'll still be able to see it up north. It'll always watch over us.'

'That's a nice feeling,' said Barney. 'Happy?'

'I'm so happy it frightens me. Oh Barney, I love you so much. It has been a wonderful day, so wonderful.'

Barney swept his wife tightly into his arms and kissed her.

Christmas morning was happy bedlam. The children were up at dawn emptying Christmas stockings and running from bedroom to bedroom in excitement, jumping on beds, hugging and kissing everyone.

Bob, wearing a knitted Christmas stocking as a nightcap and still in his pyjamas, delivered mugs of tea to everyone in bed. Then it was roll call for the present opening.

Bob had cut a large branch of sweet-smelling eucalypt and anchored it in a kerosene tin filled with dirt. The children had decorated the tree with homemade paperchains, cut-out stars and tinsel. Piled around the kero tin, now wrapped in Christmas paper, were the presents.

Bob sat back and grinned at his happy family. There were no lavish gifts, but practical clothes, useful items, novelties and books, and everyone had made something for another member of the family.

'Kevin, you're a brilliant French knitter, I love these colours,' said Gwen, holding up the multi-coloured pot holder.

'And look what the girls have made for Richie,' she said, showing Bob the tiny beribboned blue knitted booties.

'Won't be able to play football in those,' commented Bob. 'Now gather round, everyone. Time for the Christmas singalong.'

Barney and Abby exchanged a grin and Abby whispered, 'There's no escape, it's a family tradition.'

They all drew into a circle and, led by Bob, sang their favourite Christmas carols. Colleen and Shirley pulled Richie's cradle into the centre and, sitting on either side of the placid baby, the two new aunties chorused sweetly, '*Away in a manger* . . .'

Later, when everyone had stowed their bounty and the Christmas wrappings had been picked up, some being carefully smoothed for reuse, they all gathered for a big breakfast.

Gwen and Abby kept up a running supply of steak and bacon and eggs, porridge and home-made mulberry jam on toast until everyone was satisfied.

After breakfast when Abby was sitting on the verandah rocking Richie, Barney came to her with the little blue box Mrs Anderson had given him at the wedding.

'Ab, this is something very special. It's something more than a Christmas gift. It's not from me,' he said mysteriously.

Abby took the box and carefully undid the little bow that had been tied so perfectly. She opened it and took out the tiny tissue-wrapped gift. Slowly she unfolded the paper to reveal a beautiful ruby and diamond ring.

She gasped. 'Barney, it's magnificent.' She looked up and saw sadness in his eyes.

'Mum sent it over.' He choked a little as he said it.

Abby reached quickly for his hand. 'Oh Barney, darling.'

'It belonged to my grandmother, a sort of family heirloom, I guess.' He paused. 'You know what she's saying, Abby. She wants us to be part of the family. All of us.'

Abby slipped the ring over her finger alongside the simple gold wedding band, and held her hand out for Barney to admire. 'If only your father . . .' said Abby sadly, suddenly finding it unnecessary to complete the sentence for she knew that Barney was thinking exactly the same thing.

That evening at Amba, Enid put her sewing in her basket, picked up the dogs and walked slowly down the hallway to the library.

'Good night, Phillip. Merry Christmas to you.'

Phillip turned the tiny key in the door of the leadlight bookcase and looked at his wife standing in the doorway.

'Goodnight, my dear. Christmas wishes to you too. I'm going to read.'

Enid nodded and went to her room. In the darkness she stood at the window and, looking towards Anglesea, wished her son happiness.

In the library Phillip sat in the leather armchair

bathed in the light of the single lamp standing by his chair. He did not see the gold lettering on the leather jacket of the unopened book, but sat with his eyes closed, feeling very lonely and very sad.

They tucked Richie's toy train from Mr Richards in with the cases and the bundles in the back seat of the car. Eventually they ran out of things to fuss with — the car was ready, the engine and tyres checked yet again, they'd double checked the house for things left behind — and so now they had to say goodbye.

Gwen hugged Richie to her and Bob lent down and kissed his head.

The twins clung to Abby, unable to stop their tears.

'Stop blubbering,' said Kevin, who was having trouble keeping back tears himself. He shook Barney's hand and hugged Abby then turned away to take Brian's hand.

Barney stretched out his hand to Bob, who took it then gave him a solid hug. 'Look after my girl,' he muttered. Barney nodded and kissed Gwen's damp cheek and lifted Richie from her arms so she could embrace Abby.

Mother and daughter clung together for a moment. 'I love you, Mum. I hope I'll be as a good a mum as you.'

'I'll miss you so much, Ab . . . but be happy.'

Barney gently eased Abby and the baby into the car as Bob picked up Brian and put an arm about Gwen.

The calls and good wishes faded away as the car headed down the track and they all stood in silence, just little Brian waving a hand and saying almost to himself, 'Bye, bye . . .'

Two days later, Gwen had smoko ready for Bob as he came in from the paddock. He washed his hands at the sink as she poured the hot tea into a mug. Hearing a vehicle pull into the yard, Gwen put down the teapot and looked out of the door.

'Bob, you'd better come quick.' Her voice was strained and frightened and Bob hurried to her side as the police sergeant got slowly out of the car and took off his hat.

They listened as their life fell apart around them.

There were no words that could possibly make things different, so the sergeant simply stated the facts. There'd been an accident the previous night. At a level crossing. The train had hit the car and killed Barney and Abby outright. The baby had been thrown clear and was under observation in hospital, but he seemed to be all right.

The sergeant cleared his throat. 'Everything was smashed up pretty bad, but they said the baby escaped with barely a scratch — a miracle really.'

CHAPTER SEVENTEEN

ABBY AND BARNEY, WHO'D LOVED EACH OTHER
so much in life, were separated in death.

Each family claimed its own and mourned in
their own way. The Catholic church was
crowded with mourners for Abby. The following
day Barney was buried after a sombre service at
the Presbyterian church, which wasn't large
enough to accommodate the huge crowd of
mourners. Enid had to be supported by Phillip
throughout the service and while her frail physical presence was there, her heart and spirit had
fled.

The Pembertons and the Andersons attended

both services. Mrs Anderson had the sad task of telling the McBrides that Phillip preferred that none of the McBrides attend the funeral of their son. He blamed Abby and her family for taking him from them.

The town and district were devastated by the tragedy. The loss of the two young people was bad enough, but the division between the grieving families added confusing dimensions to individual and community grief. Barely concealed differences surfaced as groups discussed the deaths and their impact. Old-timers agreed that never in memory had the district been so polarised and saddened by tragedy. There were many who confided to each other that no good came of defying church, family and the unwritten rules of society. The official investigation blamed a signal failure as the cause of the accident.

Gwen barely let Richie out of her arms once he came home after being checked in the hospital. The children hovered around supportively, watching Gwen bottle feed the tiny boy and their enthusiasm for helping at bath time created an atmosphere that enabled the entire family to cope with the grief and adjust to new routines dictated by the infant. Gwen's love for her daughter was transferred to the baby with double measure.

Privately, she and Bob spent hours anguishing over their actions. Should they have stopped Abby marrying Barney? Broken hearted or not she'd be alive and with them still. Gwen thought of Abby throughout each day and dreamed of her at night. She vowed to herself that she would think of her every moment of every day as if that would keep her close to her daughter. And each night Gwen sobbed herself to sleep in Bob's arms.

With time, however, the threads of their shattered lives began to weave together. The children returned to school, suffering the stares and whispers of the other children. Bob drove himself to physical exhaustion and Gwen kept sobbing over reminders of Abby all about the house. The laughter had gone from their lives. The songs had ceased.

There was nothing to relieve the grief at Amba. Enid sank into a shadowy world, staying in her bed, her dogs clutched close to her. Her mind was troubled, her heart broken, the tenuous links that had been leading her back to her faith severed forever. There was no God. There was no hope.

Mrs Anderson tried to get her to eat, but more often than not the food trays came back untouched. Concerned, she spoke to Phillip Holten, but Phillip, locked in his own guilt and grief, could offer little help. When Mrs Anderson asked about the future of little Richie, Phillip Holten bellowed at her to 'Never mention the child ever again in this house!'

Little had changed six months later, but the joy of Richie's smiles and healthy progress brought light into the lives of the McBride family. Mrs Anderson, sometimes accompanied by Jim, visited most Sundays. Once, working in the kitchen garden at Amba she was describing Richie's latest efforts to Jim when she glanced up to see Enid standing by the door listening. Catching Mrs Anderson's eye, she turned away and walked slowly to her sitting room. The small incident cemented Enid's resolve to confront Phillip over an idea she'd been considering for some time.

'Am I interrupting, dear?'

Phillip looked up from his stamp album, surprised to see Enid out of her room — she had spent most of her time since Barney's death confined to bed. 'No. It's perfectly all right. Do come in, my dear. Is something the matter?' He noted that Enid's hands were clenched in front of her and that she was holding herself stiffly. There was something very determined about her manner as she sat down.

'I wanted to talk to you, Phillip. I have been

thinking for some time about this matter and I
have come to a decision.' She took a deep breath,
trying to still her nervous breathlessness. 'I want
us to adopt Barnard's son. I believe his place is
here. With us.'

Phillip stared at her in outright astonishment,
then his face darkened. 'You're talking nonsense,
Enid. I will never countenance such an idea. I
refused then, and I haven't changed my mind. We
must forget that girl ever existed,' he said bitterly. Then, seeing Enid's tragic face, added more
softly, 'You can't replace him, Enid. He's gone.'

'It would make me happy, Phillip.'

'My dear, you haven't the strength to take on a
child. And at our age...'

'We have the Andersons...' began Enid, but
her determination crumbled when she saw Phillip's face set hard.

'I will not hear any more of this,' he said,
holding up his hand. 'Come, sit down and have a
glass of sherry.'

Meekly, Enid sat and Phillip poured the amber
liquid into small crystal glasses.

It was Enid's last stand. From then on, her
secret feelings for Abby and her lack of resolution
with Phillip began to nurture overwhelming feelings of guilt. She kept telling herself how different it might all have been had she really stood up

to Phillip when Barney was pleading for his family's support over his marriage to Abby. She agonised endlessly and her condition quickly deteriorated.

The mood in the house took its toll on the Andersons as well and one night after dinner, Mrs Anderson confided to her husband that it was like working in a morgue. 'I don't know how much longer I can take it, Jim. It's so depressing round here. I'm more nurse than housekeeper these days.'

'We can't let Mrs Holten down. Or him for that matter. What would Barney say if we left them in the lurch, eh luv? Besides, where would we go? This has been our home far too long.'

'You're right,' sighed Mrs Anderson. 'And I couldn't bear to move too far away from that darling poppet Richie. I keep remembering Barney as a baby...' Her eyes filled with tears and her shoulders shook as Jim patted her consolingly.

Within two months Enid was in such frail health, her heartbeat so erratic, that she was admitted to hospital. Phillip spent most of each day at her bedside as she struggled for breath. The doctors were not optimistic. In lucid moments she could talk of only one thing — the baby. Phillip found it increasingly difficult and yet compassion for his wife forced him to listen and acknowledge her words.

Late one afternoon as he sat by her bed, she suddenly opened her eyes and stared at him with fierce, unnaturally bright eyes. She took his hand and gripped it with surprising strength. 'Phillip,' she said in a hoarse whisper, 'I so wanted the baby . . . so wanted to love him. He's part of me, Phillip, and you . . . Can you understand that? He needs our love.'

The effort exhausted her and her grip fell away and for a moment she seemed to fall into a sleep. Then her eyes opened and met Phillip's. 'Love is what we all need.' She took a breath. 'Love is the only real thing in this world . . . Do you understand, Phillip?'

He took her hand. 'Yes, dear,' he said quickly, anxious to please but not really understanding what she had said. 'Enid dear, don't tire yourself. Rest now.'

She closed her eyes and Phillip sat a while longer then left to find a nurse. When they returned, Enid had slipped away.

The nurse checked her pulse then looked at Phillip. 'I'm sorry, Mr Holten.'

'She wasn't in any pain,' said Phillip, unable to find any other words. He kissed his wife's forehead and, with bowed head, walked slowly out of the room.

Alone in his grief and bitterness, Phillip worked on at Amba, refusing invitations from the Pembertons and other acquaintances to visit or stay for a meal. He spoke little to the Andersons except when necessary. It seemed impossible that his life had come to this. He was now known as a recluse, a lonely and bitter old man.

The gossip in town was of his hatred for the McBride family, how he blamed them for taking away his son and now his wife. But the gossips could not know what was really consuming Phillip Holten. In the long lonely evenings in his darkened library, Phillip sat staring straight ahead into the gloom, trying to fashion a new sense of purpose out of the wreckage of his life. He kept hearing Enid's voice.

'I so wanted the baby . . . He's part of me, Phillip, and you . . . He needs our love.'

It played on his mind, over and over again, like a record with the needle stuck in a groove until he resolved to act.

Shearing was finished when a letter to the McBrides arrived from a solicitor in Sydney. As he read it, Bob's face tensed, his hands shook and his temper flared.

'He can't do this,' he shouted. 'I don't understand. He can't take Richie from us.'

Gwen quickly took the letter and read it, sitting down slowly on a cane chair on the verandah as she took in the unbelievable news — Phillip Holten was taking legal action to obtain custody of his grandson.

She looked up at Bob, speechless for a moment. She closed her eyes and said a silent prayer.

'What right has he, what right?' demanded Bob as he stamped up and down the verandah.

'Maybe as much right as us, luv,' said Gwen quietly. 'There was no will. We never asked any legal advice, we just assumed...'

'You talk as if you're going to let him go,' said Bob, puzzled. 'Aren't we going to fight...?'

'We'd better talk to Father O'Leary.'

Father O'Leary had talked to the solicitor in town and came to see the McBrides, looking gloomy. 'It could be an expensive legal fight and I don't like your chances. Holten argues he can offer the boy a better, more secure future.'

'But what about *love*, what about a mother in his life?' demanded Gwen, close to tears.

Father O'Leary patted her hand. 'He has Mrs Anderson, who raised Richie's father, plus he says he plans to have a live-in nanny and governess.'

'Why? Why is he doing this?' cried Gwen.

'He's lonely, he feels guilty, and he hates us,' answered Bob bitterly.

'Now, Bob,' Father O'Leary said soothingly, 'that won't help you or him. Prayer may help though. Will you join me?' And they bent their heads together, praying for guidance and strength for Richie, for the souls of his parents, and for Phillip Holten.

Gwen went to see Sarah Pemberton, wondering if she could help. It was less in desperation and more a quest for sharing the agony with another woman.

Sarah was sympathetic but she too emphasised the harsh reality of Phillip Holten's resources. 'He has the money, he has a lot of influence still, despite his strange behaviour, and he could make it very difficult for you all if you just tried to disappear with the baby. Look at it this way. You'll be close by Richie here and that's important . . . I know I can speak for Keith when I say you're welcome to stay on here at Anglesea.'

'Thanks, Sarah.' Gwen's mouth trembled, then she dropped her head on her arms on the table, her shoulders shaking with great sobs. Sarah let her cry out her feelings, patting her shoulder until Gwen gathered herself together.

'I'm sorry, Sarah. I guess everything got on top of me. This is so hard for us to bear . . . and also knowing it's the last thing Abby would want.'

After several weeks of frantic efforts to try and thwart Phillip Holten, it became clear to the McBrides that they were not going to be able to keep Richie with them. Gwen asked Mrs Anderson to plead their case, that it was a monstrous cruelty to take the little boy, now almost a year old, from the only family he'd known.

'You'd be wasting your breath. He's already hired the nanny and I'm not supposed to have contact with you about Richie. Once he's over here, I doubt you'll be allowed to see him at all.' Hearing the sadness in her voice, Gwen broke down.

'All I can say is that Jim and I will give him all the love we can, and keep talking about you all to him. In time Mr Holten might come round. He's a stubborn man, give it a bit of time is all I can say to you.'

It was of little comfort to Gwen. She clung to Richie, who was confused and dismayed at all the tearful attention. Gwen and Bob sat the other children down and tried to explain the situation fairly.

'We all have each other, Mr Holten doesn't have anybody, and he is Richie's grandfather too,' said Bob. 'And he can offer him a better future at Amba, schools and so on.'

'What's wrong with our life, with our school?' demanded Kevin.

The girls started to cry and so did Gwen. Brian, not fully understanding his mother's unhappiness, climbed onto her lap and hugged her.

It was a cold legal document that arrived stating the child would be collected the following Tuesday. Gwen tried to downplay the parting, telling the children they'd be seeing Richie soon for Christmas. Each child kissed and hugged Richie who happily waved as the tearful children trudged down the track to the school bus. Brian was sent up to the Pembertons' to play under Sarah's watchful eye so he wasn't around when Richie left, then Bob and Gwen quietly waited.

The car pulled up and the nanny — a plain-looking lady in her thirties — and a man in a dark suit got out of the car. Gwen was standing by the gate holding Richie in her arms. Bob walked forward, handed over the small cardboard suitcase that held Richie's clothes and few toys. He signed the papers and beckoned Gwen. The nanny smiled and reached for Richie who turned away and clung to Gwen, hiding his face in her shoulder. Gwen was crying, unable to release her grip on Abby's baby.

Bob took Richie from her. 'Don't make this harder on yourself, luv.' He kissed Richie and handed him to the nanny. 'Be a good boy, matey,' he said brokenly.

The nanny swallowed. 'He'll be well cared for, please don't worry.'

She got in the car and Richie began to scream and squirm, holding out his chubby arms to Gwen when he realised she wasn't coming with them.

Bob held Gwen's hand as the car began to pull away.

'Richie...' screamed Gwen at the sight of Richie's crying face inside the car.

Bob wrapped his arms about her and held her to him as she struggled, trying to run after the car. Finally, when the fight had left her and she stood quietly sobbing, Bob led her into the house, sat her in the kitchen and set about making tea.

It wasn't till much later that day that Gwen found they'd left behind the wooden train Mr Richards had made for Richie.

Bob put it up on the mantelpiece. 'We'll send it over. Abby cherished that train...'

It was too much for him. He rested his head against the mantelpiece and his shoulders heaved as he was overcome by his feelings of grief, frustration and loss.

CHAPTER EIGHTEEN

THREE CHRISTMASES PASSED. EACH YEAR WHEN the ruby-tipped Christmas Bush blossomed, the McBrides gathered it along with wild flowers to put on the graves of Abby and Barney. Time had eased some of the pain but their sadness surfaced again every time they thought of Richie alone at Amba, and that was often.

They had had no contact with him since the day he was taken from Gwen's arms. But Gwen and Bob kept telling the children, and themselves, that Richie was being given a great opportunity for the future. And, after all, they had each other, and Phillip Holten was all alone. Yet, despite the rationalising, Gwen ached to hold her daughter's child again.

Time had dragged so slowly and Gwen felt older than her years. She noticed, too, how sadness had deepened the lines on Bob's face. They had made repeated attempts to see Richie over the years but were always rebuffed by Phillip Holten. Richie was kept at Amba most of the time and if it hadn't been for Mrs Anderson's visits bringing news of him, Richie would have been totally lost to them.

Once, about a year ago, Gwen had been crossing the main street in town when Phillip Holten's car, driven by a man she didn't recognise, went past. She glimpsed the wistful face of the young boy in the back, and as she stood in the middle of the road she knew that it was Richie. It took all her will to stop running after the car. She wanted to catch it, hurl her shopping basket at the window, to wrench open the door and free her small grandson.

A driver tooted politely at her still standing in the road, breaking her trance. Gwen trudged across the road and sank on to a chair in the cafe. The agony of knowing he was so near yet forbidden to see his family was devastating. Gwen had had several meetings with Mrs Anderson who told her what a bright and lively boy Richie was, how he delighted the station hands with his antics, and that he had already been enrolled in boarding school which he'd start when he was eight. If Phillip Holten knew of these meetings he ignored them. For the Andersons, Richie was the light of their lives. But Phillip Holten refused to see joy in the company of the boy, continuing to agonise over the loss of his son and wife.

Phillip suffered alone. He spoke to the Andersons, the nanny and the men around the property only when necessary. He spent long lonely hours in his library during the evenings. As Richie grew older he had tried to make the evening meal his time with the boy, but although it had become habit for both of them, neither enjoyed the experience. Phillip was awkward, unable to relate to the tiny figure at the end of the formal dining table. Attempts at conversation were strained and more like a polite inquisition — Phillip asked questions and the boy responded briefly.

Richie felt awkward with the authoritarian figure who seemed devoid of warmth and humour. Phillip usually turned the occasion into an educational opportunity for instruction on manners. Richie, however, resorted to an observation game based on one Jim Anderson liked to play. He set about memorising every item in the room, each night adding another to the list. The next day, in his favourite hideaway in the barn, he would try to recite them all. Sometimes he'd select an object he didn't have a name for and would quietly ask his grandfather. 'What glass thing, Richard?' Phillip would ask in surprise, turning in his chair to look at the sideboard. 'Oh, that's called a decanter. You put port wine in it. When you are an adult you can have some port wine.' The boy wondered what port wine was but saved up the question for another day. For Phillip such brief exchanges were the highlight of the meal and would hearten him enormously.

But most nights after dinner, alone in his study, Phillip found it more and more difficult to fight off suffocating black moods. He knew his attitude to the boy should be different but could not bring himself to get too close for fear of opening the wounds that scarred his heart. The pain was easier to bear when he blamed the McBrides for the deaths of Barney and Enid. Increasingly though, the terrible thought seeped into his consciousness that he was responsible for killing both of them . . . that he had turned his back on his son and sent him to his death . . . that he had refused his wife's dearest wish and she had simply given up and died. Atonement had not been achieved by bringing Richie to Amba as he had hoped. There was no release, no peace, no easing of pain.

He thought of the stern grim father he had scarcely known, how little he had known his own son, and now his grandson. History was repeating itself and he felt powerless to stop it.

The Sunday before Christmas, Sarah Pemberton dropped into the McBrides for morning tea after church. How much a part of Anglesea they'd become. She couldn't imagine how they'd managed without them. She hoped they'd always be part of the place.

'How are the Christmas preparations coming along, Gwen? I suppose you're baking cakes for half the district again.'

Before Gwen could reply, Bob responded with more than the start of a smile, 'Yep, got another truck-load of raisins coming this afternoon.' They laughed and Bob went on with mock seriousness, 'We've decided to go into business in the city . . . a cake shop. Gwen can be the breadwinner for a change.'

'Don't you dare,' said Sarah shaking a finger at him. 'And that was a lousy pun, Bob. By the way, this Christmas will be a bit different. The CWA ladies out our way are organising Christmas Eve carols by candlelight down on the common. I think it's a great idea.'

'So long as the weather holds, it will work,'

said Gwen flatly. 'There's no way everyone would fit into the community hall if it rained.'

Bob fiddled with the makings of a smoke and Sarah knew what they were both thinking.

'You will come, won't you?' she said softly. 'It will be a lovely family night. The kids love lighting the candles and singing the carols.'

Bob and Gwen looked at each other briefly. 'Of course we'll be there,' said Bob with strength in his voice. 'The whole McBride clan will be there in fine voice.'

Gwen smiled, relieved that the decision had not been for her to make.

It was a typical Australian December morning of promised warmth, burning blue sky, birds warbling and mottled sunlight beneath the scribbly gums — the kind of day that makes all good things seem possible.

Mr Richards was humming as he drove up the track to Anglesea. It was only a dirt track but it led to a home filled with love. The thought pleased him, even though it was his first visit since the deaths of Abby and Barney and he knew that it wouldn't be the same without them.

He parked, stepped onto the verandah and was instantly ambushed by Brian and the twins who had been hiding behind the Malacca cane furniture.

They led him down the hall as he called out, 'Anybody home?'

Gwen was delighted to see him and came out of the kitchen wiping floured hands on her apron. 'Why didn't you tell us you were coming? Brian, go and find Dad and Kevin and tell them Mr Richards is here. Oh, it's so good to see you again.'

Brian, with the twins in tow, bolted off. Mr Richards looked at Gwen. The delight of seeing him had given way to other feelings. Her eyes said it all and as she crumpled, he wrapped his arms around her. He let her cry, then led her to the kitchen where they sat at the table littered with the ingredients of mince pies.

Gwen wiped her eyes with the bottom of her apron. 'Thanks for your letter,' she said between sniffs, referring to the note he had written to them shortly after the news of Abby's death had reached him. 'It was a great comfort. I still take it out and read it from time to time.'

'I'm sorry I haven't been back before this, but I've been outback working at a bit of this and a bit of that, looking up friends and so forth.' He took his pipe from his waistcoat pocket and went about tapping and lighting it. 'Bumped into Brother John from time to time. Funny bloke that fella. Still stirring up dust storms along the Birdsville track and back of Cloncurry with his motorbike.

He asked me to give you all his love.' He paused for a puff on the pipe, then asked quietly, 'How's the boy going?'

Gwen had to fight to keep control of her emotions as she told the story and tried to paint a positive picture of care and opportunities Richie had at Amba. Mr Richards listened, saying nothing, but nodding occasionally in acknowledgement of some detail. When she had finished, he took his pipe out and leaned towards her. 'But it still hurts, doesn't it? Particularly at this time of year.'

Gwen nodded in agreement, afraid to say anything in fear of breaking down in tears. Then she found some strength. 'Richie still has your train. Loves it. Mrs Anderson has told him about you.'

Mr Richards was delighted. 'Well fancy that now. I reckon I ought to call in and say hello to the boy before I move on.'

'You're not stopping for Christmas?'

'Well, I've got to see a few people up the track. A job for Brother John. But I could be back at Christmas if there's room at the table.'

'Of course there is,' replied Gwen, brightening at the thought. 'We're having carols on the common on Christmas Eve. Just the local folk from properties but it should be lovely.'

'Carols on the common. I like the sound of that. Sure, I'll be there.'

It was late in the afternoon when Mrs Anderson announced to Phillip that Mr Richards was wanting to see him. He had just come in from helping move some sheep to another paddock and was taking his boots off on the back verandah.

Phillip was surprised at how delighted he was at the news. 'Thank you, Mrs Anderson,' he said. 'Thank you.' And to her amazement he padded off in his socks to meet the visitor. 'We'll take tea in the library please,' he called over his shoulder.

He greeted Mr Richards with warmth and escorted him inside, suddenly becoming self-conscious about the socks. 'Been doing a little work with the sheep,' he explained and Mr Richards smiled.

'Honest toil, Mr Holten. And how have you been keeping?'

'Please sit down. Light up if you want to. Well, I've been keeping all right, all things considered. No coughs or colds,' said Phillip, trying to mask his evasiveness. 'And you?'

'Oh, for an old codger who can't sit still, I'm making out all right.' He raised an eyebrow. 'Reckon someone up there keeps an eye on me.'

They exchanged views on the price of wool and

livestock, the need for good summer rains to boost the pastures, and the prosperity the country as a whole was enjoying. Phillip was feeling more relaxed than he had been for ages when Mrs Anderson arrived with tea and Christmas cake.

'I took the liberty of cutting the Christmas cake a little early, Mr Holten. Seeing as how Mr Richards is such a special visitor,' explained Mrs Anderson. 'I've just called out to young Richie to come in and join you for a piece of cake and to say hello. He's just had another birthday, you know. He's grown into such a lovely little boy, Mr Richards.'

Before Phillip had time to come to terms with the slight panic that swelled up inside him, the telephone rang in the hall. He leapt to his feet. 'I'll take it, Mrs Anderson.'

As he hurried from the room, Richie appeared at the French doors that opened from the library onto the verandah and stood there looking in, clutching his wooden toy train.

'C'mon, luvy. My, look at you, been driving your train in the dirt again. Come here quick and I'll dust you down and wipe your hands on my apron.'

Richie glanced at Mr Richards out of the corner of his eye as Mrs Anderson fussed. He caught a wink and a half-smile from Mr Richards.

'There now,' said Mrs Anderson. 'Cleaned up for meeting Mr Richards and a piece of Christmas cake.'

Richie turned to face the old man and looked directly at him, taking in the weathered face, shock of grey hair, beard and clear blue eyes. He gave a quick grin.

'Well, young fella, last time I saw you you were a little bundle in a blanket. Now you're almost a jackeroo,' said Mr Richards lightly, looking the lad over. 'Ah...he has Abby's eyes and mouth but he's got Barney's strong forehead and jaw.'

'Thank you very much,' said Richie politely as Mrs Anderson handed him a piece of cake, then he went and sat on the settee beside Mr Richards, his legs swinging. Between bites, he looked up at him. 'You made my train, didn't you?'

'Yes, and I'm mighty pleased to see it's still choofing along.'

'It's my favourite toy.'

'Well I'd better choof along too and take Jim his cuppa and a bit of cake,' chuckled Mrs Anderson. 'You two can have a good old yarn together.'

'When did you make it?' asked Richie, running his hand over the train.

'Before you were born. I gave it to your mum.'

'She got killed you know. My daddy too.'

Mr Richards took his hand. 'Yes, I know,' he said softly, then brightened. 'Now, what other favourite things do you have?'

The boy hesitated, then looked up into the old man's eyes. In them he saw something that gave him courage, despite the trouble he'd been in for taking down the forbidden books in the library. He let go of the comforting hand and walked over to the bookcase, unlocked it and carefully selected a book. He stood holding it, a hand running slowly over the illustrated cover, then turned and walked back to the settee. 'This.'

'*Seven Little Australians*,' said Mr Richards, reading the title. 'And what makes this so special?'

Richie slowly turned the pages and as he did, Phillip came to the hall door. He saw instantly that the bookcase doors were open and that the two on the settee, their backs to him, were obviously looking at a book. He was stunned and confused, frozen to the spot.

'I look at the pictures,' explained Richie seriously. 'This is my best picture. I love this picture.' His lip trembled slightly as he looked at the black and white drawing of a large family happily together in a big lounge room.

'Ah now, I've read this book. It's about seven brothers and sisters in one family and they all love each very much.'

'I'd like brothers and sisters.'

'But you've got others you can love, haven't you?'

'Yes, I love Mrs A and Jim.' He paused, 'And I love Diet and Tucker.' He paused again, thinking hard. 'And I love lambs.' But no matter how hard he tried, he knew this didn't add up to a family like the one in the picture.

'And you love your grandfather.'

Richie hesitated then said very slowly, 'Y . . . es.'

'He needs a lot of love from you, you know, Richie. When your dad got killed and your grandma died, he lost his family too.'

Richie didn't have time to start to grapple with this concept before Phillip coughed and walked into the room. The boy quickly closed the book and was going to hide it behind his back when Phillip said pleasantly, 'You can keep the book if you like, Richard.'

'Really, Grandfather? Really keep it?'

'Of course, but look after it, mind.'

Richie ran over quickly and surprised his grandfather with a hug, then ran out of the room calling for Mrs Anderson to tell her the news.

The two men returned to their tea and cake. 'You've got a good lad there, Mr Holten. He's coming along real fine.'

Phillip was deeply moved but he tried to be nonchalant. 'Well, thank you for those kind remarks. It's a struggle of course with no real family around for support.'

They talked for another hour and Phillip was sorry when his guest announced he had to get on the road as he had a few hours' drive ahead of him. 'I hope you will drop by again. It's a pleasure having a talk with you, Mr Richards.'

'Well, I've promised to come back in a couple of days for the carols on the common,' he said as Richie and Mrs Anderson came in. 'Ah, here's the young jackeroo come to say goodbye.'

Holding the train close to his chest with one hand, Richie extended his other to shake hands. 'Thanks for making my train. I love my train too, you know.'

'Now that's a nice thought to take with me,' said Mr Richards. Crouching down to be at the boy's eye level, he spoke in a soft, confidential tone. 'You know what you do when you love something very much? You share it.'

'Like give someone else a go with it?' asked the boy cautiously.

'Yeah, that's the idea.' Mr Richards leaned forward and whispered briefly in Richie's ear, pulled back and winked. Richie smiled and tried to wink back.

At the evening meal Phillip was very relaxed. He had felt a warm feeling when Richie arrived for dinner and smiled as he carefully put the book on the table beside his plate. For the first time Phillip found it easy to make conversation with his grandson. They exchanged a few light remarks about Mr Richard's beard and how he looked a bit like Santa Claus, speculated about what Santa might bring Richie for Christmas, commented on the quality of the Christmas cake, and agreed that another slice before bed was in order.

Afterwards, in the study, Phillip poured himself a scotch whiskey instead of his usual port wine. He was enjoying it while looking out of the open doors at the night sky when Mrs Anderson came in to say goodnight.

'Before you go, Mrs Anderson, what are these carols on the common Mr Richards said he was coming back for?'

'Oh, it's the CWA ladies doing their bit to make Christmas Eve a little bit special this year. They're having carols by candlelight. Everyone is invited.'

'Thank you. Goodnight, Mrs Anderson,'

He settled down in his usual leather chair and was so deep in thought that he didn't notice Richie's small figure until he stood beside him.

His hair was damp, slicked in place. His cotton dressing gown was pulled tightly around him by a silk cord with tassels. He held his beloved train.

Phillip looked at him in surprise. 'You've come to say goodnight, have you?' They normally said goodnight at the dinner table.

'Mr Richards said you were sad because you lost your family,' said Richie, pausing to take a deep breath. 'Well, you've got me.' He thrust the train into Phillip's hand. 'You can have a go with it, Grandfather.'

Phillip took the battered and grubby train and lifted it up for closer examination, turning it over slowly in his hands. The hard lines of his face, the familiar set of his mouth, seemed to melt and he looked unsure and deeply moved. He could barely speak. 'Thank you,' he whispered hoarsely, putting the train on his lap and a hand on the boy's shoulder. 'Thank you very much.'

As their eyes met, Phillip realised that the needs of this boy were also his own needs and he saw how he had been denying them all his life. 'I think I'll enjoy this very much tonight. I'll give it back at breakfast if that's all right with you.'

Richie smiled, relieved. It had taken a lot to give up his train, but he sensed the gesture had finally pleased the man he'd never been able to please.

At the McBrides' everyone but Gwen was in bed. She finished wrapping some more Christmas presents and hid them at the back of the grocery cupboard on the top shelf. Then she went to the mantelpiece over the fireplace and reached behind an old tea caddy for an envelope, took out the single sheet of paper and sat down at the kitchen table. It was the pencilled note Mr Richards had sent them almost four years ago.

Dear Bob and Gwen,
The news of the great tragedy has only just reached me through my friend in the Bush Brotherhood. There are no words adequate enough to convey to you the sadness I feel at this time and the sympathy I want to send to all of you. But my prayers and thoughts are with you and I hope that they are of some help. The grief will last a long time and no doubt you will often ask 'Why?'

Brother John would explain it as 'The Lord giveth and the Lord taketh away'. You were given Richie and Abby was taken.

And apart from always asking 'Why?', you may eventually blame yourselves for what happened or blame someone else. Well I reckon that won't help much.

What will get you through this time of anguish is love. Remember the great love that Abby and Barney had for each other. Nurture it and share its memory, for when you pass on the love of those two fine people you keep them alive.

I'm sorry this is a bit of a scrawl but I'm writing by a campfire on the banks of the Cooper. There's a big star overhead and when I look up I can see the Southern Cross. Abby used to say there was something special about that part of the sky.

With kindest respects,

Mr Richards.

Gwen folded the letter carefully and put it back behind the tea caddy then went out on the verandah and looked up at the night sky and found the Southern Cross.

'Goodnight, Abby,' she whispered.

CHAPTER NINETEEN

A LOCAL FARMER TOOK HIS SLASHER TO THE COM-
mon to cut the grass; another ran an electricity
extension from the community hall for strings of
coloured lights in the pines by the creek; and a
team of youngsters set out chairs and bales of hay
in a semicircle. Ladies from the CWA prepared a
table with a crochet cloth, flowers, candlesticks
and a Bible. Back in the hall they worked on the
scones, cakes and sandwiches for supper.

The Church of England minister arrived with a
portable organ. It had been a magnificent but hot
day and as the sun dipped, the little valley which
cradled the common cooled and a soft breeze

made it a welcome oasis for the rural families that began rolling up from all directions.

There were loud greetings and excited tumbling on the grassy slopes by the younger children. The teenage boys sat on post-and-rail fences or squatted in groups exchanging gossip and glances at teenage girls, all prettied up and giggly. The adults shook hands or hugged. The men exchanged views on the weather, prices, needs and prospects; women swapped notes on their preparations for Christmas. Everyone agreed that the CWA ladies had done themselves proud. It was going to be a great Christmas Eve. Mr Richards arrived and was given a small cheer by the McBride family.

As the sun finally slipped behind the distant ridge line, the ministers of three religions, led by children carrying a cross and candles, emerged from the community hall. The little procession moved down the slope to the natural amphitheatre by the creek, followed by the steadily growing crowd.

Mrs Doherty, the organist, sitting under a halo of coloured lights, struck up with *Hark, the Herald Angels Sing*, and as everyone found seats in family groups, the sky glowed pink and purple.

The candles on the table were lit and then, when it seemed all was more or less organised, the

Church of England minister, the Reverend Charles Hill, stepped forward and nodded to the organist, who quickly worked in a closing bar.

'Thank you, Mrs Doherty,' he said at a level more to be seen than heard, then lifted his voice to pulpit strength. 'Ladies and gentlemen, boys and girls, a happy and holy welcome to you all on this wonderful occasion. I am sure that I speak for my fellow clerics in saying that we are delighted to be here. To start our round of Christmas religious celebrations with candlelight carols out here in this beautiful setting is indeed a blessing, for here it is so easy to feel the presence of God. It is such a natural feeling and it brings us joy, just as that wonderful event in a manger in Bethlehem so long ago brought joy to the world.'

He paused and looked around and grinned. 'I rather detect something like a smell of a manger here tonight.' The crowd roared with laughter. 'I mean . . . I mean . . . the smell from the bales of hay,' he added, which earned him a round of applause and sent him back to his seat well pleased with the mood he had established for the evening.

An ample lady in a floral dress and long white gloves stepped forward as conductor for the evening. 'Our first carol will be *The First Noel*.' She gave a small signal to Mrs Doherty and soon the valley filled with song. The simple faith that held strong good people together manifested itself in voices raised in joyous expression of goodwill and love.

The shimmering twilight gave way to a darkening velvet sky which began to fill with stars. Mrs Anderson glanced over at the McBride family enthusiastically singing. She knew that they must also be remembering this night so few years ago when Barney and Abby were wed on this very spot. But their faces were alight with peace and faith and they presented a picture of complete family unity and love that made her heart twist. She caught the eye of Mr Richards on the end of the aisle near Gwen and they exchanged smiles.

At the end of the first carol, Mr Hill announced that during the next item the children attending the ministers would move among the people with altar candles. They would light a candle at the end of each row and the light would be passed from person to person, candle to candle, along each row.

There was a scurrying for candles brought in handbags and string bags and the mounting of them in a variety of holders, from silver family heirlooms to simple cardboard shields decorated with coloured pencils. And, as the singing again rang over the New England hills, the little bush-land amphitheatre started to sparkle like the sky above as candle after candle was lit.

Gwen turned to Brian who was rummaging in his school bag handing out candles to the family. 'Did you remember to pack one for Mr Richards, Brian?'

'Genius that I am, of course.' He grinned and handed a candle to his father, who passed it to Gwen. She swung around. 'Here you are Mr ...' and stopped. He wasn't there. The chair beside her was empty.

She stepped out and looked down the path that divided the crowd. She saw two figures standing near the back, scanning the scene, then taking a step or two, then stopping, unsure of where they should go. She became half aware of another person suddenly appearing behind them, and for a fraction of a second she thought it might be Mr Richards, but her attention went back to them and she started to tremble.

There was no mistaking, even in the fading light, the tall straight figure of Phillip Holten and beside him, holding his hand, an excited little boy.

'Oh my God, it's Richie,' she murmured.

As she stared in disbelief, a little girl appeared at her side with the altar candle. Without taking her eyes off the boy, Gwen lit her candle, and then slowly raised it shoulder high. The man and the boy walked towards her.

'Bob,' she whispered urgently.

Phillip Holten led the boy to them and for a second they all just looked at each other.

'I'd like to wish you all a merry Christmas,' Phillip said, then bent down towards the boy. 'Richard, this is the surprise present I promised you...the rest of your family.' He looked at Gwen. 'And this is your grandmother.'

Richie smiled and held his candle up to Gwen's. 'Hello, Grandma. Can I light my candle now?'

The End

Di Morrissey
Heart of the Dreaming

At twenty-one Queenie Hanlon has the world at her feet.

Startlingly beautiful, wealthy and intelligent, she is the
only daughter of Tingulla Station, the famed outback
property in the wilds of western Queensland... and the
love of handsome bushman, TR Hamilton.

At twenty-two her life is in ruins. A series of disasters
has robbed her of everything she has ever loved.
Everything except Tingulla — her ancestral home and
her spirit's dreaming place.

Now she's about to lose that too...

A sweeping saga of thwarted love and heroic struggle,
of a brother's treachery and one man's enduring
passion, *Heart of the Dreaming* is the exciting and
triumphant story of one woman's remarkable courage
and her determination to take on the world and win.

Di Morrissey
The Last Rose of Summer

FOLLOWING THE PHENOMENAL SUCCESS OF DI MORRISSEY'S
FIRST NOVEL, *HEART OF THE DREAMING*, COMES ANOTHER
STUNNING AUSTRALIAN SAGA — THE COMPELLING STORY OF
TWO BEAUTIFUL AND REMARKABLE WOMEN ...

KATE, a strong-willed heiress determined to defy
Edwardian convention. ODETTE, a fiercely independent
and idealistic child of the sixties. Years apart yet
inextricably linked by Zanana, the magnificent mansion
they both love ...

From turn of the century India to contemporary Sydney,
The Last Rose of Summer is a spellbinding saga of
bitter struggle and jealousy; a story of love, possession
and intrigue ... and of two women connected across the
decades by the men who love them ... and the magic of
Zanana.

Di Morrissey
Follow the Morning Star

QUEENIE AND TR RETURN IN DI MORRISSEY'S BLOCK-BUSTING
SEQUEL TO *HEART OF THE DREAMING*.

Queenie Hanlon has the perfect life.

She's the mother of two adoring children, the wealthy
owner of a thriving outback station and the lover of
handsome bushman TR Hamilton.

Then one day when TR is seriously injured in a riding
accident Queenie's perfect life suddenly comes
crashing down...

Her bitter and vengeful brother returns from Italy to lay
claim to his inheritance. Her precious daughter is
seduced by her uncle into giving up all she's strived for.
And her beloved TR can no longer recall the life they
once shared.

Once before Queenie Hanlon was robbed of everything
she ever loved... surely it can't happen all over again?

Di Morrissey
Tears of the Moon

Two inspiring journeys
Two unforgettable women
One amazing story...

Broome, Australia 1893
It's the wild and passionate heyday of the pearling
industry, and when young English bride Olivia
Hennessy meets the dashing pearling master
Captain Tyndall, their lives are destined to be linked
by the mysterious power of pearls.

Sydney 1995
Lily Barton embarks on a search for her family roots
which leads her to Broome. But her quest for identity
reveals more than she could have ever imagined...

TEARS OF THE MOON IS THE STUNNING NEW
BESTSELLER FROM AUSTRALIA'S MOST POPULAR
FEMALE NOVELIST

'... a sprawling saga ... skilfully atmospheric'
THE BULLETIN